Mike

The Firefighters of Station #8

S. R. Wyatt

LOVE ENDURES

Mike: The Firefighters of Station #8

Copyright©2022, 2024 S.R. WYATT

Published by Love Endures

Paperback ISBN: 978-1-963776-05-8

Cover Design by Erin Dameron-Hill

Published in the United States of America

The Firefighters of Station #8

Mike (Book 1)
Shep (Book 2)
Jared (Book 3)

DEDICATION

To all firefighters around the world, true American heroes who put their lives in jeopardy every day. Thank you for your bravery and dedication. Although it may seem you are taken for granted, you are greatly appreciated, valued, respected and this world is blessed to have devoted souls like you. I have first-hand knowledge in a life altering experience. My own home was burned to the ground. While many made comments on the destruction, my thoughts were solely on the safety of the men who came to my aid.

I would also like to thank and give recognition to my inspiration guys who allowed me to interview them for my books. Who willingly answered my questions with enthusiasm and even allowed me into their station, access to their bay, and climb in their big fire trucks. So many wonderful, fun men who were so nice to a stranger. I did not model any character after a certain individual. Since the guys were being respectful, I had to use my imagination for the personal aspects. I combined what I learned with my own ideas and created each firefighter with his own charisma.

ACKNOWLEDGEMENTS

As always, I'd like to thank my husband who has been my main support and encouraged me every step of the way.
I'd like to thank my editor, and my cover artist who does wonderful covers.
For everyone who loves a little romance and a Hot Firefighter.
Keep the Spirit!
Samanthya

CONTENTS

CHAPTER 1

Training day.

Nestled in the middle of one-hundred-twenty acres of private farm land, backed up by three-hundred acres of plush forest, stood an empty farm house that had been scheduled for fire training. Five units were on site, including Mike's—Station Eight. His team stood ready for backup while Station Seven and Station Nine trained new recruits.

At a glance, the set up appeared as if all precautions were in order and the men in position ready to begin. Having two extra teams standing around might seem like a waste of time and manpower, but every drill offered a learning contingency. Even if they did nothing but watch, their time would not be futile.

Being thirty miles from town, the secluded property present-ed the perfect setting for an exercise without interruption. No bystanders, no chance of anyone just happening by. Those in attendance stood waiting for instruction.

Mike popped the kinks out of his neck, then hoisted an air tank onto his back.

"They're getting antsy," one of the instructors said, stepping up beside him.

"Better get started then." Mike glanced about the structure, assessing the placement of each team. Some to participate, others to watch. Even though he wasn't in charge, he checked to see that each man was where he belonged and equipped with proper gear. Trucks and crews formed a somewhat perimeter around the old wooden structure. Including one team appointed to prevent any stray sparks from igniting outside the designated area.

The old house might be scheduled for a training exercise, but Mike took every precaution as though this was any emergency call coming through dispatch. Every fire needed precise attention to detail—a controlled burn was no different.

Two men in full gear stood off to the left, holding axes. Behind them, three more had attached hoses to the ends of trucks, preparing to open nozzles. Two ladderbacks were situated at opposite ends, ready if needed. Out of habit, Mike took notice of the wind direction, logging it in the back of his mind in case he needed the data later. He glanced to the right, finding a row of men lined up, raring to go. With many entry-level firefighters on hand, the men had been divided into teams—one experienced and one new recruit. Everyone was in position.

The instructor issued the signal to begin. A firefighter, equipped with full gear, stepped forward and tossed a flame into a first-floor open window. A ball of fire surged like a thundercloud just before the house exploded. Smoke roared and bits of flaming wood sailed through the air with massive force.

What the fuck!

Mike secured his face mask and ran into the dark cloud, shouts and screams surrounding him. He headed for the firefighter who'd tossed the torch. Mike hadn't seen if the man had been knocked back or where he'd landed, but being that close to the house, the guy had to be seriously injured, if not dead. He didn't have time to speculate.

This should not have happened. He, and he was sure every man there, had expected a gradual flare. Then flames should have licked the structure. Not an explosion from hell.

Mike sucked oxygen as his steps led him forward, his instincts kicking in. His heart pounded with every breath as he searched, unbelieving of what he'd seen. Two shapes emerged in front of him. He watched as they grabbed an unconscious body and hauled a man clear of the burning structure. Mike heaved a short sigh of relief.

Black smoke bellowed in a whirling arc with ten-foot flames towering above the house. Bits of the roof had shot straight up like missiles and pieces were now hanging in the trees. In every direction, burning boards and shattered walls cluttered the ground. Firefighters scurried about the debris littering earth, some battling flames while others crouched low, dragging wounded men to safety.

Christ. They'd been too close. Fiery heat and chaos surrounded him, still he managed to examine his surroundings. Two teams rushed forward with hoses leveled at the burning building, or what was left of it. A firestorm raged like hell's furnace.

Wilson, the chief of Station Nine, shouted orders and every man scampered, doing his job. Mike stood rooted to the ground, assessing the commotion. Everything that could be done was being done. The explosion had come as a surprise, but each man had responded with proficiency. Even the emergency response medics had jumped into action.

"Mike." He turned to find Laredo at his side. "What the fuck happened?"

"Hell, if I know. But you can bet your sweet ass I'm going to find out."

"Never seen anything like that. Is there a gas line around here?"

"Cap would have checked that out before he cleared this place for training. Nothing should have been inside to cause the house to blow up."

"We were lucky." Laredo's heavy breathing punctuated each word. "Only a few men were close enough to feel the blast."

Thank God for that. But still, one man had been in the heart of the surge. Mike hoped the flame-retardant suit had done what it was supposed to.

"Wasn't Ryan the one who tossed the flame?"

"Yeah," Laredo answered. "He's with Station Nine. Tough break."

"Is he still breathing?"

"Was when the squad rolled out."

"I better call Cap." Mike adjusted his face mask as he pulled out his cell. The air heavy with smoke, he coughed, his fingers clumsily hitting the numbers on the screen. Only one ring echoed before the Captain answered. "Cap. Mike here. We've got a situation. The farmhouse blew up."

"What do you mean *blew up*?" Shep's harsh voice came back at him.

"Station Nine staged the drill," Mike shouted over the noise. "Procedures were by the book. Everything looked good. As soon as Ryan threw the torch, the damn house exploded. As if a gas line was open."

"That's not possible," Shep shouted back. "No gas. No electricity. It's a deserted house. Already cleared. Hell, even the water lines were turned off."

"Yeah," Mike said, glancing at the burning structure. "Too bad about that. We could use some extra water right now."

"What the hell happened?"

"I don't know. I can only tell you what I saw. The flame hadn't even cleared the window when a ball of fire ignited." Mike recalled the scene in his mind, rewinding it in slow motion. He'd never seen anything like it. And he hoped to never see it again. A training maneuver gone bad. Real bad.

"Anyone hurt?"

"Ryan must have been knocked back thirty feet. It took a while to find him. The medics put him on oxygen and rolled him out. A few others got hit with the blast."

"Find out everything and report back to me. You get it on film?"

Mike glanced about and found a photographer bracing a camera on his shoulder. Every training session was recorded. The films were used as the second part of training maneuvers, so firefighters could see how things were done and discuss scenarios. At least the guy had enough sense to stay out of the way. Maybe there would be something on film that could help explain what the hell happened.

"Yes sir," Mike said. "It had to be gas. I don't know what else could have made this place go up like the fourth of July."

"Station Nine is in charge. Wilson doesn't need me in his way. But I can help by getting a fire investigator on this one. Let him know."

A large van with the letters SAPD pulled up alongside one of the fire trucks. Mike swallowed a lump of dread as he recognized the bomb unit.

"Bomb crew just rolled on site."

"They'll search for explosives," Shep's voice rumbled through the phone. "Make sure the fire is out, clear everyone and wait for the results. As soon as you have something, get your ass back here."

"Right."

Mike watched the pandemonium before him that could have quickly turned into a disaster. The whole point of the exercise was to teach men how to fight fires. A system of techniques was to be followed in an orderly process, but the explosion had ambushed them. All levels of firefighters were expected to deal with the unforeseen, in both crisis and routine circumstances—by the look of things, the new recruits had dived right in along with the old dogs.

At least no one had stood around with their dick in their hands.

***

"This was a great idea," Cassie said as she shoved a chip into her mouth. After a long week of enthusiastic eight-year-olds in a classroom, she was ready for an evening of spicy sauce and beer. Her friend, Tammy, preferred a margarita, but tequila had a habit of knocking Cassie on her butt.

"Taco sauce and cheese dip is always a good idea," Tammy agreed. "I fed the boys hotdogs before I took them to the Scout Hut."

"Hot dogs?"

"Yep. Their favorite."

Hot dogs just didn't compare to Mexican food. El Puerto's was one of Cassie's favorite spots. At least once a week, the two of them would have dinner at the cozy restaurant.

She was ready to let her hair down, kick off her shoes and wiggle her cramped toes. She'd love to wear tennis shoes to school, but being a teacher, she felt the need to give some care to her appearance. Most days she wore a comfortable dress. Sandals might work in the summer, but tennis shoes were definitely not part of business casual attire.

While Tammy talked about her two boys, a red image appeared in Cassie's peripheral vision. She glanced out the restaurant window and zeroed in on a Staunton fire truck. Right in front of the building. When another one appeared behind the first, Tammy's voice faded away.

A silent alarm went off in Cassie's brain—the same way it did every time she heard a siren or saw any emergency vehicle roaring down the road. Ever since that night, when she'd awoken in her cousin's house to a room filled with smoke. The night she'd felt her way down the hall in a panic because she couldn't see and she'd needed to find her cousin's son, who thankfully had already made it outside. She'd stumbled to the door and a pair of arms had grabbed her and carried her into the fresh night air. When she'd finally calmed, the shock of flames climbing from the windows and above the roof had paralyzed her and brought reality crashing down. She could have burned to death.

Her chest squeezed just as it had that night two years ago. Would the time come when she could breathe normally and not cringe when she heard a siren?

She thought she heard a voice penetrate the fog she'd drifted into.

"Cassie! Are you all right?"

She blinked. Her pulse raced, her throat felt dry and she immediately realized she needed to calm down. Her gaze returned to the sun gleaming off the shiny vehicle. The truck was not racing, nor did she hear a siren. She willed the tension from her muscles, chastising herself.

"Cassie?"

"I'm all right. I just ... my mind wandered for a moment." Still, a little pang of fear hovered. She shot another glance outside. The fire engine had disappeared. She dropped her gaze. The taco salad had lost its appeal.

"What's got you so quiet?"

When Cassie raised her head, she noticed a streak of yellow in the long window facing the parking lot. Her attention averted again, she stared at the front of an engine as the doors swung open and two men climbed out. Then a red SUV, clearly labeled Fire-Chief, pulled up beside them. From the other side of the lot, a second yellow engine rolled in.

Her pulse sped up. She quickly scanned the inside of the restaurant. "Is the kitchen on fire?"

"What?" Tammy squeaked.

"Either there's a fire or these guys are having a convention." She motioned outside just as more uniforms came into view.

"Damn. Would you look at that," Tammy said as she gawked out the window. "Six, no eight gorgeous hunks."

"How can you think about sex when the building might be on fire?"

"So, *that's* what's bothering you." Tammy turned around with a look of concern. "Look. There's no siren. These guys are not racing in here. They don't have on their bulky equipment. Although there is definitely some bulk on their bodies. Look at that guy."

Cassie looked in the direction where Tammy pointed to the side parking lot where the firemen gathered. She studied the driver of the red vehicle. His blond hair had that wind-blown look. Black sunglasses shielded his eyes from the sun but gave him a sexy movie star-type guise. When he laughed, the knot in Cassie's chest eased. If there was an alarm, these men wouldn't be standing in the parking lot laughing.

She felt like a fool. A child fearing the big bad monster. When would she grow out of this? Her chest heaved as she released her frustration. "Obviously, these firefighters are not here to put out a fire."

"But, by their good looks, bulging forearms and rigid buns, they could sure start a few."

Tammy's teasing remark made Cassie grin.

"Mmm, mmm. I could sit here and watch that all day." As if she meant to do just that, Tammy propped her elbow on the end of the table and brazenly stared.

Cassie shook her head. Her friend's flirty behavior was the best medicine for Cassie's state of mind. No one could be around Tammy and not smile. So, she looked out the window and enjoyed the view.

Navy blue shirts stretched across tight abs and exhibited some pretty hearty muscles. Matching pants covered impressive thighs, not as constricting as their shirts, but damn distracting. Two males were taller than the others, but each guy stood at least six feet. Cassie relaxed as her previous apprehension slowly developed into carnal appreciation. Her gaze landed on the man she'd first spotted. Mr. Sunglasses. The sun brought out highlights in his hair, strands fluttering over his black shades. And his smile, all teeth with a lazy slanted grin. That guy had danger written all over him.

She hoped no one noticed the two of them ogling the firefighters outside. But then, the group of hot men was drawing a lot of attention. She hadn't dated in quite a while and had no interest in changing that, but she could appreciate a fine specimen of all man. Usually, men with dark hair held her attention, like the guy standing beside Mr. Sunglasses. Coal black hair, brooding looks, and big arms. Mr. Muscles. Yep, she definitely preferred Mr. Muscles to Mr. Sunglasses. With biceps like his, the guy had to work out every day.

"A lot to be said for a man in uniform," Cassie said with a sigh.

"Bet he benches five hundred pounds." Tammy sounded breathless.

Cassie searched her friend's face. "How do you know which one I was looking at?"

"Easy." Tammy's gaze turned to hers. "You always go for the dark-haired ones."

Cassie smiled and glanced back to the men in blue. "There's too many to choose from." She threw the comment out as a jest. In reality, she held no belief that any of those guys would pay attention to her.

"And they're coming in here." Tammy said excitedly as she nodded toward the glass.

Sure enough, the entire group headed to the restaurant. Caught up in Tammy's enthusiasm, Cassie couldn't help but ogle the swaggering male hips. The men ranged in age from twenty something to probably forty, since one had some gray at his temples.

Silence filled the room, the firemen drawing the attention of every customer. When the door opened, the sound of the men's voices carried throughout the quiet space of the restaurant. They'd caused quite a stir. Cassie forced her eyes forward. Tammy, of course, watched the activity with a total lack of inhibition.

By sheer willpower, Cassie resisted the urge to whirl around and gape like everyone else. She narrowed her eyes and bit her bottom lip.

"What?" Tammy asked, seeing Cassie's scowl. "Did I suddenly grow a wart on my chin?"

Cassie had been trying so hard not to stare at the guys that she'd been completely unaware she was glaring at her friend. Tammy's perplexed face came into focus and Cassie frowned. "Sorry."

Tammy laughed. "Why don't you bite the bullet and feast your eyes?"

"I don't want to be transparently obvious." Cassie stabbed at her lettuce.

"Why not? Everyone else is." Tammy placed her elbows on the table and rested her chin on her hands, ogling the men in uniform.

"You don't have to be so blatant about it."

"I've never seen so much male testosterone in one place. Eight of them. Right here in the middle of this room."

Jealousy prompted Cassie to suggest, "You could trade places with me."

"Not a chance." Tammy's smile grew bigger.

"You're embarrassing me." Actually, she'd embarrassed herself with her senseless envy. Because, if she was to be honest with herself, she wished she had Tammy's self-confidence. Cassie placed her fork beside her plate. "Now I've really lost my appetite."

"Mine just increased." Tammy's eyes twinkled with mischief.

Cassie resented her friend's taunting. "Can you tone it down a bit?" She grabbed her beer bottle by the long neck.

Green eyes shot to hers. Their sparkle of glee now glinted with annoyance. "It's been a while, okay? I may have two challenging boys, but I'm far from over-the-hill. I'm in my prime."

Guilt made Cassie's face flush. Who was she to criticize when—if she had the guts—she'd do the same thing? Tammy was her best friend. A single mom, she was pretty with strawberry hair, green lively eyes, and a face that always held a welcoming warmth. She loved food, had no willpower and was thirty pounds heavier than she wanted to be. They came to the Mexican restaurant on an average of once a week, which anyone with an ounce of good judgment knew that was no way to lose weight. Cassie had ordered a salad tonight, but she loved El Puerto's food. With the chips and salsa, she would have to run an extra mile on the treadmill.

Expecting to exercise tonight, she had pulled her hair back into a ponytail. She suddenly wished she'd left it down where it could flow over her shoulders, so the lights in the ceiling would bring out the golden highlights of her natural blonde hair.

Her fingers tapped a rhythm on the wooden table while she sat there, looking daggers at her friend. She refused to turn around and display barefaced interest in the men who'd drawn such attention.

Oh, hell.

She was dying to have another look.

CHAPTER 2

This happened every time a bunch of the guys got together. People would stop whatever they were doing and watch. The clientele of this restaurant stared in awe like they'd never seen a firefighter before. Or a group of men in uniform having dinner, or drinking a beer instead of putting out a fire.

Hell, Mike was human just like anybody else. His job happened to be putting out fires. Saving lives, if it came down to it. He should be used to the attention but being called a hero made him feel uncomfortable. Since he'd been a little kid, he'd wanted to be a fireman and ride on a big red truck, like his dad. Of course, children only saw the glamor and excitement. Once he'd joined the fire department, he learned a whole new respect for the term *firefighter*.

After the day he'd had, he needed a beer more than food. Even though both shifts had come to eat, only the guys off duty would be drinking. His shift officially over, he was allowed. He ordered a combination platter and grabbed one of the bottles Laredo brought to the table. He took a long pull, allowing the frosty chill to sooth his dry throat.

The back of Mike's neck prickled. He'd felt a singe earlier but chalked it up to patrons checking out the uniforms. Jared sat across from him, staring over Mike's shoulder, giving one of his leering grins. Without a doubt, women had to be the reason.

Jared couldn't help his pretty boy looks, and he had the charm to go with them. Since the team already had a Casanova in the group, the guys at the station called Jared *Pretty Boy.* He craved action, enjoyed life in the fast lane, and was not the type one usually found applying for a fire-fighting position. But he'd been an asset to the department. One thing Mike shared with him—there was nothing he valued more than his bachelorhood.

He lifted one hand and rubbed the skin on the back of his neck above his collar. Jared scrutinized him with a smirk.

"You've already found someone to hit on?" Mike asked.

"Can't stand it, can you? Might as well turn around. She's a real looker."

"She must be. You've been staring ever since we sat down."

"There's two. One for each of us." Jared flashed a smile. "The blonde only peeked once. She must be shy. Bet I could liven her up."

"Maybe she doesn't like *pretty boys.*" Although Mike had yet to meet a woman who could resist Jared's charm.

"Whoa," Jared said and dropped his chair back on all four legs. "Think I might change my mind. The blonde is the looker, but damn, that smile."

"I heard that." Cooper, the youngest and newest member of their group, spoke up.

"Good sign you aren't deaf." Jared took another pull of his beer and kept his gaze on the woman he'd been observing.

Cooper lifted his glass of iced tea. "Lucky you. You're off duty."

"You're still in uniform," Mike reminded Jared.

"Short stuff, here, can drive the rig back to the station." Jared slapped Cooper on the back.

Cooper's eyes lit up like the lights on a Christmas tree. The boy's dream was to be the next man in line for driving the quint, so he jumped at the chance to drive one of the engines.

Cooper mimicked Jared and surveyed the two women. His eyes grew heavy-lidded and the boy's admiring gleam drew Mike's interest, finally making him curious enough to turn around and satisfy his own inquisitive mind.

A woman stared at him with a mixture of intrigue and apprehension. He shifted in his chair, just before her gaze darted away. The woman virtually had wrenched his gut. Jared was right. She was a looker. A beauty with blonde hair, a picture-perfect oval face, translucent eyes and full pouting lips. He guessed her to be in her late twenties, a few years younger than him. She didn't seem to welcome the attention. If anything, she seemed cautious. Did she not know how striking she was? The look in her eyes said she did not. His libido gave a slight jump.

Damn.

"Get your own date," Jared said with some potency and slid out of his chair.

Shit. Mike had been caught drooling. The redhead jerked with noticeable excitement and fluttered like a teenager. She said something to her companion. The blonde turned her disillusioned gaze to him. No invitation there.

But Mike had seen her earlier flicker of interest. She darted a glance at Jared, who, without wasting any more time and with the grace of a predator, swaggered across the floor to the ladies table.

Mike couldn't hear their conversation from where he sat, but by their tone, and knowing his friend, there was a lot of flirting going on. With every moment that passed, he wanted to sneak another look, feast his eyes on the woman to see if he'd get the same reaction as before. He angled his chair so he could see them from the corner of his eye.

"She's got to be the prettiest woman I've ever seen," Cooper sighed with the admiration of a star-struck teenager. "She might be older than me, hard to tell with that ponytail, but—"

"Down, pup." Mike's voice came out more forceful than he'd intended. Shoving out of his chair, he stood and wondered what the hell he was doing.

"That's right." Jared laughed, entirely too cozy with the two women. He noticed Mike's approach and waved a beer in his direction. "Hey buddy. Meet Tammy and Cassie."

Mike gave a warm smile to an unmistakably delighted Tammy. "Hello," he said, then turned to the golden blonde on the opposite side of the booth. Her smile was breathtaking. Maybe more reserved than her friend, but he'd bet this woman was not unapproachable. Her posture and keen scrutiny indicated she could handle anything and anyone. She'd evidently sized Jared up and was now doing the same to him. Her light green eyes sparkled and her lips curved in challenge. As if silently communicating, *I know what you're about*.

Cooper was right. The blonde had to be the most beautiful woman he'd ever seen. He allowed his gaze to roam lower. A tight shirt displayed full breasts with a hint of some serious cleavage. Not wanting to be rude, he allowed his consideration to linger only a moment before putting on his game face.

"Hope my friend, here, has been behaving himself."

"He sure has. I'm Tammy." The redhead waved a hand with bright-red tipped nails. "This is Cassie. Would you like to sit down?"

Cassie's eyes flashed with surprise and possibly annoyance, but her friend ignored her. Jared slid into the booth beside the agreeable redhead. At the blonde's reaction, Mike hesitated.

"Do you mind? We don't want to interrupt your dinner." He sure as hell wouldn't move in where he wasn't wanted. After a few seconds, Cassie slid over. It wasn't the welcome he normally received, but he found himself relieved, so he scooted into the booth next to her. An alluring fragrance assaulted his senses. Not sweet, not floral, but damn ... irresistible.

Out of consideration, he kept a suitable amount of space between them. The devil side of him threatened to squeeze closer and watch her squirm.

"This place sure livened up when you boys strolled in. How did so many uniforms manage to take a break at the same time?" Tammy asked.

"Training maneuvers this week. We deserve a treat at the end of a long day." Jared eased back, propping one arm on the back cushion.

After the fiasco at the training site, they all needed a good stiff drink. At least they knew Ryan would be okay. The men were drained. Back at the fire house, they'd washed off the grime and hashed out the incident, going over the hellish episode again and again. The shaking of heads was getting them no answers, and the guys were hungry. No one had been in the mood to cook. They'd decided to go out.

"I see." Tammy beamed.

Usually Jared went for the swimsuit-model type, but Mike could see the attraction. Tammy had a gleeful charm and a welcoming friendliness.

"What if there is a fire somewhere?" Cassie drew his attention. He took that as his cue.

"There are other departments and we left a skeleton crew at the station. Some of these guys are off duty."

"Like me and Mike," Jared said. "Since we have our trucks with us, if a call comes in, the guys are prepared to respond."

"You must really like your job. I'm in awe that you risk your safety." Her throaty voice swamped Mike's nerve endings. And who could resist those compelling eyes?

Jared turned on the charm. "All in the line of duty, ma'am."

Mike was ready to punch his buddy back to reality. But Jared had impressed the woman next to him. She giggled and her face lit up like she was sitting next to a superhero.

Mike turned to Cassie. "A few of these guys are still on shift. The rest will head home."

"That's a lot of trucks out there." Tammy fluttered her eyelashes and tilted her head to gaze up at Jared. "Which one is yours?"

"Well now, funny you should ask. That's my baby right there." Jared pointed to a truck in the parking lot.

"The one with the long ladder?"

"Yep. That's the one."

Like hell. The quint was Laredo's baby and he wouldn't let anyone else touch it. Although, in all fairness, Jared had driven the quint before Laredo had joined Station Eight.

"It's so long. How do you drive that thing in the city or around sharp turns?"

"Long arms," he said, setting down his beer and extending one arm. "And lots of practice. I take care of her, give her what she needs, whether it's a bath or a quart of oil, and she purrs like a little kitten."

Oh Christ. Jared was pouring it on a bit thick.

"I just give the wheel a spin and she cuddles right up. Never lets me down." Jared bared his pearly whites.

"Wow. It's long and—"

"Fire," Cassie sputtered. "Uh, ladder. I mean, it reaches up how many floors?"

Mike wanted to laugh at the double entendre. Tammy flirted just as outrageously as Jared. When she mentioned *long*, Cassie had jumped in as though she had to save Tammy from herself.

"That one is eighty-five feet," Jared said, but Cassie continued as if he had not answered.

"Tammy. David and Christopher."

Who were David and Christopher? Husbands?

Mike searched for rings on the girls' fingers. Neither one had a gold band or a diamond. Cassie seemed nervous and her eyes were definitely trying to relay some message.

Tammy raised her arm and glanced at her watch. "Oh. Uh. I need to be going."

"Another engagement?" Jared asked her.

"You have your duty. I have mine." She gave an apologetic smile and reached for her purse.

Mike knew an evasive answer when he heard one. He guessed Jared had the same thought, for he stood without any coaxing.

"Nice to meet you, ladies. Maybe we'll see you again sometime."

"I hope so," Tammy replied.

Mike turned to Cassie, wondering if she felt the same as her friend. He wouldn't mind seeing her again. "I would like that."

When she didn't answer, he rose, making a point of brushing against her with his thigh. He heard her intake of breath and inwardly smiled.

Awareness.

Should he ask for her number—or take a chance of running into her at the restaurant again? Since she stared at the table, he decided he'd leave things up to her.

***

The guy was Don Juan in blue jeans. Cassie knew the type. Impossibly handsome, with a chest that indicated he spent many hours in the gym, or doing some other physical activity. Judging by every uniform at the firefighters' table, an exceptional physique may well have been a requirement—or an end result. Who knew putting out fires could shape a man's body like an Adonis?

Mr. Muscles had phenomenal shoulders. He looked like a line-backer. And his eyes had penetrated hers when they met. His gaze seemed to be searching for secrets or waiting for ... for what? For her to give him her phone number?

"You ladies be careful driving home." His deep voice soothed and, at the same time, generated electric shocks dancing along her spine.

"I have to go. But Cassie does not," Tammy stated firmly.

Cassie could have killed her. Tammy was the one who had drawn the guys over. Now she intended to go on her merry way and leave Cassie to the wolves? If Jared's smile grew any bigger, she was sure fangs would emerge. Mike seemed less sinister, but her attraction to him screamed *danger*.

"Is that so?" Jared prepared to climb back into the booth, but Tammy pushed him as she climbed from her seat.

"Haven't you ever heard, three is a crowd?" She grabbed his arm and tugged. "Gotta go." Then the traitor held her hand up with thumb and pinky extended and mouthed the words *call me*.

If Cassie could have gotten her hands around ...

She wanted to crawl under the table.

The sparkle in Mike's eyes matched his teasing smile. At least he had the wisdom to slip into the seat on the opposite side. What kept him from bursting with laughter, she had no idea, because he looked like he was holding back. Her cheek suffered her embarrassment—she nearly chewed the inside of the damn thing off.

"If you could see your face," he said before he laughed. A deep vibrating sound that sizzled her already sensitized skin.

"Don't feel like you need to stay because of what Tammy said." Gee, that sounded mature.

He spoke in a lazy drawl. "The funny thing is, Jared came over first and I'm the one still here."

Funny? Not to her. At the moment, she was sweltering in a sea of embarrassment—part from Tammy's obvious match-making and the other part from her own traitorous thoughts. The guy was seriously hot. She mentally shook herself. Was he making fun of her?

"Is this a contest? Am I some sort of prize?"

"What?" His brow scrunched up in a frown. "No. I only meant that Jared is usually the one who gets the girl. Now he's gone. And before you say anything else, I know I don't need to stay. But I want to."

His eyes were a gorgeous shade of deep blue. She almost lost herself in them, until his gaze dropped to her cleavage.

Blood rushed to her face. Her looks had been a curse in high school. Others had told her she was pretty. At one point, she'd believed them. But she'd been cursed with big breasts, and girls with big boobs attracted all the jocks with only one thing on their minds. Being burned once was enough. She had no desire to repeat her mistake. She rarely dated and if a guy was focused on her chest ...

"Do you mind if I stay?"

She raised her head and found his eyes locked on hers.

"Let's start over. Hi. I'm Mike. I'd like to get to know you." He leaned forward with his forearms braced on the edge of the table. His warm smile conveyed tenderness and held a hint of promised excitement. Add his actions, his voice and his kind eyes peeling away her barriers, she slowly dissolved into a puddle. Somewhere a little voice niggled the back of her brain, *do not fall under his spell.*

He must have read her thoughts or guessed her vulnerability, for he lifted his arms from the table and leaned back against the cushioned booth. Keeping his gaze on her, he took a sip of his beer. Transfixed, she watched the knot in his neck bob as he swallowed. Heat flared below her belly button. She resisted the urge to close her eyes.

A man's physique had never affected her this way. Wasn't there a saying that went, *things that seemed too good to be true, usually were*? This guy looked like sin, smelled like heaven, and made her want to jump into his lap.

She reached for her drink and hoped her hand would not shake.

"Okay. What would you like to know?"

"Everything." His voice lowered to tantalizing pitch. She focused on his mouth as his lips tempted, beguiled.

This was getting too deep. She attempted to lighten things up. "How much time have you got?"

"Forever."

Sensations swamped her that she'd never experienced before. On impulse, she wanted to tell him everything, give him everything. That knowledge frazzled her. She laughed to cover her nervousness. This guy was a smooth talker and probably had used the same approach with many women.

"Some pick-up line."

He arched a dark eyebrow, his expression vulnerable. "I thought we were starting over."

And just like that, she fell under his spell.

"I work at a school. Not much of a paycheck to brag about, but I love kids." Was it her imagination, or had he winced? Good grief. She wasn't asking the guy to father her children.

He gestured around the room. "And this is where you go after work?"

"Mexican food is my weakness. Tammy and I come here every once in a while."

"My good fortune you chose today."

Really? "Your friend did come over first."

"Jared can't pass up a pretty face. He must be losing his touch. He left the prettiest one for me."

Pretty. Beautiful. A man used flattery when he wanted something. In her younger years, she'd wanted to be pretty, but her sister had crushed those fanciful thoughts. She'd constantly told Cassie she was unattractive. True, her skin was creamy smooth, but her blonde hair was too pale, her nose too round, her eyes were more green than blue. Vulnerable and shy, she'd been convinced that guys only wanted one thing.

"Hey. There's nothing wrong with these eyes." He tapped a finger at his temple. "And I like what I see."

What a flatterer. Yet, the way he said it, she wanted to believe him. Just because he had mouthwatering good looks didn't mean he had a motive. Besides, his mesmerizing eyes were already melting her inhibitions. She couldn't remember ever being so relaxed with a man.

"When you were a little boy, did you want to be a fireman?"

A shadow crossed his face so quickly she wondered if she could have imagined it.

"My dad was a fireman. Today we use the term firefighter. That's all I ever wanted to be. Guess it's in the blood."

"How about brothers or sisters?" she asked, then took a sip of her beer. Having the bottle in her hand grounded her.

"None" he said with a shake of his head. "How about you?"

"A sister." A jealous, overbearing sister who had dominated her youth and still attempted to run her life. Feeling her body tense, Cassie shook off her thoughts and picked at the label on her bottle.

Beep. Beep. Twang.

Mike jerked to attention. He glanced down at his belt.

Someone yelled from across the room. "Mike."

He banged the glass bottle on the wood table and scooted from the booth. "My ride's leaving." He stepped to her and bent close.

The breath caught in her lungs for fear he was going to kiss her. She couldn't move. Taking her hand, he brushed his lips over the skin at her wrist.

"Till we meet again, pretty lady."

And then he was gone.

Chapter 3

Mike gritted his teeth against the burn and pushed, straining his muscles to their limit. Nothing gained without hard work. Results were all that mattered. His father had drilled that lesson into him long ago.

He sucked air in his nostrils and blew out his mouth, pushing his body harder. Thirty years later and he still believed his father's words to be true. It had been just the two of them for so long.

That's what kept him awake. Thinking things that were unobtainable. Dreams that had no likelihood of ever becoming a reality. Still, knowing they were impossible didn't stop him from thinking about Cassie's smile or the way she tilted her head when she listened. Or the way her eyes assessed his every word while she tried to hide her own secrets. She kept her thoughts private, but he'd seen a glimpse of the woman underneath. Enough to kindle his interest.

"Man, I thought I'd be the first one here." Cooper dropped his towel and stood beside the weight bench.

Mike's chest heaved.

"You got a lot of weight on there. Why don't you have a spotter?" Cooper asked, his tone uneasy. Mike didn't need anyone hovering over him.

"What makes you think I need one?" he hissed through his teeth. "Maybe a scrawny little runt like you needs a spotter."

"Four hundred and fifty pounds? Hell, Hoss. Even the Jolly Green Giant—"

Gasping, Mike lifted the silver bar higher. Cooper grabbed the center and helped to place the weights in their holder.

"Christ, man. How long you been at this?"

Sweat ran into Mike's eye. He swiped at it with the back of his hand. He took a quick glance about the room, glad no one else had entered.

For two long weeks, Cassie had plagued him. No woman had ever stayed in his mind so long. She'd seeped in and circled his brain like a spellbinding mist. Sensual images of her had kept him awake through every long night since he'd met her. Long before the sun rose this morning, he'd finally given up. He'd headed to the weight room with the idea that pumping iron would tire him out, exhaust his body enough he'd have to sleep.

Right.

When he closed his eyes, Prussian gems stared back at him. Blonde hair, the shade no bottle could ever achieve. A perfectly rounded nose he ached to kiss. Pouting lips he wanted to taste. He willed the sandman to take him, to no avail. His mind revisited her curvaceous breasts and imagined long sexy legs wrapped around him while her cries of ecstasy reverberated in his ears.

"Mike!" Cooper's bellow jerked him to awareness.

"I'm not deaf." Mike raked a hand through his short hair, causing it to spike up.

"Well, when you put it like that … where did you go?" Cooper threw a towel on Mike's chest, then stepped over to the next bench and laid back.

"Where's *your* spotter?"

"Gee, Hoss. I'm benching a couple hundred pounds less than you."

Mike shrugged, wiping sweat from his face and shoulders. He'd grown used to the nickname. When he asked Cooper where he'd come up with it, Cooper told Mike about a western TV show on an old rerun station. One of the characters was big guy who reminded Cooper of Mike.

"You'll grow up one day, *pup*." Cooper was younger, lanky and always tried to keep up with the rest of the guys on the team. He stood over six feet, was twenty-two, and Mike still thought of the newest member as a young'un'. Reminded him of a puppy trying to run with the big dogs.

"You didn't answer," Cooper said. "You look like you've been in here all night."

Mike glanced at the kid who was only eight years younger than himself. "That's the advantage of having this equipment at the station. We can use it anytime."

"Better than having to pay a gym. I can use my hard-earned money for other things." Cooper lifted his bar from its holder and pumped out a set.

"Yeah? Like what?"

Coop finished counting before he answered. "Oh, luxuries like food, rent." Then he replaced the iron in its holder.

Mike had seen no evidence of the kid struggling. Maybe he should keep a closer eye out.

"You spend a lot of time in here."

He didn't reply. The kid didn't need to know everything, even if he thought he did. Maybe Mike did spend a lot of time pumping iron. He found it the only recourse to push through his pain, push through the memories. Convince himself that his life was good. Things were fine the way they were. He had a job, a home, good health. What else could he expect?

Cooper lifted the bar for a second set, pumped a few times and then placed the weights back with a clank.

"So, what kept you awake?"

Long blonde hair. Turquoise eyes. A body that promised him heaven.

"Must be a broad," Cooper said.

"People still use that word?" Mike shot the kid a glance.

"In my family, men ruled. Broad and babe were words used in everyday language." Coop's face colored. "I won't mention what else I heard in my house."

For the first time Mike wondered what kind of household the kid had grown up in. Cooper had showed up out of the blue, wanting to join the fire department. Never said much about his family or where he'd hailed from. Did he have a family? Did he have enough money to live on?

"Besides, you just changed the subject. Why are you keeping her to yourself? She a secret?"

"Who said there was a woman?" If Mike admitted Cassie filled most of his thoughts, the kid would never let up.

"Makes sense. Jared has a new girl every week. Laredo talks about *hit and run* sex."

"Hit and what?"

Cooper sat up. "You know. Hit it and run before she gets her hooks into you."

Christ. What has the kid been learning? At the firehouse, no less.

"First Jared and now Laredo. You shouldn't listen to those two. You're still at an impressionable age."

"I'm not a kid." Cooper's face flushed red. "What kid could work with you guys and handle the things I've seen?"

True. Every member of their team pulled their weight. A firefighter required a man's physique and a man's mind. Every emergency call, in all likelihood, presented life-threatening probabilities that made some men puke. Cooper had seen and carried out his duties with admirable responsibility. And he'd done so without whining.

"Sorry, Coop." Mike stood and rolled his shoulders. "You're the youngest—that makes you a kid."

"I was old enough for Uncle Sam at eighteen. Old enough to drink at twenty-one. At twenty-two, I'm still a freakin' kid at Station Eight."

"It's called life, pup." Mike snapped his towel around his neck. "I think I'll go take a nap."

***

Today had started out just like any other. This morning, Cassie woke up to the alarm, showered, dressed for school and prepared for the onslaught of twenty-three children. Actually, they were pretty good kids. She loved teaching third grade. Her students were old enough to have learned the basics and were ready to begin challenging their minds.

The problem was *her* mind. The blasted thing refused to focus on teaching. Her attention remained on a certain man in a navy-blue uniform. From his short, black hair all the way down his rocking, hot body to his fire boots. Six feet plus of male perfection filled every brain cell in her head.

When he'd slid into the booth beside her, her pulse had kicked into overdrive. She'd known not to get excited—more than likely he was just like every other guy. Out for a good time, score, then drop you like a hot potato. Although, Mike's actions had been more considerate. She'd sensed a moment of hesitancy, as if he were as uncertain of her as she was of him.

He'd smelled *so* good. Her nose had tingled at the aroma of musk and something she couldn't identify. And then he'd gone and melted her heart when he'd told her he'd like to get to know her. He'd even kissed her wrist, sending a shock jolting through her system. It was damn near impossible to teach children when she kept imagining Mike with his clothes off.

Would she see him again? He hadn't asked for her number. He didn't know her last name. She couldn't very well drag Tammy to the Mexican restaurant every night.

Fourteen days she'd dwelled on the firefighter. Sure, he had an awesome profession, but she always looked deeper to find the person underneath the layer they showed the world. Something told her Mike had a few layers he kept hidden.

Then there were her fantasies. Mike had a hot body. She couldn't help but be drawn by his magnetic blue eyes. His massive chest and bulging arms. His short black hair that she wanted to stroke and comb her fingers though. She wasn't one to jump into bed with a guy. She spent most of her time avoiding men. But this one ... Mike had looked at her as if he wanted to know her rather than a guy looking for a hook up. The vibes coming from him made her wonder. Would he be gentle? Would he care enough to see her for who she was and not just for sex? He made her want to let down her guard.

This has to stop.

She jerked open her carry-bag and stuffed papers inside. Grading student tests would take care of part of her Friday evening. That still left the weekend.

"Hey. Are you ready to leave?" Tammy's voice carried from the doorway.

"I'm packing up now." Cassie slung her jacket over an arm and grabbed her purse. "Ready."

"You want to hit El Puerto's tonight?" Tammy asked as they exited the building.

So, Tammy had been thinking the same thing.

"Are we taking your boys with us?" Cassie asked.

"Heavens, no. They're going to their dad's. It's his weekend." Tammy's ex-husband was a decent dad—he just didn't know how to stay faithful. She'd finally divorced him two years previously when the twins, David and Christopher, had been four. They seemed to be doing well and were now in first grade.

"I don't know, Tammy. I really don't want to stake out the place. We've already been there twice this week." Her stomach revolted at the idea of a regular dose of hot salsa. Not to mention the weight she would gain.

"I can't believe you let him get away without your number."

After reflection, neither could she. "We don't know anything about those guys."

"Well, they can't be serial killers if they're firemen." Tammy's grin was pretty persuasive.

Cassie slipped on her sun glasses and adjusted her purse strap over her shoulder. A gust of wind brushed her face as they headed out the side door. "I've got a ton of papers to grade."

"It's the weekend. That's just an excuse."

"I don't want to go." If she kept repeating that phrase, maybe at some point she would begin to believe it.

Tammy stopped in the middle of the sidewalk, blocking Cassie's progress. "Sure, you do."

Oh brother. She looked away, unable to meet her friend's gaze while she lied. "No, I don't. I'm tired."

Tammy glared at her as if she'd just grown horns. "Look. We're going and that's that." Then, without warning, she grabbed Cassie's arm and hauled her through the staff parking lot. She didn't stop until she reached her car.

"Oh, all right. We're just setting ourselves up, you know."

"No, I don't know. It's Friday night. They might show up. Or someone else might catch our eye. Either way, we'll have fun. I'm not staying home when I have a night free."

They both were free. Cassie had no desire to sit at her apartment alone, either. What would she do? Stare at four walls? Chances were her six-foot hunk would invade her thoughts, just as he had every other evening this week.

Besides, who was she kidding? If there was a possibility Mike would show up, she wanted to be there.

"Six?" she asked.

"Six is fine. That will give me plenty of time to primp." Tammy made a grand gesture of patting her hair. Wearing a satisfied look, she pushed the button on her key ring to unlock her doors. After the beep signaled them open, she turned back. "I'll pick you up."

"Okay. I'll be ready." Now that Cassie had finally agreed, her shoulders felt lighter. The more she thought about going out this evening, the more she looked forward to it. "Would a little black skirt and stilettos be too much?"

"That's my girl." Tammy laughed.

CHAPTER 4

Jared accompanied Mike this evening to Wendy's. The bar, not the hamburger joint. Wendy provided good food along with plenty of beer, a jukebox and a pool table. Place was always packed. The guys weren't too rowdy, but the only women that frequented Wendy's were liberal or biker gals. Not that he preferred any female this evening—he had one too many running loose in his head now.

Trying to forget the luscious blonde, Mike had been drinking more than normal. One chance meeting and the woman lodged in his mind like she'd been embedded there.

He shoved the door open and stepped into the cool night air. "I'll take your keys."

Mike glanced up and realized Jared was speaking to him. Mike stiffened his spine and braced his hands on his hips. "No need, Jared. I'm fine."

"You've had a bit to drink. As a matter of fact, I've never seen you put away alcohol like that. Something bothering you?"

"Nothing is bothering me." Except an itch he'd like a certain blonde to scratch. He may have overindulged, but he still had a clear head.

And he was smart enough not to drive.

He glanced over his shoulder at the brunette standing twenty feet away. "Don't you have someone waiting for you?"

A lecherous smile lit Pretty Boy's face. "Sure thing, Hoss. First, I'll take you home. She'll keep."

"Don't let me interrupt your night."

Jared chuckled. "She suggested I drive you before I had a chance to mention it. And she's willing to wait."

"She is, huh?" Mike took in her smiling face, thinking the woman pretty and considerate. Unusual traits for a woman picked up in a bar.

Mike shrugged and turned to walk off. He could find a ride. Jared stopped him.

"Something's got under your skin. If I had to guess, I'd say a female. Maybe one of those gals we met at the Mexican restaurant." He cocked his head and one corner of his mouth lifted in a taunting grin. "I left you alone with that blonde. I have to wonder, Mike. That babe was smokin'."

Resentment struck him. An unknown feeling, a lot like jealously. "Keep your blasted mind where it belongs," he barked in a sharp tone.

Jared didn't take offense. He smiled, as if Mike had just revealed something he shouldn't have.

"Come on." Jared clapped him on the back. "Let's get you home."

"I'm not drunk. And I'm not some child you have to take care of."

"No one said you were. You'd do the same thing if it were one of the guys."

Ass. Didn't matter that he was right.

Mike fitted his frame into his truck on the passenger side. "What makes you think you're fit to drive?"

Jared started the engine. "You know me. I spend most of my time sipping on one bottle and checking out the women." As he pulled into traffic, he continued, "I know. Sipping is for ladies. Not men."

"Hell. If it works ..." Mike never paid much attention other than Jared always had a bottle in his hand. Although, Mike had never seen Jared drunk. Always in control. Never made a scene. His pretty boy face had women flocking around him like chicken after feed. Even in the dark, Mike saw Jared's teeth flash in an invigorating grin.

Mike pushed a button on the dash and Hank Williams, Jr. blared in the cab. He turned the volume down to a reasonable level. When he was by himself, he usually had the windows down and the wind in his hair, so the music had to be cranked up just to be heard. Lately, the volume hadn't mattered. His attention had been elsewhere. Damn, if Cassie didn't have the most arresting eyes.

"Are you going to share?" Jared's question came from out of nowhere.

"Share what," Mike growled. He'd never shared a woman and damned if he would start now.

"Information, you dope. Not the woman you obviously have on your mind." Jared's chuckle filled the cab.

Hell. He'd jumped the gun. If the woman wasn't constantly in his head—

"She's what's got you preoccupied, isn't she? You haven't been yourself for days."

Mike had never let a female get under his skin. He sighed as if the weight of the world rested on his shoulders. He scrubbed a hand over his face. Confession time.

"Yeah. Cassie."

"Cassie? The blonde from the Mexican restaurant."

"Yep." Mike put his window down and rested his elbow in the open space. "Can't stop thinking about her."

"She is a looker. Nice jugs, too."

A flame of resentment shot through Mike, but he quickly shook it off. Any man with eyes would look. He turned in his seat. "How come you didn't make a play for her?"

Jared glanced out his window, put on the turn signal and pulled over in the next lane of traffic. "She wasn't interested. Now the redhead, she's another story."

"You seemed to hit it off with Tammy."

"She could give as good as she got." Jared checked his rearview mirror. "But we didn't hook up. She seems like a nice girl and I'm not into nice."

Nice—as in, doesn't sleep around.

"I know what you mean. Cassie is nice." Which didn't mean a damn, because he still wanted her. Redheads, brunettes, blondes, he'd worshipped them all at one time or another. Yet here he sat, like a lovesick fool pining about a woman he didn't know and couldn't have.

Forget her.

How?

"You drooled over her like a man looking at his last meal. So, cut the bullshit. It's obvious you want her."

Mike conjured an image of long blonde hair draped over his chest. The same vision that haunted his dreams. Whether he was awake or asleep, Cassie occupied his mind. Her feminine curves pressed between his muscled thighs. Lust pounded in his groin the way it did every time he thought of her. He forced her vision away before he drowned in his own desire.

Jared punched him on the shoulder. "You got it bad, man. Either find—shit! Look at that!"

Up ahead, a vehicle lie sprawled on its side in the middle of the road. Flames creeped from under the hood and a stream of smoke spiraled upward.

"Christ. Pull over."

"What the hell do you think I'm trying to do?" Jared snapped.

When the truck jerked to a stop, Mike grabbed the handle and flung open the door. "There's gear in the back."

Jared called dispatch while Mike ran to the tailgate. He flipped the latch and jerked open the tool chest where he kept spare equipment for emergencies. He grabbed a set of fireproof gloves and jogged to the burning SUV. "Move those people back!" Flames threatened to send them all to hell, but a woman's echoing screams chilled him to his bones.

"This is going to be a bitch with the truck on its side," Jared shouted.

The job would be risky enough even with a fire crew and proper equipment. They couldn't wait. Mike grabbed a hunk of metal and jerked. The vehicle wobbled, but held. Watching his footing, he climbed.

Jared crouched as close to the driver's window as he could, calling out to the woman. "We're with the fire department. Trucks and rescue will be here any second. We're going to get you out."

Mike crawled over the metal, now hot from the flames escaping beneath the hood. Thankfully, the window on the passenger's side was down. He stuck his head inside, finding a young female he guessed to be about nineteen.

"Hi. My name is Mike and I'm going to get you out. What's your name?"

"Sandy. Please help me." She shoved hair from her face, exposing terror filled eyes—but not panic. Victims who panicked were unpredictable, and most times, a dangerous lot. Fatalities occurred from freaked-out people who lost control. The tone of her voice exhibited strength. She might be anxious, but she'd asked for his help and her eyes begged him to rescue her.

"I will. Now listen carefully and do exactly what I say." He took in every factor, from the top of her head to the bits of broken glass sprinkled about the cab—on the seats, on the dash and across her lap. Thank Christ, she was the only occupant. Blood trickled down her forehead. From his position, and the way she moved, he suspected no broken bones, no sign of a fatal injury. "First. Are you all right? Can you tell if anything is broken?"

She glanced down and whimpered. "I don't think so. My hip and my arm hurts like hell. I slammed on my side. I hit my head, too. All I can see is smoke. Please. Get me out!"

"Take it easy." He crawled inside, as far as his size allowed, with most of his body braced on the car door. "Can you move?"

She stretched awkwardly at first. "Yes. But I can't reach the latch of my seatbelt."

Shit.

The clock was ticking and he didn't have time for mishaps. He jerked off his gloves and tugged on the seatbelt strap. It didn't budge.

"Try pulling on the steering wheel and lift your hips. Hold yourself up as much as you can."

She grabbed the wheel and seemed unable to move. Tears rolled down her cheeks as she started to cry.

"Come on, Sandy. I know you can do it." Sweat dripped from his nose. Heat from the flames crawled closer and he feared time was running out.

The click of the latch resounded like a gunshot to his impatient ears. He reached for her. "Take my hands. I'll pull you up."

A look of horror crossed her face. "What? How? I don't ..."

"Move it," Jared shouted, which meant *move your ass.*

"Take my hands. Now!"

When she extended her trembling arms, Mike stretched. "A little more."

Tears streamed down her face. "I'm ... trying."

Dammit. A little more.

"Mike!"

"Come on, Sandy! Reach!"

As soon as their fingers touched, he grasped her hand and firmed a good grip. He jerked her up and pulled her free. Then immediately slipped an arm around her back and lifted, practically throwing her in Jared's arms.

The fire trucks had arrived. Men scurried with hoses and rushed to the burning vehicle. Heat seared Mike's back. Blustery fire drew way too close and he knew time had run out. He jumped. Two firefighters caught his arms, breaking his fall.

"Hey, man. Are you okay? You got her out of there just in time."

Mike turned to find the SUV engulfed in flames. Trucks from Station Nine rolled in and more men scrambled, immediately hooking up hoses and spraying the burning vehicle.

"Better get that looked at." A firefighter pointed to Mike's side. He glanced down. Blood oozed through his torn shirt. In all the excitement, he hadn't noticed. Exhausted and drained, he gave a nod.

A medic met Mike and escorted him to the back of an ambulance. His shoulder stung. He figured he'd scraped it crawling up the underside. Now that she was out, the girl, Sandy, was crying hysterically and kept repeating, "He saved me. He saved me." At least she'd held herself together when it counted. He'd seen countless victims fall apart right after the crisis was over.

All in a day's work.

He tried to swallow and choked on a cough. *Shit.* He needed something to drink. A bottle of water was shoved into his hand.

***

"Well, this was a bust." Tammy dipped a nacho chip into a dish of sauce and popped it into her mouth.

"How can you eat any more? My God, we've been here for hours."

Why am I still here?

Cassie glanced around the packed dining room. Loud voices and laughter came from a group clinking glasses, obviously celebrating a special occasion. By the bar, a fat guy gave her a flirty nod for the hundredth time. She quickly turned, reminding herself not to look over there again.

"We got stood up," Tammy said.

"How poignant since we didn't have dates to begin with." Cassie rolled her eyes. "And I'm not coming back here again tomorrow or any other night. The men in here will think we're on the prowl."

"We are." Tammy grinned.

"You know what I mean. Who knows when our guys in uniform will show up again?" It was a long shot. A pathetic attempt, hoping the gorgeous men in navy blue would sweep in and carry them away.

"Jared did say they'd been in some sort of regional training that night. Like it only happened once or twice a year."

"In six months, we can try again," Cassie said flippantly.

"You're depressing," Tammy said with a glare. "We came here to have fun."

"We came here looking for men in uniform." Cassie gave an exaggerated sigh.

"You scared him off."

Where had that come from?

"I what?"

"You had to mention the boys. You're the one who scared him off."

"Good grief. I did not scare anyone off. I simply tried to remind you of the time. You had to pick the boys up from the Scout Hut. And if something as critical as children scared those guys, then good riddance."

"I had a lust brain-fart. Ignore what I said." Tammy took a gulp of her margarita.

Cassie laughed. "I know how much you love your boys. And I know you talk through the side of your mouth sometimes."

"I'm lonely, Cassie." Tammy's eyes grew sad and her expression bordered on pained. "I'm still young. My boys are the most important thing in my life. I just want a little romance to help me remember I'm a woman."

"Oh, honey. I'm sorry that SOB deserted you." Tammy's husband had been a hound dog. "You're pretty. You're funny. Any man would be glad to have you."

Tammy made a great show of glancing to the empty space beside her. "But there's none around."

God love her. Tammy was a good woman and Cassie's closest friend. Tammy would do anything for anyone. She was kind hearted, loved her boys and never let a day go by without smiling. That's why Cassie hated to see her so down.

"Don't be in such a hurry. You'll find the right guy."

"I'm not interested in the right guy at the moment. Just a living, breathing one. Someone to spice things up a bit. Even flirting is enough for me." Tammy gave a slight shrug while running her finger around the rim of her glass. "I don't need a relationship. I want some fun. Like our dreamboats in uniform."

"Mr. Sunglasses?"

"Man, he was hot. Too much for me to handle, but he was a lot of fun. It may have been a short sojourn, but flirting with him made my night."

Cassie waved the waitress over to their table. "Two more please."

"Who's going to drive us home?"

"The next one is coffee."

They ordered more food to absorb some of the alcohol they'd consumed and later, true to her word, Cassie ordered coffee.

Tammy stared down into her cup as she stirred in some sugar. "The crowd has come and gone. It's a wonder they didn't throw us out. People were standing, waiting for tables."

"We're paying for this table. We're eating their food. Drinking their alcohol."

"I think I've had enough." Tammy opened her purse and pulled out her wallet. "Let's go."

Cassie climbed from the booth with a numb butt. If she looked back, she'd probably find an imprint on the cushion. Why had she agreed to wait so long?

Hope.

Yes, she'd been as excited and eager as her friend. This was so out of her comfort zone. For nearly two years, she hadn't cared if she dated or not. Guys were too eager to take her out, but she'd turned them down, making one excuse or another. Now she felt like she couldn't wait to see Mike again. Sure, they'd flirted. But he seemed ... different. Jared embodied a playboy, anyone could see that. Maybe Mike wasn't the type to stick with one woman. But she was a big girl. Although, she did not believe in meaningless sex, in his case—

Right.

If he didn't stir something in her she would not be having these thoughts. The man was hot. Lethal. He'd had her hormones active from the moment he'd sat beside her.

Cassie shook off her thoughts and followed Tammy to the front doors. She glanced at her watch as soon as they stepped into the night. "We were in there for four hours. Do you believe that?"

"Pathetic, isn't it?" Tammy locked her arm around Cassie's as they trudged forward.

"These are the actions of desperate women," Cassie scoffed.

"Not desperate. Determined." Tammy whirled her hand about. "Optimistic."

"Rash." She shook her head. "I can't believe I sat in El Puerto's for a delusion."

"Want to come back again tomorrow night?" Tammy teased, but her voice also held a note of hope.

Cassie closed her eyes in exasperation. "I want to go home."

"Just kidding." Tammy pressed the button on her key remote and unlocked her car doors.

Cassie crawled in and leaned her head back against the headrest. "When I get home, I'm going to get involved in a steamy book. At least the heroine will get her man."

Tammy turned on her headlights and pulled into traffic. "What a way to spend a Friday night."

"I'd like to see Mike again, but sitting in a Mexican restaurant for hours is ludicrous. I've never done such a thing. Even in high school and college, boys chased me. Not the other way around." She crossed her arms over her ample chest. She had lingered like one of the tortilla chips in a basket, waiting for someone to pick her up. Unbelievable.

"So, now what? Forget him or go looking for him?"

"Why on earth would I do that?"

"Come on. That's the first *man*—and I use the term specifically—who has snagged your interest in—oh no. Someone's had an accident." Tammy's anxious voice jerked Cassie's attention.

Flashing lights lit up the dark. Police cars and fire trucks blocked the lanes of traffic. Firefighters hosed water on a burning car. The fear that normally attacked her when she saw a fire truck hovered, but a stronger fear pushed to the front of her mind.

Mike. Could he be fighting a fire?

"I wonder what happened," Cassie said, hoping no one had been hurt.

"Oh my God," Tammy shouted. "Look. There's a man on top of that SUV. It's on fire."

Cassie stared in horror as a man fell from the burning car. Her heart leaped into her throat. "Stop! Stop!"

"All right, already." Carefully, Tammy eased her car to the side of the highway and found a spot to park. "Cassie, what is it? Do you recognize him?"

Her gut clenched. She took a steadying breath and leaped out of the car. A compelling need drove her. She had to see. Had to know.

"Cassie, wait."

Smoke rolled into the sky. Gas and exhaust fumes filled the air. A large crowd had gathered and police kept the people back. Several trucks, a rescue squad, and firefighters were scattered around the scene. She threaded through the crowd, fear crushing her chest. Her heart pounding with each step as terror ate at her insides, stabbing her brain. Then she saw him.

Jared.

She almost didn't recognize him without a full set of teeth flashing in a smile. But then, why would anyone be smiling at a vehicle accident?

"There's Jared," she said, feeling Tammy's presence behind her.

"He's not in uniform. Or in a fireman's suit." Tammy called to him. The second time he heard her. Then Jared stepped back and Cassie saw—*Mike.*

Her legs nearly buckled.

His head hung, his shirt had blood on it and she couldn't see the rest of his body. *Oh my God.* Had he been in the wreck?

Jared motioned to a policeman to let them through. She hurried forward, closing the distance to the medic squad, fearing the worst and praying he was all right.

"Mike?"

His head jerked up. Glazed eyes bore into hers.

"Hey, girls," Jared said. "Just the medicine my ole buddy needs."

Cassie's eyes soaked up every inch of Mike. Black smudged his face and he looked a mess, but he was the most wonderful sight to her. When he smiled, she started breathing again. She wanted to touch him, be sure he was safe and unharmed.

"Are you okay?" she managed to get out. "What happened?"

"I'm fine."

He didn't sound fine.

"Jared and I saw the SUV on its side and stopped to help." His deep voice grated, rolling over her, making her already shaky nerves tremble.

"Mike, here, saved the driver," Jared explained.

Tammy gestured to the ambulance pulling away. "Is he okay?"

"She," Jared corrected. "Mike pulled her out."

With Cassie taking in every detail of Mike, Jared's words barely registered. When they did, she wanted to scream.

"Out of that?" She pointed to the car that now sizzled with steam. Her gaze locked on Mike. She swallowed a cry of horror, knowing only moments before he'd been in a burning death trap.

"I got her out before the flames engulfed the car."

She would not cry. But God, how she wanted to hold him. Run her fingers over his face, through his hair. Assure herself that he was all right. She clasped her hands together in an iron grip to keep from reaching for him.

Mike's gaze consumed her. To the point where her fear slowly dissipated. A budding heat grew in its place and threatened to develop into a full-blown fever. Damn. He made her hot. And he looked like something a tomcat dragged to your back door.

"Was that you we saw fall from the demolished car?" Tammy's worried voice jolted Cassie back to reality.

"He didn't fall," Jared said. "He jumped."

Cassie gaped at Jared. "Jumped?"

Mike didn't move.

"Would you mind taking him home? He's refusing to go to the hospital."

CHAPTER 5

Cassie bent to examine Mike's side. Burnt cloth stuck to his skin, making her want to cringe. The smell of smoke was so strong she covered her mouth with the back of her hand.

"Mike, you're hurt." She wanted to sob. He'd pulled a woman out of a burning car without a second thought. He acted like it was no big deal. She knew men who would take credit for anything just to get into a girl's pants. Not Mike. He pushed it aside. Said it was his job.

Cassie shivered. Knowing Mike was the man on top of the burning SUV ... she'd never been so terrified. What if ... what if ... The chilling thought was too horrible to contemplate. Cassie slowly breathed in. The last thing she needed was her dreadful imaginings paralyzing her.

"It's nothing," Mike said.

She glared at him in disbelief. "A burn is nothing to mess with. It can get infected."

"I'll take care of it." He brushed her concern aside.

"How?" she demanded. His casual demeanor pissed her off. A burn was serious. *Men*. Maybe he didn't want to be labeled a hero, but his refusal to go to a hospital was just stupid. Jared and

Tammy had disappeared, giving Cassie time to convince Mike. She wasn't having any luck.

"I'll go to the clinic in the morning." The tone of his voice revealed how much the ordeal had taken out of him. He seemed more weary than aggravated. Even though he clearly could take care of himself, he'd been injured. He needed care.

"You're unsteady on your feet. Jared said you've been drinking. I promised him I'd take care of you."

"I don't need a babysitter."

She had to handle this carefully and be sure not to injure his misplaced pride.

"But you do need a ride. And if you're not going to the hospital, someone needs to look at your side." As a teacher, she'd received some training from the nurse in the school clinic. Although, skinned knees and splinters from the playground were not the same thing as burns. Mike needed care. Jared said he'd been drinking. He shouldn't drive. She inhaled a deep breath and took the plunge. "You'll stay with me tonight. I'll hear no argument."

His eyes glimmered, sucking the breath out of her body. All sorts of thoughts flashed in their depths.

She could look at this as a perfect opportunity, to have him in her care, be able to touch him, spend time with him. But in all honesty, she just wanted to help him and she feared he would go home and not take care of his wound. At least not as well as he should.

After a long silence, he relented. "I'll probably regret this."

She wasn't sure if he meant for her to hear. She released her breath and did a happy dance in her head.

With a grunt, Mike stood and led her to a large, shiny-black truck. He handed her a set of keys, then slid into the passenger side. Most men treated their trucks like gold and this one looked brand new. He must really be hurting if he allowed a mere female to drive his big four-wheel-drive.

Without grumbling or giving her instructions on how to drive, he calmly buckled up and leaned back. He didn't even tell her to be careful with his baby. A glow of warmth filled her insides. This was one nice—big—truck. Not too big for her to handle. She glanced to Mike as she cranked the engine. Excitement flowed through her knowing he was hers to take care of until morning. Nerves danced in her stomach as she turned on the headlights and maneuvered onto the highway.

He fell asleep not long after. Tempted, she almost headed to the hospital. Since he'd refused to go earlier, she didn't want to take the chance he might get mad at her, so she decided to take him home and see how much damage had been done.

When she'd seen the fire trucks at the accident, she had immediately thought of her fire guy. A little conversation, a light flirtation, and she couldn't get the man out of her mind. No one else had ever lingered in her thoughts. She hadn't had a real boyfriend since high school—not since she'd found out boys were jerks.

Taking a quick peek, she glanced at the sleeping man beside her. A flood of emotion filled her chest. Did she dare go down this path? Should she be scared of him? Or should she embrace this sudden attraction? For even though Mike radiated sex appeal, and his eyes promised forbidden delights, he'd been reserved.

At the restaurant, he'd looked at her the way a man looks when he's interested. She thought he'd wanted to see her again. Then tonight, when she'd offered to take him home, he'd been reluctant. But he had agreed to go with her.

It wasn't long before she pulled into her apartment complex.

"Mike." She grazed his shoulder. "We're here."

His eyes fluttered open.

Oh God. Smoky, drowsy, bedroom eyes. Fire lit her lower belly. Desire settled between her legs.

"What?" The husky sound stroked her burn.

She was in over her head. "Come on. Let's get you inside."

He made it into the building on his own. She shuddered, thinking of how it would feel with the towering man leaning on her. Cozying up with her. She pushed those thoughts to the back of her mind. Right now, he needed care.

Conscious of his breath on the back of her neck, she inserted a key into the lock, then pushed the door open and flipped the light switch. "Here we are."

Mike stepped inside and did a slow turn, observing her living space. She watched him, holding her breath. The room seemed much smaller with his large frame in the middle of it. He glanced at her and held out both arms.

"Okay. I'm all yours." His raspy, sensual voice slithered up her spine.

For a second, she allowed his words to caress her needy mind. Wondering if he realized what they implied.

Jerking her mind back to his injury, she led him into the kitchen. "Sit down and let me tend to that."

"You don't have to bother."

"It's no bother. Since you won't go to the ER, I want to look at it." Her chest tightened with worry. He'd lost some blood—the wound probably needed stitches, but the burn was what worried her most. She pointed to a chair. "Sit."

When he obeyed, she turned and stepped to the sink.

Hot or cold. I guess cold since it's a burn.

She turned on the faucet and glanced over her shoulder—and froze. Hot smoldering eyes glimmered back at her. Hot with passion? Or hot with pain? It was difficult to distinguish which.

Cautiously, she placed the bowl of water and a rag on the table.

"Let's get you out of that shirt."

Mike slid her a lopsided grin as he unbuttoned his shirt. She inhaled softly. Black springing curls spread across his sculpted chest, with pecs and abs that would make any woman drool. She wiped her mouth with the back of her hand and realized how ridiculous the gesture looked. Still, she couldn't prevent her tongue from sliding across her dry lips.

Willing her hands to be steady, she dipped the cloth in the cool water and dabbed at the dark spot on his shirt, hoping the moisture would loosen the cloth bonded to his side. He winced.

Her gaze flew to his, but he stared at the floor. He'd been hurt more than he wanted her to know.

Biting her tongue, she soaked the cloth again and squeezed, allowing the water to dribble over his shirt. Once it was completely saturated, the fabric peeled away. She tried to hide her alarm. The marred flesh looked raw and open—the shirt had ripped the skin away. Mike had to be in pain. And he'd not made a sound.

Mentally, she went over the items in her medicine cabinet. Nothing for a burn. All she could think of was cold water. That's what was used on burns.

"Mike. Please let me take you to the hospital."

"I've had worse."

Being a firefighter, he should know. She carefully lifted one arm and eased the shirt from his shoulder. His bulky, muscled, breath-snatching shoulder.

Good Lord, the man was ripped.

His muscles bunched and tightened as he pulled one arm through the sleeve. She stepped around him and bit her lip, watching the ripples expand on his back as he twisted the second arm free.

The breath caught in her throat. Never had she seen more contours on a man. Damn, he was pure sex appeal. Her hands shook. *Get a grip.*

She wet the cloth again and dabbed around the wound. "You really had me scared. Maybe it's not as bad as I thought. But you should still see a doctor."

Mike had known he would eventually see revulsion on Cassie's face. And tonight, he had. At the accident. A shocking expression of horror and distress. The same expression he'd seen on his mother's face every time an alarm sounded. Every time the scanner went off. The way she'd stare at the door after his dad had closed it behind him on his way to a fire. The fear and panic she could not deal with. She'd left his father. But she'd also left him.

He ought to say the hell with it. A man has needs. And here was a woman for the taking. Every move she made screamed sexuality. She didn't do a very good job of hiding her emotions. Maybe she didn't want to hide her interest. Maybe she wanted him to make the first move.

Before he could change his mind, his hand lashed out capturing her wrist. He searched her eyes for long moments before his gaze lowered to full, plush lips. Her pulse leaped beneath his fingers, and he jerked his gaze back to hers. Heavy lids drooped, not enough to hide her desire. He rubbed his thumb in a circle over her flesh—teasing—caressing.

Slowly, he tugged her closer. The sweet smell he remembered from their first meeting invaded his senses. Her chest expanded when her leg brushed his inner thigh. Encouraged by her response, he drew her nearer still, until she was close enough for them to breathe each other in.

Suddenly he was starving. Hungry for a buxom blonde with green yearning eyes. She leaned forward and he sank his hands in her thick, silky strands. Mouths opened, tongues tangled, and he lost himself in the fervor of her kiss. She moaned, the sound going straight to his erection. He tightened his arms and shifted, forcing his knees between her thighs and settling her on his lap. She gripped his shoulders as he squeezed her bottom, expertly positioning her intimately against the bulge of his arousal.

Pain – an instant flash of fire to his side. "Arrrr ..."

"Oh my God. I've hurt you."

He'd never seen a woman move so fast. One minute, she was as deep in the throes of passion as he, and the next she'd jumped off his lap like her pants were on fire. Right when they both had been about to go up in flames.

"I'm sorry."

"Don't ... apologize," he gritted through his teeth. He flung back his head and took a few calming breaths, waiting for the nausea to clear.

"Oh, God. What do I do? I'm sorry ..."

"I said don't," he barked as he scowled at her. He just needed a minute.

Her concerned expression turned into one of disbelief. Now he'd gone and done it. She'd burst into tears any minute.

He was wrong.

Her eyes lit up like glistening diamonds. She placed her trim hands on her perfectly rounded hips and gave him a cold look that clearly indicated this woman was pissed.

"Don't what? Don't say I'm sorry you're hurt? Or don't make an idiot of myself by falling all over you?"

Was she kidding?

He'd like nothing more than to have her fall all over him. Around him. In him. Him in her. That wasn't going to happen if she got up on her high horse.

Mike believed in quick action. As a firefighter, his life depended on it. He needed to defuse this temperamental situation fast. He grabbed her again, jerked her onto his lap, being mindful of his side, and firmly planted his mouth on hers. Her struggles didn't last long. His thumb added just the right amount of pressure on the bone in front of her ear, making her mouth open, and he took full advantage.

He traced the shape of her lips, tasted her sweetness, and slowly slid one hand over her ribs, caressing, nudging the underside of her plush breast. Her fingers roamed through his hair and danced across the back of his neck, drawing him in deeper. He could kiss her forever.

Suddenly she stiffened, sending his instincts on full alert. He feared opening his eyes, but did so anyway. She leaned back and sucked in a deep breath. When her eyes opened, her blue-green orbs glowed with passion. With a gentle touch, she trailed a fingertip down his right cheek.

"I don't want to hurt you again." Before he could protest, she placed the tip of her finger to his lips. "Let's clean you up. And then we can get more comfortable."

More comfortable?

He wondered if they had the same idea of *comfortable*. She'd already felt the bulge in his jeans.

She climbed from his lap and he reluctantly let her go. He watched as she turned back to the pan of water while uttering words of comfort, her voice low and her eyes on her task. He had to admire her control. She might try to act as if nothing had happened, but her trembling hands suggested she had been shaken. Hell, his head was still reeling.

Hot. Passionate. How could she go from instant arousal to poised and unruffled? He couldn't turn need off like a damn light switch. And she couldn't hide her desire.

"Will you tell me what happened?" Her voice a tad shaky, she went back to the task at hand. "I saw you on top of that SUV ... I thought you fell. Jared said you jumped."

Talking about something other than that kiss might be a good idea. He remembered her reaction at the crash. Clearly, she'd been scared.

"I was just doing my job."

"You weren't on duty. Jared said you'd been to a bar." Her tone was not accusing. Only concerned.

"Yeah. We had a few drinks."

As if she needed to keep her hands busy, she twisted the cloth, water dribbling into the pan. "Even though you weren't on call, you risked your life to save a woman."

He loved being a firefighter, but he didn't like being put in the role of hero. He hiked a brow and watched her from beneath his lowered lids, gauging her reaction.

"It's what I do."

"You do it well." She smiled and pressed the cool cloth to his feverish skin.

The wailing sirens, the flash of red fire trucks, were exciting to a kid. Even now the roar of the engine, the blast of the horn, shot adrenaline through his blood stream. Not only the excitement, but the thrill of saving someone or helping people gave him a satisfaction beyond anything else. Nothing compared to the high.

"When I saw you on top of that car, I didn't know it was you at first. Then when I realized ..."

Expecting to find aversion or anxiety, he swallowed his disappointment and pushed her arm away. "That's enough."

"You do this every day," she whispered.

"I told you. It's my job."

"It's more than a job to you, isn't it?" The catch in her voice caused him to glance up. Was she going to talk his profession to death? This was just what he'd been afraid of. He needed to set things straight.

"It's my life," he said holding her gaze. The strength of his conviction resounding in his voice. "It will never change. That's what I do and what I want to do. What I'll always do."

"You're dedicated," she said with a smile. Her pleased expression threw him for a loop. "You save people, like that woman tonight."

Was that approval he heard? Cassie confused his brain. Her sweet face lit up like ...

Ah hell.

He didn't want to be a symbol. He wanted between her thighs, but not if she gave herself as some damn hero devotee.

He scowled. "I'm not a hero. I'm just a man."

"Oh, really?" She gave him a smirking grin. "I hadn't noticed."

"You have a smart mouth on you." He'd like to taste it again. And every inch of her.

"And you look like the devil incarnate."

He frowned. Guess he did look pretty rough. Although that hadn't stopped her a moment ago.

She pressed the cool cloth to his side. Earlier, he hadn't even realized he'd been burned. Hurt like a bitch, now. She was right. He should get it checked in the morning.

"This cut could probably use a few stitches." Her gentle hands pressed a bandage to his side and lightly applied tape. Soft hands. He imagined them caressing the rest of him. Her fingers crawling across his chest. Her naked body lying atop his.

Their legs intertwined. He already had a semi-erection, now it stiffened to an iron rod. He glanced at her to see if she noticed.

Her eyes focused on the bandage, the tip of her tongue slipped between her teeth. Boiling heat pierced his abdomen and spread up his neck. His hands flexed. He could grab her and make his imaginings real.

"There. All done." She stood staring at him.

Now what? Hadn't she said something about spending the night? Desire fired in his belly. Slowly, he pulled her onto his lap, giving her plenty of time to resist.

She didn't.

Although, she did brace her arms on his shoulders, keeping her body back several inches to keep from brushing his wound.

"You're going to hurt yourself."

"I'll switch you to my good side." His hands eased up to gently rub the tight cords in her back. "You're tense."

"You've had a rough night and you say *I'm* tense."

"There's nothing wrong with my legs or my arms. Is this the more comfortable part?"

Her laugh poured over him like warm honey. He wanted to kiss her senseless.

"I had something else in mind."

"Like what?" One hand massaged her back while his other hand teased its way under her shirt to her abdomen. Her skin reminded him of silk. She slid her hands behind his neck and played with his hair. Nerves he didn't know he had tingled. He needed to kiss her again.

She rested her forehead against his. "Maybe you should shower while I scrounge up something for you to eat."

Hell. He probably had grime on his face and stunk like charred metal. He basked in the scent of her hair, the warmth on his brow, her breath skimming his chest. Unable to stop himself, he brushed his knuckles down the slender column of her neck.

"As wonderful as this feels, what do you say we put this on hold. For a little while." With the gentlest of touches, she gave him a quick peck on his brow.

As long as you pick up where you left off.

When she stood, he felt cold all over.

"I can offer you a shower, but I'm afraid I don't have any clothes for you. I have a washer, so if you can make do with something, I can have your things clean by morning."

He didn't give a rip about his clothes. His brain latched on to staying with her till morning.

"You'll let me spend the night?" he asked, not hiding the hopeful smile that curved his lips.

"I'm not about to let you go." A teasing glint entered her eyes. "We'll talk about where you sleep later."

Damn. The night wasn't over yet. And if he didn't have any clothes, the evening promised to get very interesting.

CHAPTER 6

"Make yourself at home," Cassie said and closed the spare bedroom door behind her. She leaned against its wooden surface, the hungry look in Mike's eyes imprinted in her mind. It took all of her strength not to march right back in there and take care of that bulge in the front of his jeans. Mike's hot looks and easygoing manner made a woman want to tear off her clothes.

She shoved away from the wall and released a heavy breath. Her apartment had two king size bedrooms, each with a private shower, which was what had sold her on this place. She kept it stocked with soap and shampoo, all the necessities for when her mom visited. She didn't need to think about Mike and all his naked muscles in that shower.

Was she being stupid? She wanted him. He didn't hide the fact that he wanted her. She still couldn't believe her thoughts or the way her body had responded. And that kiss. She hadn't wanted to stop. Usually, she pushed men away. So why was she behaving so irrationally with Mike?

She swiped her hair from her face and went back to the kitchen to clean up. She'd give him a few minutes and then gather his clothes.

The smell of smoke lingered in the kitchen. She lifted Mike's soiled shirt and took it to the laundry room, thinking it belonged in the trash. After tidying up, she searched the refrigerator for an idea of what to fix him to eat. Omelets or cheese and crackers with a sausage roll. He probably wouldn't want anything much heavier.

His behavior disturbed her. Firefighters were fit and most were conscientious. Jared fit the roll of playboy. Mike did not, even though he'd flirted and he was hot enough to attract any woman. Given the vibe earlier, he could have taken her right in this kitchen. He was a prime example of a hot-blooded male, yet he'd been respectful and controlled his passion, even when she'd pushed him while squirming in his lap. Their attraction was mutual and she'd been as hungry as he. She hadn't denied him—much. She'd been tempted almost beyond endurance, but his pain-filled groan had stopped her cold.

What had she been thinking? She didn't do things like that—throw herself at a man. Did she want Mike to think her easy?

She gathered food from the refrigerator and placed the items on the counter. She pulled a large knife from the wooden holder and cut into the sausage roll with vigor. Mike should be undressed by now. He would be getting into the shower. Should she remind him not to get the bandage wet? Maybe he needed more towels. He was a big man, after all.

Once the smoke was gone, what would he smell like? She tried to recapture his scent from the Mexican restaurant. A tantalizing aroma, all male. Spicy and man. She slammed the knife down in frustration, snatched a paper-towel and wiped her hands, then abandoned the food and charged down the hall to the towel closet. She grabbed two more towels, shut the door and hurried to the spare room. Easing the door open, she glanced about and heard the shower running. Her gaze landed on the partially open door to the bathroom.

Her pulse raced. Did she dare take a peek? She had extra towels for him. If he caught her ... She had an excuse—that she came to pick up his dirty clothes.

She crept closer to the bathroom door, a matter of inches separated it from the closure. How in the world would she explain if she got caught spying on him in his shower? The idea of being noticed had her swallowing with apprehension. Then she spotted a hazy outline of his reflection in the bathroom mirror and the crazy notion of joining him pricked her brain.

Damn. This wasn't like her.

Mike was the type of guy who'd put lustful thoughts in any girl's head. Fighting her inner demons, she leaned her head against the doorjamb. When the water stopped, she jerked back. She could not get caught lurking. She dropped the towels on the bed, grabbed his belongings and fled.

She'd missed her chance.

After tossing his clothes into the wash, she headed back to the kitchen. The food prepared, she set two plates and silverware on the table. The aroma of fresh coffee filtered through the room. Suddenly, the back of her neck tingled, alerting her to his presence.

"I decided on omelets. There's also a plate of sliced cheese and sausage," she said as she turned. Whatever else she'd been about to say died in her throat.

Braced on one arm, Mike leaned against the doorjamb—looking powerfully male. Wet, dark hair spiked about his head as if he'd rubbed it vigorously to get it dry. Inky lashes curved above his glazed blue eyes and his sculpted cheeks crinkled in a wolfish grin. Her gaze lowered and she gasped. Black, wisps of hair dusted his tanned skin, streaming a trail over perfectly shaped abs, down his sculpted belly to where his hips formed that jaw-dropping angle.

She licked her dry lips and wondered if she would ever breathe normally again.

The towel covered a pair of sturdy thighs, well-shaped knees and calves, again with dark curling hair and ... how could a man have nice looking feet?

"You were saying?" His smooth voice held a trace of mirth.

Her mouth worked, but she couldn't get words past her lips. In her mind, she saw him step forward, tear off the offending wrap, and catch her as she flew into his naked arms.

She couldn't move.

She simply drank in his natural sexuality. A throbbing began in her center and threatened to wet her panties. She stood agog as he shoved away from the wood and slowly came toward her.

"Omelets?" He stepped around her and pulled out a chair. "Mmm. Smells delicious."

You're delicious.

Forcing her drooling tongue back in her mouth, she lifted two mugs from the counter and joined him. After she slid onto her chair, she raised her face to his—the rascal had a shit-eating grin plastered on his lips.

He knew exactly how his state of dress—or undress—affected her. If he wanted to tease her, let him. It might be fun to see what he might do with only a towel to cover his manly parts.

"Help yourself," she said in a throaty voice meant to entice.

Mike's gut jerked. He'd like to *help himself*. Cassie had no idea how much control it took for him not to act on her words. If she knew how he longed to throw her on this table and bury himself in her heat, she wouldn't be openly ogling him. He wondered if she'd follow through if he took her up on her unspoken invitation. Wearing only a towel, he expected her probing gaze to ignite the thing in flames. He already burned.

Although he was enjoying her scrutiny, he held back. Aching with need, his balls would probably turn blue in sheer disbelief that he'd denied them when he should have seized her and skipped the meal. He lowered himself to the chair. *Damn.* With his size, the towel was barely long enough to shield his bare cheeks against the smooth wood.

It might be brazen, but what other choice did he have? When he'd finished his shower, he'd known Cassie had been in the bedroom. If the towels on the bed and the disappearance of his clothes weren't enough to convince him, her scent would erase any doubt. The bathroom door had been partially open. Had she lingered? Had she given in to her desires and looked? What healthy woman wouldn't?

That thought tightened his balls. Cassie sneaking into his room, maybe even his shower. The bath towel on his lap lifted. At least with the table between them, she couldn't see.

And if she did? Hell. She looked ready to burst into flames as it was. He smiled. Yeah. This should definitely be one interesting night.

"I thought you might be hungry. If you'd like something else, just let me know." As soon as the words left her mouth, her face flushed. She quickly averted her eyes, realizing her statement had sounded suggestive.

Oh, he wanted something else, all right. And she knew what it was. He scarfed down a bit of food. He'd need his strength. Meeting her gaze, he lifted his mouth in a grin.

"I know it's late, but I thought you might want the caffeine," she said.

"You thought right," he said and gave her one of his sensual grins. Her hand shook. Good. Anticipation was the best part.

He took a gulp of coffee. "It tastes good." He stared at her lips while he ran his tongue over his. "Not as good as you."

Her eyes glazed over. He glanced down to her breasts and right on cue, her nipples puckered. The towel leaped again. His dick had become a yoyo.

And then, we can get more comfortable.

"How's your side?" Her scrutiny made him hot, but her velvety voice fueled his yearning.

"It'll do." He managed to keep his hands to himself and finish the rest of his food. He settled back in the chair and rubbed his stomach, loving the way her eyes were fixed on his chest. "Is now the *comfortable* part?"

"What?"

He held in a chuckle at her surprised, yet innocent, expression. She'd forgotten.

"You said earlier we could get more comfortable."

The vein in her neck pulsed and her throat worked as she swallowed. "I'd say you are pretty darn comfortable in nothing but a towel."

A thrill of satisfaction settled in his chest. Cassie was antsy. Fidgety. He liked that.

"Since you brought that up, maybe you have something a little larger." With both hands, he angled his thumbs toward the lower part of his body.

"Oh ..." She quickly pushed out of her chair. "Of, of course."

When she disappeared, he chuckled. Clasping his temporary garment, he stepped to the living room and flopped on the couch. Carefully, he arranged the towel so his family jewels wouldn't hang out.

He took the time to study Cassie's living room. Cozy. Just what he would imagine her place to be. Soft colors on the walls, with a matching sofa and chair in blue. Noticing the pillows scattered about, he wondered if she often fell asleep on the couch at night while watching TV. An assortment of shelves lined one wall holding little figurines and whatnots. He guessed women liked collecting those sorts of things. It had been just him and his dad, growing up. They hadn't had much use for knickknacks.

A row of pictures lined the top shelf. He supposed they were of her family. One of an older couple, most likely her parents. One of her, evidently her graduation photo. One of her and Tammy. And one of her and another girl, making him wonder if she had a sister.

Cassie sprinted through the living room and didn't see him. She came to a sudden stop, then retreated two steps back, jerking her head in his direction. She tossed a blanket at him.

"Thanks." He patted the space beside him.

"I should get you a new bandage since you've gotten that one wet." Her arms stiff at her sides, less poised, as if she wasn't sure what to do.

"Okay." It wasn't that bad, but if she wanted to tend to it that suited him fine.

Blinking, she lowered her gaze and then it darted back, as if she needed to take another look before she could move. "Oh," she said distractedly, then dashed down the hall.

He smiled at her reaction. All nerves and jittery. The woman wanted him. He'd have to be dead not to notice.

She came back with supplies and sat down on the low table directly in front of the couch. He stared at her flushed cheeks as she cut a square of gauze. When she leaned forward, her knees slid between his. He silently thanked the blanket for hiding his immediate reaction.

His chest squeezed from the touch of her fingers smoothing over his skin. He watched her in silence, admiring her slanted eyes, her slightly curved nose, her full, plush lips, wanting to devour them. A fragrance between sweet and sinful drifted, acute enough to draw him, entice him.

"There. Butterfly strips. It's better than nothing if you don't want to go get stitches."

She gathered the items and padded back down the hall, he appreciated her tight buns in her washed-out jeans. When she came back, she stood in the middle of the room as if she was afraid to come near him.

"Well, uh, it's late." She bit her bottom lip, sending another surge to his groin.

"Come here," he said in a coaxing voice, barely above a whisper. He held out a hand, palm up. She slowly closed the distance and placed her fingers in his. He didn't want to rush her, so he gave a slight tug and waited. After a moment's hesitation, she slumped on the couch next to him. He placed his arm around her, and pulled her close. Holding her felt so right.

He didn't make another move. Giving her time to adjust, he wanted to assure her he was not going to pounce, even though she smelled good enough to eat.

After a few moments, she gingerly placed her hand on his chest, above the bandage. Her fingers soft against his skin, electrifying the desire in his body. Her sweet scent enveloped him. He rested his head on top of hers and savored the feeling as she snuggled into him.

Now *this* was *comfortable*.

Except her hand was damn hot.

It felt like a branding iron pressed into his skin. A slight sigh fell from her lips as she curled into his side. He inhaled a deep breath and felt his shoulders unwind. He couldn't remember ever feeling so peaceful.

He nuzzled her temple.

She lifted her face as if seeking his kiss. She had the most expressive eyes and he fell into their depths. Her hot breaths were shallow—still they scorched his skin. He cupped her cheek, brushing her lips once, twice, then he slanted his mouth over hers. His tongue swept past the seam of her lips and she welcomed him, seeming eager for his invasion. She tasted like sugar and warmth and everything he desired. He kissed her gently at first. Then thoroughly. With long strokes, he explored her mouth. The more he stroked, the more he wanted. She tasted divine. She gripped the back of his neck and he turned up the heat.

Sliding his fingers in her hair, he moaned and kissed her until neither one of them could breathe. He pulled back long enough to stare into her eyes. Pools of jade sparkled back at him, longing, craving. He kissed her again. Tenderly, with teasing strokes, building her passion. He couldn't get enough of her mouth. She tasted so damn good, better than anything he'd experienced in a long time. Maybe never.

With a will of their own, his hands roamed over her body and it wasn't enough. He could spend hours kissing her, but he wanted more. He wanted to peel every layer of clothing and then run his tongue over her delectable skin.

Again, he paused, locking his gaze with hers. "You have beautiful eyes."

Need flashed in her gorgeous green orbs, showing him what he so desperately wanted to see. Her hands slid up his chest, her sensual touch making his entire body come alive. He wanted to rip off her clothes, take her over and over until they both succumbed to exhaustion. Fear of pushing her too fast brought him back from the brink of abandoning his control.

He drew in a ragged breath and willed his body to slow. Finding the hem of her shirt, he slid one hand under the fabric. Warm, soft flesh greeted his searching fingers. She ran her tongue over her bottom lip, flaming the very desire he tried to restrain. Suddenly, he needed her as naked as he.

Impulsively, he pushed her top up and over her shoulders. His eyes feasted on the creamy flesh above her lacy covering and her hair trickling over her shoulder to lie against the curve of one full breast. He focused on her eyes and the raw desire he saw in them. With the tip of his finger, he traced her collar bone, then slid to the swell of her breasts. Turquoise darkened to a deeper teal and she held her breath, as if waiting to see what he might do next. He flicked the clasp of her bra, peeled the flimsy thing off and tossed it over his shoulder. The fullness of her breasts spilled onto her chest.

"Exquisite," he whispered, his eyes drinking their fill.

Leaning down, he swiped his tongue over one nipple, then smiled when it budded up tight. The rate of her breathing increased. She buried her hands into his hair, moving her body against him, turning him on beyond belief.

He palmed the twin globes and watched her eyes roll back. The sound of her sigh had him bending forward, burying his face in her perfect cleavage. He slid his hands over her bare ribs, then cupped the undersides of her breasts, holding their weight, adoring the precious treasure. She gripped his hair, inciting him. He kneaded and squeezed, pinching her nipples and rolling the tight buds between his thumb and forefinger. God, she was beautiful.

He took one beaded nipple into his mouth, laving it with his tongue. She tasted so good. She groaned, the sound prompting him to suck harder.

She offered herself up to him, moaning, heaving, her body responding faster than his brain. He moved to her other breast, ravishing it as he had its twin. Her fingers tightened in his hair and she gripped with a vengeance, which only heightened his arousal.

Her movements grew more frenzied and the desire to kiss her became unbearable. He captured her lips, anchoring her mouth beneath him in a kiss meant to possess.

He thrust his tongue into her mouth again and again, showing her what he wanted to do to her body. The kiss devoured as he eased her back onto the cushions, his elbows bracketed her in, keeping most of his weight off her.

Cassie was the sweetest thing he'd ever tasted. Her tongue dueled with his while her fingers played with his hair, her moans causing him to shudder. She gripped his head, tugging him forward. Unable to hold back, his hips collided with hers, his erection burrowing into her stomach. She clung to him like he was the most important thing in her world.

Moving his hand over her belly and lower, he cupped her. Her instant reaction made him harden to steel. She pushed her lower body against him, her contented *hmmm* growing deeper as she rocked, sending his blood thrumming through his veins. They'd crossed some line. All he could think of was more. They both needed more.

His fingers moved to the band of her jeans and dipped inside, her smooth skin summoning him to explore further. The confining material needed to come off.

He could barely catch his breath long enough to say what he wanted.

"I swore if I was lucky enough to have you, I would make love to you properly and savor you for hours. But I ..."

The brilliance in her eyes made him pause. His need so fierce, he thought he might explode.

"Say yes," he whispered. "Please, say yes."

CHAPTER 7

"Yes, Mike. Yes."

A shudder went through him. He gave Cassie a scorching kiss, then lifted her. "Help me get these off."

He quickly unfastened her jeans and dragged them down the longest legs he'd ever seen. Cassie was beyond beautiful. He savored the view splayed out before him like an incredible feast, his erection hardened to steel. First with his eyes, then with his touch, he appreciated her smooth skin. Taking his time, he slid his hand upward, over her calf and behind her knee. When he grazed the inside of her thigh, her gasp rang like music in his ears. He glanced up to see her teeth sinking into the flesh of her bottom lip, rousing his desire. He nearly ripped her panties in his haste to remove them. The blanket and towel long forgotten, he tossed her scrap of lace to the mounting heap on the floor.

His throat went dry at her magnificence. He had no words. The woman was beautiful beyond imagination.

He craved the feel of skin against skin. Mindlessly, he moved without thinking, pressing his chest to hers, hungry for her touch—he hissed at the stabbing pain in his side.

"Mike, your burn."

"Forget the burn. I'm fine." It hurt like a mother, but nothing would dissuade him from his goal.

With gentle pressure, he massaged her stomach, his fingers drifting lower on her belly. Reaching, mapping a path to promised delights.

She rolled her hips. A signal that she wanted more.

With slow precision, he smoothed one hand over her hip and downward, slipping his fingers behind her knee. He lifted one trim leg and kissed the inside of her silken thigh. She trembled. He took a peek at her face and found her passionate gaze locked on his. The look in her eyes begged him to continue and he was damn sure going to do just that.

He licked his lips and relished her hunger. Without words, he elevated the opposite leg, placing open-mouth kisses on her exquisite flesh. He hadn't touched anyone like this in a long time. The sound of her gasps drove him, fueled his desire. He moved slowly, nibbling higher and higher, nuzzling her silky flesh.

The pliable patch of hair lured him. He blew a gentle breath over her curls, then flicked his fingers over her. She was wet, and ready. Slowly, he slipped a finger into her slick folds. Her whimper of delight fired his burning need. Blood roared in his ears. He wanted her. Now.

He delved and tasted, thoroughly enjoying the sensation of burrowing into her softness. She was so wet. So needy. So delicious. He used his tongue to drive her wild, working her pebble until she writhed. He massaged her bud while she flung her head from side to side, little moans escaping her lips.

He knew exactly what she needed and he took great satisfaction in giving it to her. He dipped one finger inside her exquisite sheath as he feasted. Her body tightened and her legs trembled. He needed to see her face.

He watched her—her emotions bare. Unable to lie still, she twisted and jerked, still he plunged, loving her reaction. Every little moan ratched his lust up a notch.

Suddenly, her eyes clouded over, her body tightened and a half groan, half scream escaped her throat. He'd never enjoyed watching a woman more than this moment. Immense pleasure filled his chest as he watched her spiral out of control.

God, she was beautiful. Wild and hot and unbelievable. And he was iron hard.

As she floated back to earth, the corners of her mouth lifted in a satisfied smile. Her eyes fluttered open.

"You're beautiful."

"Mike ... please." She spoke in a just loved, satisfied voice.

Taking his time, he kissed his way up her body, nuzzling her curves, gliding over every inch of her skin until he found the sensitive flesh behind her ear.

"What baby?" he whispered. "Please what?"

"I need you."

He wanted to make love to her, give her every pleasure imaginable, everything her heart desired. He'd been hanging on by a thread and she'd just said she needed him.

"Mike," she uttered, barely above a whisper.

He lowered his head and took one nipple into his mouth. His tongue laved and swirled while his hands caressed, needing to touch her body, arousing her back to life.

"Oh, God. You're teasing me," she whimpered. He loved the little sounds she made.

"You want this? You're sure?" he grunted between his teeth. If she denied him now, she'd kill him.

"There's no way you can stop now. Make love to me."

He wasted no time snatching his wallet from the coffee table. He tore the packet open with his teeth and quickly sheathed himself. He glanced up. Cassie's eyes were fixed on his erection. He was a big man and this part of him was no exception. When she ran her tongue over her lips, savage need raced down his spine.

He shifted his body and positioned himself between her legs. "Don't think," he rasped out. "Kiss me."

Bracing most of his weight on his elbows, he licked her lips and when she opened, he took her mouth passionately. A rising tide of desire swept him into its current. She tangled her tongue with his while her nails raked his back, her appetite enflaming him, causing him to groan and press her deeper into the couch.

Her fingers gripped his buttocks. Desire pounded his temples. Unable to hold back any longer, he tilted her upward and buried himself in her welcoming heat.

He lost all sense of coherent thought.

Waves of liquid fire licked through his body, setting every nerve on edge, unlike anything he'd ever known and could not describe. Sensation rocked him to his core.

Another moan fed his desire, urging him to move. He pulled out as far as he dared and slowly, maddeningly, thrust back in with just enough force to let her feel all of him. The friction fired his blood. The muscles in his arms bunched as he held himself above her. She wrapped her legs around his, her back arching. With long slick strokes, he drove in and out, sliding deep. He never expected this to feel so erotic. So fucking good.

Their kiss intense, he growled into her mouth with rising hunger, then broke free. Passion propelling him, he increased the tempo.

"Come, baby," he gasped, his breathing ragged. "Come for me."

"Oh, God. Yes!" she shrieked, her eyes tightly closed. Her nails dug into his back as she rocked with him, riding the waves of passion.

Overwhelming pleasure shot through him fast and hot. He bit back a yell as her spasms gripped him, sending him over the edge. He threw his head back as burning lava poured through his veins, his chest heaving and his lungs panting at his throbbing release.

Unable to hold himself up any longer, he dropped his frame, his body sinking into a puddle of softness, his mind swimming in a pool of ecstasy.

A little shocked at his intense climax, he couldn't move. His chest heaved as he listened to the sound of their harsh breathing. Moments passed before he realized he must be crushing her, yet when he moved, she grasped his neck.

"I'm too heavy for you."

"No."

He chuckled. "Yes I am. And I need to move to my good side." Shifting his weight, he eased himself out. Her gasp nearly had him shoving back in. He rolled to her side.

Damn couch wasn't big enough.

His bandage was hanging half off.

"Mike. Your burn."

"What burn?" he said drawing Cassie next to his heart.

"You know what burn. Your side must be aching."

"Hard to tell. My whole body is throbbing." With the most remarkable sensation he'd ever experienced. When she made to move, he tightened his arms, then pressed his lips to her forehead. "I'm good."

He relished a few moments of bliss and realized he needed to get up. He shifted again and managed to stand, smiling at her moan of disappointment. He slipped to the bathroom, then hurried back, not wanting to be away from her a moment more than necessary. Lifting her up, he held her exquisite body against his and carried her down the hall.

"Umm." She rubbed her cheek in the grove of his neck.

"Yes, I know. Mmm." He padded into her room and placed her on the bed.

With her arms locked around his neck, she tugged him to her. He stretched out beside her and brought the comforter over them, nestling into a cocoon of warmth. She curled her body into his as if they were one. He thought of the pleasure they'd just shared, and now a tender moment of sweetness he'd never felt before. She'd kindled his emotions, triggering his protective instincts. Her passion surprised him, roused him to unimaginable heights. He'd never been a possessive man, but he suddenly found he wanted Cassie to be his. She felt good. This felt good.

She had the face of an angel and a body made for sin. He'd been completely captivated and already he wanted her again. He massaged her thigh with one hand while the fingers of the other stroked lazily over the smooth skin of her shoulder, wondering what the morning would bring.

Before long, he realized she'd drifted off. He never liked his dates to sleep over and he rarely spent the night with them. Yet, here he was all snug in Cassie's bed, with no intention of leaving. He didn't want to be anywhere but exactly where he was.

A calming peace settled over him. Cassie had given him a serenity he hadn't known he needed or wanted. This sensual woman belonged here, in his arms.

At least, for now.

***

The sun rose finding Mike already out of bed. He braced a hip against the kitchen counter and wondered what the hell had come over him. People usually saw sense in the light of day. Yet after two cups of strong coffee, the elation he felt had not weakened. They'd shared great sex. And when she'd nestled right up against him in bed, he'd been damn content.

He could get used to this.

Hell. Who was he kidding? It was one night of sex. Hopefully a lot more. But not a lifetime. What woman would stay for the long haul? He shook his head in disgust. His mother sure hadn't.

He was a firefighter. That would never change. Some guys lived for the thrill. With him, the job held more meaning. Saving lives. Giving help to those who needed assistance. Sometimes the job offered more grief than reward. Finding horror in a burning house, a fatality at a collision on a freeway, or seeing anguish on a family member's face ripped his guts out now and again. Still, firefighters were his lineage. His grandfather, his father, dauntless and daring had been bred in his blood.

He cringed when people called him a hero. He just did his job.

It felt good when a burning house held no victims or a car went into a river without its occupants. He couldn't describe the relief when he felt a pulse or saw a chest rise after a near death encounter. And then there were the days he experienced immense satisfaction knowing his team had survived unharmed. Many nights he'd catch a few hours' sleep before he had to jump back in a truck when the alarm sounded again.

For some relatives, the occupation predestined doom. The danger, the threat, the waiting for your man to come home ... Women couldn't handle the pressure long term. He better well remember that.

"Got another cup?"

Deep in his musing, he hadn't heard Cassie slip into the kitchen. A whistle died behind his teeth. Blonde hair mussed, eyes bright as the morning sun, she gave him a smile that made him want to take her right back to bed.

Wearing a T-shirt that hung midway on her shapely, bare legs, she leaned her shoulder against the door frame. One knee bent and the toes of her foot curled on the instep of her opposite foot while she shot him a sultry smile. Damn, the woman was hot. Provocative. She had the sexiest legs and last night they'd been wrapped around him.

His shaft thickened.

He'd never done the morning after, so he hesitated on what to do. His first instinct—nail her to the door frame. The more rational side reminded him this was new and he didn't want to scare her away.

"Sure thing," he said and opened a cabinet door to retrieve another mug. After pouring coffee into the cup, he counted to five before turning to face the intoxicating creature again. Being on edge was alien to him. And damn irritating. He wasn't a player like Jared, but he'd never experienced this kind of agitation over a female.

She finger-combed her long thick hair, drawing his gaze to her neck. The sudden urge to kiss that tantalizing spot behind her ear kicked him in the gut. Remembering how soft her skin had felt against his lips last night, he thought he might die if he didn't make love to her again. Now.

"Thanks."

He blinked. "Uh, cream? Sugar?"

"Maybe a dab of milk. I'll get it."

She opened the fridge and he hoped she would bend over so he could see if she wore anything underneath that skimpy shirt.

His tongue swelled in his suddenly dry mouth. She grabbed the carton, poured some milk into her cup, and placed the container on the counter. Then, she lifted her mug and blew at the top.

Damn.

"I need my morning coffee to make me feel human again."

"Lady. After last night, I know exactly how you feel. I could use several evocative adjectives ..."

Her cheeks flushed red. He'd not meant to embarrass her, but the words were out of his mouth before he knew it. His voice had been gruff. It was a wonder he could speak at all with lust crowding his mind.

If anything, Cassie grew bolder. She sipped her coffee and stared at him, inviting him with her eyes.

He waited. Her move.

"Okay, handsome. I'm all ears."

He gave a slow perusal down her body and back up again. She electrified him and stroked his ego. He took a step forward. "Perhaps I could demonstrate."

She drew in a quick breath. Her reaction to his nearness pleased him, and he hadn't even touched her—yet. Grasping a lock of her honey hair, he inhaled, then curled it around his finger. Smooth like silk. He stared into her turquoise eyes and stroked one finger down the side of her face. He sketched a path over her chin, tracing the vein in her neck, feeling her pulse speed up. Her eyes blazed with heat, latched onto his as he drew one finger across her collarbone. Her chest rose in apparent anticipation. He slid a hand to the plumpness of her breast and palmed the nipple through her shirt. Her eyes fluttered closed. The breath hissed from her lungs.

"Soft," he murmured. "So soft."

She slumped against the counter. He slid his arm around her waist and brought her body flush against his chest. His chin resting on her head, he whispered, "Shall I go further?"

Cassie lifted her arms around his neck. "Please, Mike. Yes."

His lips crushed hers, giving her the mother of all kisses. Open mouth, and lots of tongue. She gave back, lick for lick. When neither one could breathe, he broke the kiss and swept her into his arms.

Beep. Beep.

Damn it.

He gently lowered Cassie to the floor. He shook his head, amazed at how fast he'd succumbed to desire. With a flare of frustration, he grabbed his phone. "Yes. What's up? Right. Thirty minutes tops."

He shoved his phone in his pants pocket and glanced up, knowing what he'd find. The heat in her eyes had turned to concern.

"Bad timing," he grumbled.

"Right." He heard the disappointment in her voice. The unease.

Even though her actions had been predictable, it hurt more than it should. He'd just been jerked back to reality. She'd be pissed because they were interrupted. Because he had to leave. Why should he expect anything else?

This is my life, Darlin'.

"Duty calls." He shrugged and spun around.

Her small hand clasped his upper arm. "Mike?"

He didn't want to turn back and see fear in her eyes. Or worse, rejection. He bit the bullet and faced her.

"Be careful." And then she smiled.

Smiled. Confusion danced in his brain.

"You know where I live now. So don't be a stranger." Her eyes danced and her sensual mouth curved into a teasing pout.

Hell yeah. He'd be back. If she could accept his occupation without hang-ups. It was bound to happen. Until then ... he'd return again, and again.

"I'll call you," he heard himself say.

And he would.

CHAPTER 8

Cassie drew air into her lungs until they were near to bursting and then let it all out in one gigantic sigh.

Last night, she'd exercised muscles she hadn't used in years. Maybe ever. Sad commentary on the state of her life. No wonder she'd had the best experience ever. With a man she wasn't even sure liked her very much.

Oh, yeah. Mike loved sex—he'd made that pretty obvious. He'd blown her ever lovin' mind. This morning, her body felt truly loved and exhausted. A giving lover, he'd touched her in all the right places and made her squirm to the very edge of oblivion. Oh, how she wanted to go there again.

How had she been so lucky to attract a guy like that? Sure, the man was sexy, but his caring touch was what charmed her. His arms had wrapped her in a haven of warmth, making her crave more of this tantalizing man.

Last night he'd saved a woman from burning in her car. Then acted like it was no big deal. A true hero. He didn't like the title or the attention it brought. That told her everything she needed to know.

She placed the last cup in the dishwasher just as the doorbell rang. She grabbed a towel and dried her hands on the way to open the door.

"Hi." Tammy held up her hand and jingled a set of keys.

"Hi. Come on in." Cassie left the door open and turned to go back to the kitchen, expecting her friend to follow.

"Is he gone already? I didn't see a truck outside," Tammy said as she closed the door.

"What truck?"

Tammy braced a hand on each of her plump hips. "The one you drove off in last night, genius. Or did something happen to wipe out your memory? Mine is just fine."

"You don't have to glare at me." Cassie spun around and strode through the living room. "Yes. He's gone."

Hot on her heels, Tammy's shoes smacked on the hardwood floor. "Did he stay all night? What happened? I'm dying to know."

"Gee. It took you all of, what, thirty seconds?" Cassie made a point of glancing at her arm where her watch should be. She hadn't put it on yet this morning. "Want some coffee?"

"Better put on a new pot. Unless I'm wrong, this conversation may take some time." Tammy pulled out a chair and plopped down. She placed her elbows on the table and rested her head in her hands while her expression said, *I'm waiting*.

Cassie couldn't keep from smiling, at her friend and at the remembered experience of last night. Wow. She'd probably trip over her tongue trying to apprise Tammy about her evening, without divulging details, of course. She poured water into the carafe, scooped the coffee and pushed a button.

"Quit stalling," Tammy scoffed. "Begin when you drove off in the hero's truck."

Cassie remembered Mike's reaction. "I don't think he likes being called a hero. From what I can see, he thinks he's doing his job and that's that."

"Did you have sex or did you psychoanalyze him while he relaxed on your couch?"

"We *talked*."

"With a hunk like him, yeah, I believe you." Tammy waved her hand, obviously not buying it for one minute.

Tammy was one of a kind. A person who would do anything in the world for you. They didn't come any nicer. The first time they'd met, Tammy had treated her like they'd known each other forever and they'd remained good friends ever since. If she meddled, it was from the goodness of her heart.

"He got burned last night," Cassie inwardly cringed, remembering the raw skin.

Tammy straightened and her face grew serious. "How bad was it? Is he okay?"

"It wasn't very big, but still a burn, and a cut." She collapsed into the same chair she'd sat in last night. "I cleaned it. He refused to see a doctor. I hope he gets it checked today."

"When I saw him on top of that car—admittedly we didn't know then it was Mike—I thought the car was going to explode." Tammy's eyes grew big as she gestured with her hands. "You know. Like on TV. Then when he fell, I thought he was a goner."

The image flashed in Cassie's mind and fear lanced her chest as fresh as when she'd seen him fall—*jump*.

"I remember now," Tammy said. "Jared said he refused to go to the hospital when we met him at the rescue squad."

"That's why I brought Mike home with me."

"One reason, anyway." Tammy's hand covered hers. "He's okay now, right?"

He's more than okay. He's dynamite. Pure adrenaline. Toxic.

Tammy arched her eyebrow. "By the dreamy look on your face, he must be. Now get to the hot and panting part." She leaned back and crossed her arms.

"He's hot. As in *very*." Cassie couldn't help teasing, but her words came out breathless.

"No. No. Start at the beginning." Tammy waved her hand again, a habit of hers. "When you pulled in your driveway will work. Unless something happened before you got home."

Scooting to the edge of her chair, Cassie remembered how the sight of his sculpted chest had taken her breath. How her fingers had itched and begged to touch. How her pulse had leaped with excitement and the urge to jump his bones had pierced her chest. Then the dread when she'd seen the burn and torn skin.

"His shirt was stuck to his burn, so I had to soak the material. But it wasn't too bad. Not once did he complain, and he looked"—she took a breath—"damn good sitting there with his shirt hanging open."

"Probably tasted good, too." Tammy rose and headed for the coffee pot.

Yeah, Cassie breathed out a sigh.

"Like I said, I put on a bandage and offered him my shower." Heat flushed her face. She wasn't ready to admit sneaking into the guest room and almost into the shower with Mike. If Tammy had been paying attention instead of pouring coffee, she would have dragged it out of her.

"You offered him your shower?" Tammy mumbled incredulously as she slid Cassie's coffee toward her. "A man like that? I would have joined him."

After last night, Cassie thought she still might get the chance.

"Mike came out in a towel."

Tammy clanked her mug on the table. "Good Lord." She fell into her chair, her breath caught as if the wind had been knocked out of her. Tammy rarely shut up. Seeing her mouth hang open and no words coming out was completely out of character.

"All wind and no sail?" Cassie teased.

"I would have loved to have seen that. A girl can dream. And if she doesn't get any action, she uses her imagination. But now I don't have to. Give."

Cassie made her wait while taking a sip of the fresh coffee. She really should show some pity and put Tammy out of her snooping misery.

"All muscles, wet spiky hair, a day's growth of beard—add lifesaving in the mix, and you've got one whopping man."

"So, he whisked you in his arms and you set the sheets on fire," Tammy added breathlessly.

"You're getting ahead of me."

Her eyes flew wide in eagerness and surprise. "Sorry. Go on."

"While I stood there drooling, he walked *around* me to the food."

"Huh?" Tammy's dazed expression was comical, making it difficult for Cassie to keep a straight face.

"I threw together something to eat and had it on the table. He strolled by me as if he had no interest in me. As if he paraded in a towel around women every day."

"With nothing but a towel," Tammy said dubiously.

"Yep," Cassie answered, remembering the image of the towel drawn tight around his buns.

"Maybe he wears a towel often. Or goes around butt naked. Bet all those fire guys do.

Taking a sip of coffee, Cassie gazed over the top of her cup. Tammy looked like a hungry puppy with a bone dangling just out of reach.

"Was anything peeking out?"

"I have large towels." Cassie lowered her mug and leaned forward as if about to whisper a dark secret. "But he's a large man."

"Oh God, I've died and gone to heaven." Tammy dramatically flung her arm over her forehead and slumped in her chair. A short moment passed before she suddenly jumped. "You had to imagine his—you know—on the wood. No way the towel covered his buns."

"Tammy!"

"Well," she said with indignation, then took a deliberate sip of her coffee. "So, you fixed him food, ate. Then what?" She placed her elbow on the table and propped her chin in the palm of her hand.

"He asked for a blanket." At Tammy's raised brows, Cassie hurried to explain, but Tammy held up her hand.

"Cassie. This story is not as exciting as I anticipated. Please tell me it did get good at some point."

"You wanted details."

"*Juicy* details."

Cassie giggled. "Okay. He mentioned he needed something bigger for covering, so I sprinted for a blanket. By the time I got back, he'd moved to the living room on the couch."

"Butt naked," Tammy said hopefully.

"He had the towel concealing the important part."

"What is wrong with you?" Tammy exclaimed slamming her hands down on the wood. "The man has a body like an immortal God and you bring him a blanket? Girl, you definitely have to get back in the game. You've been without a man too long."

"And what about you? In the two years you and Steve have been divorced, you haven't even dated."

"I have two boys. We're not talking about me. Besides, you've had the same dry spell.'

"By my choice." Cassie had made the mistake of dating guys who only wanted to take her out because of her ample chest. In her heart, she craved a strong pair of arms to hold her each and every night. One man for the rest of her life. A man who wanted only one woman. Who would want her for herself. Who looked deeper than her physical assets. After last night, she hoped she'd found him.

Mike had touched something within her that she didn't even know was there. The most profound feeling she'd ever experienced with a man. He'd claimed a part of her soul.

Hopefully Mike was a one-woman man. Not like his buddy, Jared. Anyone could see that guy was a born philanderer. Her gut told her Mike would be so much more. She desperately wanted to find out.

"Earth to Cassie." Tammy's voice brought Cassie from her musings. She studied her friend, knowing Tammy was no more promiscuous than Cassie. Tammy liked to joke and tease, but most of her experience had been with her husband. Look how that turned out. Naturally, she wanted to hear anything sensational in someone else's private life.

"He, uh, patted the couch beside him. So, I joined him and we talked." Cassie glared, daring Tammy to pounce since she'd used the word *talk* again. After a moment, she continued. "He put his arm around me and the electricity surged. From there on, use your imagination, 'cause that's all the specifics you're gonna get."

Tammy's smile nearly split her face. "You deserve a good roll in the hay. I knew he'd be good for you."

"I'd use the word *great*." Cassie picked up her mug.

"That good, huh?" Tammy laughed. "He must have been. Girl, you're glowing."

"I want to see him again. Not because he's great in bed. There's a depth to him that is intriguing. I want to know more." Cassie shook her head in amazement. "He has these moments where I feel like he's thinking, you know, analyzing, trying to decide whether or not he should tell me. There's something he's hiding."

"Like what? He's a fireman. He can't be a serial killer."

"Well then, suppressing. Like something is bothering him." She swallowed and placed her mug on the table, her hands enfolding the glass.

"Maybe he's a sexual deviant. He didn't want to scare you so he held back."

Cassie laughed at Tammy's wiggling brows. "You need to find your own boy toy. Then maybe your sex starved mind will settle down."

"Like playboy Jared? Nope. Don't think so." Tammy shook her head before bringing her cup to her lips.

"You flirted pretty hard at the restaurant."

"That's just flirting. I had fun. He's a little too lively for anything else."

"What about last night? He'd been with Mike and we took his truck. Did you take Jared home?"

"No, he left with the other fire guys."

Cassie stared at her in disbelief.

"What?" Tammy bristled. "You think I don't want someone special? I have my boys to think of. I'd like a real man."

"I think Jared would be insulted."

"That's not what I meant. He could give me a night of the best sex I've ever had, but that's not what I want."

Cassie didn't hide her surprise. "Oh? Every woman secretly wishes for a man who will rock her world."

"Including me. For goodness sake, Cassie, I know I joke a lot. It's been a long time. My ex left when the boys were four."

"Has there been anyone since?"

"Are you kidding? When would I have the time?" Tammy leaned closer. "*Boys*, Cassie. As in full throttle, non-stop mischief. *Two* of them." She sank back and slumped in her chair. "Any free time I am fortunate to have, I spend with you. The only action I get is reading a romance novel."

Cassie and Tammy both loved their romance novels. Most of the teachers at school read them. There was a cabinet in the break room full of books they swapped out.

"At least now things are looking up for you."

Cassie hoped so. She couldn't wait to see Mike again.

"I had a ball flirting with Jared, but that's just fun. For a partner, I'm looking for stability. The opposite of my ex." Tammy held her mug between her hands and stared into space. "I had a man who thought he was Casanova. Where is he now? Gone. That's where," she said with disgust. "With his bimbos."

"You've done a great job with them," Cassie said, meaning her boys. "The twins are happy. They seem to be handling the separation well."

"They think it's cool to visit their dad. He was never home much anyway. They probably see more of him now than before the divorce."

Cassie prodded. "And you?"

Tammy's gaze met hers, that familiar glimmer back in her eyes. "I'm great. Life is good." She turned up her mug. After a swallow, she set it down and gave a slight shrug. "One of these days my prince will come along. I'm not in any hurry. Like I said. I need to think of my boys."

"You need to think of yourself, too. You're a lovely woman. Funny, sharp."

"What do I need a man for? I have you to fill me in on all the dirty stuff I'm missing."

Cassie rose to get more coffee. She brought the pot to the table and warmed both cups. "I'm not sharing."

"You don't have to share the man. Only the good stuff. Come on. I'm living my fantasy through you. At least tell me I'm having a good time." Tammy laughed so hard she started to cough.

Cassie patted her on the back. "Like I said, get your own toy."

"Humph." Tammy sat back with a pout.

Chapter 9

Mike stepped on the accelerator and cursed. He needed to pay more attention to his driving and less on the best night of his life. He should have told Jared to take a hike, but the guy had gotten stuck in court. Mike had to rush home, shower, shave, and now he was late. He'd never been late. Even staying up all night and going to work bone weary, he arrived on schedule. Not today.

He slammed on the brake, jerking his truck to a halt. His fingers gripped the steering wheel so tight it was a wonder he didn't bend the damn thing. At this rate, he would need to buy a new set of tires by spring. He listened to the radio as the announcer broadcasted the time. *Shit.* Shep would have his ass. Glaring at the light wouldn't make it change any faster.

Finally, red changed to green. He stomped on the gas and took off. Before he'd gone two hundred feet, a siren wailed and blinking lights showed in his rear-view mirror.

Damn.

He pulled his truck over to the side and waited for the cop to approach. As the officer stepped alongside, Mike lowered the window.

The officer removed his sunglasses. "Hey Mike. Where's the fire?"

"Hey Chuck. I'm on my way to the station."

"A fire?"

"No. But Shep is waiting for me."

"Must be in a hurry. Spun out back there at the light."

"Yeah." Mike scrubbed his hand over his freshly shaven face. "Afraid I had my mind on something else."

"We usually do when we don't pay attention to our driving." Chuck braced one arm on top of Mike's truck. "Hey. I heard about the wreck last night, where you pulled that woman out of her SUV."

And immediately had hero worship sex with one classy lady.

"Jared told me," Chuck added.

"Jared? When did you see him?"

"At the courthouse this morning. He also said you were hurt."

"Nothing serious."

"My sister says EMTs make the worst patients, right on the list after doctors. She still works in ER over at Mercy."

Mike knew where this was going. Chuck aimed to please his sister by fixing them up. Mike had no intention of dating the sister, cousin or any family member of one of his friends. That could get messy. Especially when the time came where he ended the affair and the partner had other ideas. He liked his friends and wanted to keep them.

"Tell her hi for me," Mike said politely.

Chuck hesitated as if he was trying to decide whether or not he should say anything else.

"The reason I stopped you, I got those tickets to the Spurs game."

Mike had forgotten about those. He breathed a sigh of relief.

"I've already got someone else asking. Still want them?"

Hell yeah. But I'm not taking your sister.

He concealed his excitement as he answered, "Sure do. Got 'em with you?"

"I'll get them to you later. I need to stop by and see Shep anyway."

Good Lord, don't tell me Shep is on your sister's radar. Not that she wasn't attractive. She was just too risqué for a man like his boss. Speaking of Shep, Mike needed to get his ass to the firehouse.

"Sounds good. Am I free to go?"

Chuck smiled as he put on his shades. He stuck his thumbs inside his wide leather belt, drawing Mike's eyes to the gun at his side. "You're free to go." Then Chuck gave him a two-finger salute, a grin that showed his perfect white teeth, and strode to his vehicle.

Mike glanced at his watch. Really late.

When he pulled up to the station, Laredo stood hosing down one of the trucks. Somewhere inside the bay a radio blared out rock and roll music.

"Hey, Laredo."

"Hey, man. What are you doing here?"

"Covering for Jared."

Laredo made an exaggerated presentation of displaying his watch.

"I know." Mike should have left Cassie's place the second Jared called. Then Chuck had pulled him over. Cap wouldn't want to hear excuses. "Where's Shep?"

"Inside. He may not even notice. He's been locked up in there since he came in an hour ago. Ain't said nothing to nobody."

One of the most easygoing men Mike knew, Shep kept every-one else in the department sane. He expected his men to do their job to the best of their ability, so he left them alone unless they screwed up. His leadership skills were spot on and his friendly manner put his employees at ease. The best part, he supported his men and championed anyone backed into a corner. If you didn't pull your weight though, he could skewer you on the spot.

Mike stepped inside and headed upstairs to the room where he stored his gear. He passed Shep's office along the way. Hes-itating, Mike listened. Normally, he didn't spy on others, but Shep being secluded behind closed doors bothered him. Hear-ing nothing, he rapped twice, opened the door and stuck his head inside.

"Hey, Cap."

Shep reclined on the couch with his arm flung over his head. Slowly, he sat up. "Come on in."

Unusual to see his boss sacked out on the couch. "Everything okay?"

"Sure. Just clearing some of the cobwebs from my brain." He stood and stretched. "I wondered if you'd come in today."

"I'm filling in for Jared. He's stuck at court."

"Hmmm."

Mike studied Shep, wondering if the guy even knew the time. Something was off. Mike figured it best to avoid asking if any-thing was wrong. If Shep wanted to talk about what was on his mind, let him bring it up. Mike wasn't about to offer his head on the chopping block if Shep didn't already have a beef with him being late.

"I got a call this morning before I left my house," Shep said as he sat down behind his desk.

"Bad news?"

"Why did I have to hear from upstairs about your rescue last night?"

Ah, shit.

Upstairs meant the chief. Since Shep got up at five every morning and arrived at the station before six thirty, the chief must have called at the crack of dawn.

"It was nothing."

"Not according to the morning papers." Shep's expression remained neutral, but Mike knew the man had a real talent for hiding his emotions.

"The paper?"

"You saved a woman from burning to death."

"Part of the job."

Shep pushed the newspaper across the wooden surface. "It says right here, the hero was off duty."

A flash of heat raced up Mike's spine. "Look, Cap. I don't know how they got that. I never said a word to anyone."

"Obviously, someone did."

Mike glanced at the front page. A photo of him standing on the SUV. He glanced at the title. A stone of dread settled in his gut.

Hero.

"I look like a man gone wild."

Shep removed his finger from the print and leaned forward, bracing his forearms on the corner of his desk. His eyes alight with interest. "Didn't know you were the publicity type."

"I'm not and you know it," Mike growled. He flexed his hands and gripped the back of a chair positioned between him and Shep's desk.

"Indulge me." Shep gestured for him to sit in the chair. "And don't gloss over the details."

Mike released his grip and stepped around to sit. He related everything as he remembered it, including the fact that Jared had been with him. Intentionally, he never mentioned Cassie. Nobody's business about his fantastic night of incredible sex.

"Did you get checked out this morning?"

"Not yet." With Jared calling him to fill in and then with being late, he'd forgotten about going to the doctor.

"Make sure you do." Again, Shep leveled his gaze on Mike. "I want a report before you go on any more runs."

Hell. Shep meant now.

"Guess I better get going then." As Mike put his hands on the arms of the chair, his boss continued.

"Jared said a female took you home."

Mike noticed the glint in his boss's eyes. He should have known Jared wouldn't keep his mouth shut.

"Jared made that arrangement."

Shep laughed. "He can't make you do anything you don't want to." Then his face clouded over like someone kicked his dog. The same look he'd had when he'd risen from the sofa. Right before he'd masked it. Whatever bothered him, the conversation they'd just had hadn't had a damn thing to do with it.

"The lady was persuasive." At least Shep didn't ask the lady's name.

"The blonde from the Mexican restaurant?"

Christ. Did everyone know?

"Jared has a big mouth."

Shep never stuck his nose in anyone business. He placed a high value on friendship. His door was always open and he kept a confidence like bearing a cross. The two of them had shared some personal things and for that reason, he felt safe poking at Mike.

Shep leaned back in his chair, lifted his arms above his head and propped his feet on his scarred desk. "So, tell me about it."

Why not? Talking about her might oust her from his mind. *Sure.*

"She took me home. Patched me up." The clock on the wall ticked the seconds of dead silence in the room.

"That it?"

"Pretty much." Mike wasn't about to give details.

"She a one-night stand?"

Anger filled his chest so fast it caught him by surprise. He flexed his hands to calm his pulse, wondering at his quick reaction. Cassie was too good for a one-night stand. Too good for him. He scrubbed a hand over his face.

"Didn't think so," Shep said with a shake of his head. "What's the problem?"

Mike glared. He hated talking about *the problem.* Forcing his uneasiness down, he settled back and crossed one booted foot over the opposite knee. Grasping his ankle gave him something to steady his hand.

Several moments passed before he glanced up. Shep had the patience of a saint.

"She's great," Mike said in a gruff voice, barely controlling his emotion. "She's perfect. But a one-night stand is all it can be."

"Why?"

"I don't do relationships. She's the type to want one. You've never married. You won't take the risk either."

Shadows filled Shep's eyes. "I'm not single for the reason you believe. Maybe I haven't found the right woman. I haven't rejected the idea of marriage completely."

"You're pushing forty. You can't tell me this job has nothing to do with it."

"I'm not there yet. And this job has everything to do with it. Not all women can handle being the wife of a firefighter."

"Which I know all too well." He'd confided his own personal skeleton to Shep a long time back.

"I said *not all* women."

"She would still leave."

Shep's feet hit the floor with a thud. "That was your mother. You can't judge all women by the actions of one. The balance is finding the right woman at the right time. You'll never find out if you don't give someone the chance."

Give someone the chance to rip his heart out the way his mom had? No thanks.

"Hell, Shep. You're not that much older than me. These days, guys don't get married until they're fifty."

More than one emotion had flashed over Shep's face during his little speech. He may have hinted on the thing that had weighed on his mind earlier. Could it be a female?

"Have you found someone?" Mike cautiously asked.

Shep's eyes narrowed and he clammed up.

Who? Where? When? The guy never went out. He arrived at the office early and stayed late. Most of his time, he spent alone.

"No." Shep stood, which was usually a sign of dismissal.

He had the gall to get Mike to spill his guts, but when the conversation turned to him, the damn guy got tight-lipped.

"No?" Mike echoed.

"Don't turn this around on me. You have a classy lady at your fingertips."

Classy, sexy. The woman sure knew how to kiss. And those delicate fingers did some pretty naughty things. He wanted them caressing and stroking him again. Heat filled his belly at the image of Cassie's body spread open for him. He squeezed his legs together and willed his growing erection down. He cleared his throat and stood.

A hard knock on the door saved him from saying anything. The door opened and Cooper stuck his head in.

"Hey, boss. You wanted to see me?"

"Yes. Come in."

Mike took this as his cue to leave. "I've got work to do."

"Gee, Hoss. You gonna leave me high and dry?" Cooper rolled his eyes toward Shep. "What if I need back up, here?"

Mike slapped Cooper on the shoulder. "You're on your own, pup."

"Get to the hospital," Shep commanded.

Cooper's eyes grew wide as he swung his head from the Captain to him. "Thought you were okay. Did you get hurt?"

"A cut. A slight burn." Mike shrugged.

"I want that report." When Shep gave an order in that voice, you got your ass in gear.

"Yes, sir."

Fuck. Mike headed to the hospital.

CHAPTER 10

The ER had been crowded with a dozen people in line before Mike. The waiting room was packed. For a Saturday morning, he didn't know if this was the norm or if there'd been an accident close by. An elderly couple holding hands sat in one corner. Next to them sat a woman with her arms crossed and the man beside her looked like he wanted to be anywhere but here. Two guys with their heads together gave him the impression they were partners. On the other wall, Mike spotted an empty chair beside a boy about ten or twelve years old. Since Cap had insisted he bring back proof, Mike had to wait.

He took the seat next to the kid. As soon as he sat down, he noticed blood caked on a rag tied around the boy's calf. From what he could see, the kid's sock had soaked up a good portion and it looked like the injury might still be bleeding.

"Hey, sport. What happened to you?"

The woman next to him, who Mike figured was his mother, turned with fear in her eyes. Yep, she had to be the boy's mom.

"Fell out of a tree."

Mike pointed to the bloody piece of cloth. "What did you land on?"

"A saw."

Jesus Christ. What the hell was this kid doing with a saw? What kind of saw? Electric? Did he have supervision? Mike thought back to when he was a kid. Hell, he'd done a lot of things without his dad knowing.

"Tough break," he said with a calm voice so as not to excite the kid, or the mom.

"Don't think I broke it, but it sure did bleed."

"A lot of blood," the nervous woman chimed in. She fidgeted in her seat and her eyes darted about, following the activity in the room. "They're taking so long."

"Are you his mother?"

"Yes." She looked like she was ready to jump out of her skin. "I'm Donna Williams."

"My name is Mike. I'm an EMT with the fire department."

Her eyes lit up like she'd won the lottery.

"Are you a fireman?"

"I'm a firefighter," Mike answered the boy with a nod. "What's your name?"

"Todd. My dad said it should be Evel Knievel."

Mike laughed. Then noticed the bright red oozing down the boy's leg. "You should have that propped up. Did you say you landed on a saw?"

"Yeah. I'm building a club house. Well, actually adding on to it. My dad built me a tree house a long time ago, but now that I'm bigger and my friends have grown up, we need more space."

"Your father told you not to use the saw while he was gone. And you shouldn't have taken it out of the garage."

"Aww, Mom."

"Don't you *aww Mom*, me. Wait till your father gets home."

Mike had heard other people say that, but not at his house. It had been just him and his dad.

"I'll be fine by the time Dad gets back," the boy told his mother.

"I called him. He's on his way to the airport to catch a flight home today."

"Aww, Mom. You didn't have to call Dad."

The woman looked at the boy as if he'd suddenly grown horns.

"Of course, I called your father. You could have cut off your leg."

The boy wilted under his mother's stare. Mike wondered what kind of man his dad was. Mean? Harsh? If he called the kid *Evel Knievel*, he couldn't be but so bad. Maybe the mother was overreacting.

Worry filled the woman's anxious gaze. "What's taking them so long?" The woman would wear out her seat. Mike understood her worry, but if she kept that up, the boy would get nervous too. They didn't need that. Although the kid looked pretty tough. And he seemed pretty casual sitting there waiting for his turn.

"Let me have a look at that, sport."

Mike pulled the knot loose and tried to hide his reaction. The cut was deep and there was blood still seeping from the wound. He quickly rewrapped the cloth. "Sit tight, buddy."

Mike rose from his chair and walked to the ER check-in desk. "Excuse me."

"Mike? What are you doing here?" He spun at the sound of his name.

"Hey, Tracey," he said, relieved that he'd found someone he knew. "There's a kid over there who should be seen right away."

"Which one?" she asked as she turned, scanning the group of people.

"The kid with the bloody rag on his leg." It wasn't hard to miss the anxious mom sitting beside him. "They've been waiting. The mom is antsy."

Tracey spotted Todd and headed in his direction. Mike fell into step behind her.

"Hello there. My name is Tracey," she spoke to Todd, then smiled at his mom.

"Hi. My name is Todd and this is my mom." Todd spoke right away. His mom smiled in greeting.

"He fell out of a tree. I'm not sure where else he might be hurt. He walked into the house with blood running down his leg and nearly gave me a heart attack."

The kid fell out of a tree, cut his leg, deep, and *walked* into his house on his own? Mike had thought the kid strong—he'd had no idea.

"Give me just a moment and we'll take a look at your leg." Tracey glanced to Mike with a silent message in her eyes. She'd noticed the fresh blood, too. "I'll get a wheelchair."

Mike didn't want to waste time. "No need for that. Come on, champ." He scooped the kid up.

"Awesome. I can walk, but this is more fun. I want to be a firefighter."

Mike chuckled. The kid had spunk. Not one complaint or moan of pain. The cut had to hurt. He marched to the examining room behind Tracey.

"Bet it's great to ride in a big fire truck."

"Tell you what, sport. You get fixed up and then one day, get your mom to bring you to the firehouse. Station Eight. I'll let you see one for yourself."

"Wow. Do you mean it?"

"Sure do. Remember. Station Eight."

"I'll remember. Hey, Mom. Mike said I can go to his firehouse and see a real fire engine."

He didn't think the mother's eyes could get any brighter with tears glimmering in them, but her smile only made them glow more. He read the appreciative gleam and that gave him all the thanks he needed.

Tracey led them to a private room. Inside, Mike put the boy down and stepped back. Tracey removed the wrapping and cleaned the boy up. He never moved. Never let out a peep. Definitely needed stitches. A man entered, wearing scrubs, a stethoscope hanging around his neck.

"What do we have here?" The doctor's smile put Todd's mom right at ease. She was lucky to have such a trooper for a son.

While the doctor talked with Todd's mom, Tracey pulled Mike to the side.

"I heard you pulled a woman from a burning car last night. While you were off duty."

News traveled fast. Word had a way of spreading like fire among the emergency crew.

"Yeah. That's why I'm here."

Her forehead creased in a confused frown.

"I, uh, need to get checked out."

"Did you get hurt?" Tracey asked, tugging him into the next room.

"I got a scratch. Shep sent me here." He gave a self-conscious shrug. "You know the drill."

"I know if Shep sent you to the ER, there must have been a reason. Let's have a look."

Mike cautiously peeled off his shirt, then faced Tracey. Her fingers were gentle as she removed the gauze and tape from his burned side.

She gasped.

"This is no scratch." She glared at him, irritation radiating in her eyes. "Mike Armstrong. You should have been in here last night." She turned to a cabinet and retrieved more gauze and ointment.

"Welcome to the club."

"Excuse me?"

"You sound like everyone else."

"Well at lease *everyone else* has the God given sense that you don't. Get on the table."

"Can't you—"

Her glare had him groaning and hiking his hip up on the examining board.

Fifteen minutes later, he stepped from the hospital out into bright sunshine. He glanced at the paper in his hand and then the other holding his prescription. Tracey could be intense. Although he could have done without the lecture.

Next stop, the station. Mike shoved his shades on his face and sprinted down the front steps.

Traffic was calm at this time of the day, with most everyone at work and kids in school. Last week, a school bus had wrecked. With heavy morning traffic, he'd feared the worst. Dispatch calls involving children frightened him the most. The entire team had been on edge. Thank God, when the crew had gotten to the accident sight, they found all the kids were okay.

He unlocked his truck, then climbed into the cab. Just before he turned the key, he caught a hint of something sweet. Cassie's perfume. She'd driven his truck home last night and her scent still lingered in the cab. He'd gotten a good dose of her fragrance. It was one of the fixations that drew him. He couldn't get enough of her alluring scent, her softness, her little moans ...

God. He couldn't stop thinking about the woman. He wanted to see her again.

Damn. He slammed his hand on the steering wheel. With his pager going off at her place, he'd dashed out of there without getting her phone number. No way of getting in touch with her, other than driving by her apartment. Would she mind if he showed up without warning? She'd been sweet and caring, even interesting. After the night they'd shared, though, he wondered if she'd be one of those females who'd sit by the phone expecting him to call.

Shit. How the hell did he get himself into these things? He liked free and easy. No attachments. He didn't need a woman clinging to him.

But Cassie didn't strike him as the clinging type. The woman was a knockout, yet she seemed unaware of it. She had a rack that any man would praise, but more than that drew him to her. When Mike looked at Cassie, the first thing he saw was her eyes. Green with a hint of blue. Expressive. So telling, he could read every sincere thought in her head. So significant, he could feel every emotion they conveyed.

He did want to see her again. She was fun and smart and grabbed him right in his gut.

That should alarm him. He considered it for a moment, then shook his head. No woman had ever led him around by the balls and none ever would. Why was this one stuck in his head?

As he drove, he took advantage of the quiet to get his thoughts in order. When he pulled into the lot beside the firehouse, he saw the bay doors open and Laredo out front spraying down the quint. His baby. You'd think the guy had nothing more to do than wash the rigs. This time, the radio blared to a tune of John Cougar Mellencamp, one of Mike's favorites. If Jared had been out there, he'd turn it to a country station just to piss Laredo off. Knowing Laredo wouldn't hear him, Mike waved, grabbed the bag of food he'd picked up and carted the groceries inside.

Shep stood at the counter, already busy cutting up tomatoes.

"Your turn to cook?" Mike asked.

"Got something for me?" Shep glanced up and lifted his brows. "And I'm not speaking about that bag of groceries."

Mike pulled the release paper from his back pocket. "Signed, sealed and delivered."

Shep gave a nod and went back to chopping.

"Hey Cap. Mike. What are we having tonight?" Cooper strode into the kitchen, leaned over Shep's shoulder and snatched a slice of tomato. Shep smacked his fingers with his blade.

"Dude!"

"Keep your fingers out of the food."

Cooper caught Mike's eye and smiled, oblivious to Shep's scolding.

Cooper arrived on the scene close to two years earlier. In less than one, he'd captured the respect of the entire team. All the guys gave Coop a rash of shit because he was the new guy. If they didn't like him, they wouldn't needle the kid. Cooper fit the team like a finger on a glove.

As for Shep, Cooper had won him over with hard work and dedication. It was good to see the easy camaraderie the kid had with the Captain.

"We're having chicken fettuccini and salad," Shep said.

"You're the best, Cap." Before Cooper cleared the doorway, Shep stopped him.

"Finished with the tanks?"

"Yep. Full and ready for the next run. Spares are gaged and loaded on the shelves."

"Then you can stay and heat up the sauce pan."

"Come on, Cap. No one can make the sauce like you."

"It's time you learned." Shep turned to Mike. "What did you bring?"

"I figured we could use some fresh fruit." He called out the items as he unloaded the bag. "I got apples, bananas and oranges. Picked up some butter and mayo. Have you got everything you need for your fettuccine?"

"Yes. Cooper. Use the butter from the fridge before we open this one."

"Like I wouldn't," Cooper said, rolling his eyes. He took the container Mike brought and asked, "What about rolls?"

"Ms. Daniels brought a supply of rolls."

Mike locked eyes with Cooper as he flashed a knowing grin.

Alice Daniels was a real estate agent who'd set her sights on Shep. The two mixed about as well as oil and water. The woman showed up anytime of the day, right out of the blue, making it clear who held her interest. She brought food most times, so the men liked her well enough. Shep tolerated her, but no matter how many hints he threw her way, she never got the message he just wasn't interested.

"Al-lice," Cooper purred in a sing-song tone.

Shep ignored him.

"She tried sneaking by me while I was loading the tanks. I pretended to be busy. Figured she wanted some alone time with the Captain," Cooper explained to Mike.

"That woman has a nasty habit of sneaking up undetected. I'm going to have to insert security alarms." Shep frowned. "Cooper. Get the pot boiling." The kid jumped to execute his duty.

"Do they have booty-call alarms?"

Shep shot Cooper a look meant to kill.

"Just asking?"

"Don't you mean *booty forewarning*?" Mike couldn't help himself. Cooper hooted.

"Knock it off, you two."

"Come on, Cap. You don't have to worry about getting lucky. She's doing the chasing."

"Alice is attractive, but too aggressive for my taste," Shep grumbled.

"She's got a one tract mind and I don't see it changing." Mike grinned at Shep, having fun tormenting his boss. "How are you going to handle that?"

"Security alarms," Cooper answered for Shep and received another glare.

"I'm trying. The woman refuses to understand I'm not going out with her."

"Then, I guess she will keep coming here," Mike said.

"Okay with me as long as she brings food." Cooper snitched a slice of cheese and dodged before Shep could catch him.

"You're not the one she's after."

"Who's after who?" Jared asked as he came in the kitchen.

"Alice is after Shep," Cooper answered.

"You decide to show up?" Shep asked. Jared ignored him.

"She been by here again?" Jared aimed his question to Cooper. "Someone should give the woman a suit and teach her how to fight fires."

"Shep thinks she's here too much already." Cooper's grin was infectious.

"That was my point."

"But she does bring us food."

"She's a real estate agent. Doesn't look the part of Susie homemaker to me."

"She doesn't bake." The group stared at Cooper. He shrugged. "She picks the stuff up over at Mason's Bakery."

"How do you know that?" Jared asked.

"Seen her over there." Cooper grabbed a bottle of water from the fridge. He tossed it to Mike, pulled out one for Jared and then got one for himself. Shep already had one on the counter. "After she left, I went in and asked old man Mason."

"You sly, young dog." Jared sniggered.

"The stuff she brings in here isn't from his place," Mike said with a frown. "None of it has his packaging. And she comes back later to pick up her dishes."

Cooper made a sign of crossing his heart. "I swear. The old man told me she comes in there every week. I asked him what all she got and it's the same stuff she brings here. Probably takes it home and puts it in her own glassware."

"Which gives her the excuse she needs to make another trip to the station." Jared hiked his brow and smirked. "She gets her dish and gets another shot at Shep."

"Didn't you notice the apple cobbler was cut up and squished in the corners?" Cooper nudged Mike.

"I just figured that's the way she did it. Didn't matter to me. Tasted great," Jared added. "All this time I was in love with her cooking ... You know what, Cap?"

"I'm afraid to ask," Shep said in a droll tone and kept his eyes on his task.

"If we can get rolls and stuff at the bakery, we don't need her."

Shep hiked a brow. "We don't need her period."

"Then you're the one who's got to tell her to stop coming here."

"But she brings us food," Cooper piped up.

"Just marry the woman and put her out of her misery," Jared told Shep with a shrug.

That did it. Shep looked ready to blow up.

"Who's getting married?" Laredo's voice cracked in the room.

"Shep," Cooper answered. The boy might be young, but he gave as good as he got.

"I'm not—"

"You?! And I'm just now hearing about it?" Laredo's voice bellowed and his eyes grew big in their sockets.

Mike laughed out loud. That's what happened when one walked in on the tail end of a conversation. When these guys found a target, the whole gang jumped on the bandwagon.

"Oh, for God's sake," Shep exclaimed. "Will you guys give me a break? Why don't you hound Mike about why he was late this morning?"

Thrown to the dogs.

Shep must be flustered. He wouldn't normally squeal on another guy. The silence in the room was almost deafening. Laredo and Cooper stared at him with puzzled expressions while Jared grinned like the cat that swallowed the canary.

"All right, big guy. Where were you?" Naturally, Laredo had to ask.

"Couldn't take the heat?" Mike grumbled, glaring at Shep who busied himself with stirring the sauce.

"Come on, Mike," Cooper cajoled. "We never hear any stories about you."

"Does this have anything to do with that hot babe at the Mexican restaurant?" Laredo asked with a leering grin.

"Hey man. I saw her first."

"Down, pup." Mike turned his glare on Cooper. "You did not see her first, and I'm the one who went over and talked to her."

Cooper gave him a shit-eating grin, making Mike aware of what he'd just admitted. "So, it is her. The hot blonde."

"Of course, it's her," Jared agreed. "What I want to know is why you were *late*."

"Bet you did more than talk." Cooper grinned like a stupid idiot. If he stood closer, Mike would wallop the kid.

An uncomfortable wave smacked Mike in his gut. He'd had a wonderful night with Cassie and had no intention of enlightening these jugheads.

"Only thing in the world that would make *me* late would be a wild night of sex," Jared boasted.

"Did he come in all wet?" Cooper asked.

"Shower sex." Laredo joined in the fun. "Great in the morning."

"Knock it off," Mike said, his voice heavy with irritation.

"Dish it out but can't take it?" Jared teased.

"Someone doesn't like sharing."

"Not this," Mike snapped at Laredo. "Cassie is a class act and I'm not sharing a damn thing." He knew the guys were just razzing on him, like they always did. But Cassie was unique. His time with her special.

"Okay, bro." Jared slapped him on the back. "We're just funnin'. Cassie huh? She is a beautiful woman and nice, too."

"Yeah, man. I think you like her. Like, *really like* her."

Mike glanced at Cooper. The kid was smarter than he looked.

"You guys got me. Yes, I was with Cassie. I wasn't scheduled to be here in the first place. Yes, I was running late. But I sure as hell am not telling you *why*."

"There's my answer. Right there." Laredo nodded to the others.

"You guys ready to eat?" Shep, the instigator. The one who set the wolves on him.

"I'll get the plates," Cooper said as he opened a cabinet door.

"Who else has a girl keeping them up all night?" Jared asked as he took a seat at the table.

"Not me," Cooper answered.

Jared glanced around the table. "You mean Shep and Mike are the only ones getting action?"

Laredo hooted. "I think you better rephrase that one. Every man at this table is getting action."

"Don't include me in that category. Alice Daniels will have to focus her attention on someone else."

"Come on, Cap. Alice is a fine-looking woman."

"I'll be sure and tell her you said that the next time she stops by," Shep said with a pointed stare.

"Oh, no. Don't pawn your girlfriend off on me."

"She's not my—"

"Don't you like her, Cap?" Cooper kept a straight face, but Mike knew the mischief-maker's question was far from innocent.

"Why does everyone keep interrupting me?" Shep braced his arms on the table. "All joking aside, I need to find a way to rid myself of that woman. She's becoming a nuisance."

"She brings us food," Laredo said after sucking down a mouthful of noodles.

"Hey, dude. She brings stuff from Mason's Bakery, passing it off as her own.

Laredo hiked a brow then gave a shrug. "It's still food."

So much for the serious approach.

"I see what you mean," Mike said to Shep. "If the woman goes out of her way to pawn off another person's cooking and claim it as her own, who knows what she might try next?"

"You mean, she could be like *fatal attraction*?"

Guess everyone had seen that movie, even Cooper.

"There's that. And if she's hanging around, it could interfere with Shep's actual love life."

All heads turned to Shep. Each one sizing him up, trying to decide if he was seeing a woman they didn't know about.

"Hmm. Never thought of that." Laredo shrugged and took a bite of pasta.

"That's because you guys are always joking," Mike informed him.

"Would you rather we were a bunch of cranky old farts?" Jared asked.

"It's harmless," Laredo added.

"Hey. Wait a minute." Cooper put down his fork and a puzzled expression crossed his face. "You got a new woman, Cap?"

Activity at the table stopped. Jared froze with his fork mere inches from his mouth. Laredo's expression turned from mocking to one of surprise. Each man waited for Shep to answer.

He didn't. Shep forked a gob of food and stuffed his mouth, making it clear he wasn't about to.

"Is that why you turned the heat on the big guy?" Laredo prodded.

Shep glanced at Mike. "Sorry about that. It just slipped out."

Nothing ever just slipped out with Shep. If he'd gotten flustered, there'd been a reason. Shep had been acting a bit off this past week.

"I've got big shoulders. I can take it."

"Didn't appear that way when you told us to knock it off."

"Down, pup."

"You talk to me like I'm a dog."

"Sometimes you act like one."

"Yeah, always sniffing around ..." Laredo laughed. Mike and Jared joined in.

Shep never did reply to Cooper's question. He ate his food and washed it down with coffee rather than answer. Did Shep have a woman he's been hiding?

Naw. The guy hadn't had time.

But something was on his mind.

Chapter 11

Several days after the nightmare of training day, some of the guys from Station Eight had visited Ryan in the hospital. His wife had been sitting faithfully by his bed, holding his bandaged hand. He'd been doped up on pain meds and bandages covered ninety percent of his face. He didn't even know his visitors were there. With all the tubes and monitors Ryan had been hooked up to, the guys prayed daily for his recovery.

After a three week stay in the hospital, he'd finally been released to go home. Jared and Mike rode to Ryan's house to see if he was ready for visitors. His wife greeted them at the door.

"I hope we're not interrupting," Jared said.

"Certainly not. Come on in. Ryan's in the den. I'm sure he'll be glad to see you."

Mike and Jared wiped their boots, then stepped inside and followed—he'd forgotten the wife's name—to a cozy room where Ryan reclined in an easy chair.

"Hi, Mike. Jared."

"How's it going, Ryan?" He did not offer his hand. Jared and Mike were both conscious of Ryan's injuries and purposefully sat without touching him. Both could see that Ryan had endured a rough road and neither of them wanted to make him uncomfortable. The bandages were gone from his face, leaving red, raw tissue in their place. A cast covered one arm from wrist to elbow, and Mike wondered what the blanket on his lap was hiding.

"Can't complain too much. Had the shit knocked out of me, but I'm lucky to be alive."

Mike darted a glance to the doorway, making sure Ryan's wife wasn't within earshot. The guys spoke more freely without the family listening. "I believe so, too. When that house exploded, you flew through the air like a cannonball."

"Still feels as though a giant beat me with a sledge hammer. Some training exercise. Did someone forget to tell me the plan?"

"At least you can joke about it."

Ryan gave a shrug. "I've done that same maneuver a hundred times. Never had a house knock me on my ass like that before." Ryan had been with the fire department for fifteen years. Excellent at his job, he had instructed several training exercises.

"Damn, I'm sorry man."

"Weren't your fault."

Jared filled in the lapse of silence. "We visited you at the hospital, but you were pretty out of it."

"Sorry, guys. I didn't know. The drugs made me sleepy, and the doctors said sleep was the best thing I could do."

"How bad was it?" Maybe he shouldn't ask, but Ryan didn't seem to mind talking about his injuries. As a firefighter, Mike knew the team would want to know.

"My injuries were worse from the power of the blast than the burns. The suit protected my body, but the burst went under my mask." Ryan lifted his hand toward his face. "You can see for yourself I'm not as pretty as I used to be."

Ryan hadn't lost his sense of humor.

"They had to dig a piece of metal out of my thigh. I've got staples from my knee to my groin. Broken arm, a few broken ribs."

"Christ, man." Jared blew out in a huff.

Ryan looked Mike in the eye. "They told me no one else was hurt. Is that true?"

"Not seriously. A few bruises, a few scrapes. The new recruits tackled the scene like true firefighters doing their job. Good thing, since we needed every man."

"What the hell happened?"

Mike and Jared looked at each other.

"Come on guys. Don't hold out on me. Anybody with half a brain would know that was a fucked-up disaster."

"Hooley is on the case," Mike replied.

Ryan gave a nod and Jared continued where Mike left off.

"We've knocked this scenario between our heads over and over again. Every guy on our team has studied and dissected the events of that day. We came up with shit. Someone had to tamper with the training site. We just can't figure out how."

"The place is taped off. No one is allowed back on site. If you ask me, the way things happened, the explosion was deliberate." Mike shook his head. "I can't believe any of our firefighters had anything to do with it."

"Me neither," Jared added.

Ryan rubbed a spot behind his ear. "I hate to think someone deliberately set out to kill one of us. But I've had plenty of time to go over it. Every guy on site was in full gear." He zeroed in on Mike, then moved his gaze to Jared. "I don't want to believe it either."

Mike couldn't finish that disturbing train of thought. Until he had proof, he refused to acknowledge a firefighter may have intentionally devised that explosion.

Before long, Jared and Mike left. As soon as Jared cranked the engine, he spoke.

"You know, Mike. I have a few questions of my own."

"You thinking the same thing I am?"

Jared pushed the call button on his steering wheel."

"*Hola.*"

"Laredo. It's me."

"What's up?"

"Mike and I just left Ryan's place. We're figuring to go back to the training site. You in?"

"Hell yeah. I'll call Coop."

***

In the distance, Mike followed the horizon where the mountains met a blue sky. Clouds so low, they swallowed a good portion of green making the tips look like archways winding to heaven. He loved the country. What he wouldn't give for even a little corner of the Wimer land. He dreamed of a place like Shep's. A big house, comfortable, with a window large enough to see the landscape of the Blue Ridge Mountains. Nothing was prettier than the forest green in the spring, the orange and gold leaves in the fall, or the snow-capped mountains along the Parkway in wintertime. The Wimer property ran in the opposite direction, toward the Shenandoah Mountain. It would be a perfect place for a stretch of land.

As Jared sped down the road, a fresh country breeze whooshed through the open window.

"There's the turnoff," Mike said, pointing to a side road.

Two miles down the lane, another turn took them to the spot of the training site. Jared's Dodge bumped along the rutted road.

"Better back up, man. I think you missed one," Cooper said.

"Yeah, Jared. I'd like to keep my teeth from cracking together."

"Pussies."

Laredo flipped him the bird.

As the truck crested a hill, Mike saw a big sign. *Posted. Keep out.* To the right of it was another one. *This means you.*

Jared pulled next to the yellow tape, which sectioned off a huge chunk of land a good two hundred yards from the house. What was left of it, anyway.

The guys climbed from the truck.

"Damn. There's shit everywhere," Cooper said as he slammed his door.

Laredo whistled through his teeth. "I don't remember the house being in the trees."

"With everything going on that day, we all missed a lot." Mike took in the debris still scattered about. Not only did the tape contain the strewn pieces of the house, but a perimeter had been set up enclosing fifty yards of nothing beyond the wreckage. He figured that was to keep anyone from getting too close.

"Let's go." Jared held up a length of caution tape and motioned for the others to climb under.

As Mike neared some burned lumber, the images of that day came rushing back. He saw Ryan flying through the air, heard roaring in his ears just before men shouted and scurried into action. There had been black all around, he couldn't see ten feet in front of him. Flames, thunder, shadows, then outlines of men. Confusion racking his brain. Adrenaline kicking in when he needed to act.

"You okay, Hoss?"

He jerked his head. "I'm fine, pup. Worry about yourself." He'd spoken sharper than he'd intended. But a man didn't like to admit to weakness.

"We all know we're not supposed to be here, so don't touch anything. If you do, use gloves." Jared produced a bag of latex gloves.

"Where the hell did you get those?"

"Out of my ass. You want any or not?"

Cooper shrugged. "Just saying, I didn't see you get them out of the truck."

"None of us were paying attention to anything other than this mess." Mike spoke to Cooper, trying to make up for his sharpness earlier. "If you see anything suspicious, call out. Just be careful."

"Come on, Hoss. We're out of grade school."

The kid may have worn a devil-may-care grin, but he knew the ropes. Cooper wasn't afraid of anything and he rushed head-first into any situation. Not without caution. He used his training and handled himself with expertise.

The four divided and searched in different directions. Mike stepped over boards, split timber and thousands of pieces he could only assume were bits of the walls and flooring. He'd been on a few scenes where a house had exploded from a leak in a gas line. This scene resembled the same destruction. No ordinary flame or procedures of a controlled burn could do this damage. The only thing that could rip the guts out of a building and leave this kind of wreckage would be a gas line, some source of fuel, or a substance charge.

Forty yards away, a mound of ruins lay where the house had been. From there to where Mike stood, fragments of wood, pipe, and glass were strewn across the ground. Bits of frames that had once been windows were the only recognizable items. Nothing was left of the walls or main structure. The old house had more than likely existed of wood and not much more. Four by four posts and a few pillars were detectable—bits of a tin roof, everything else lay in shambles or hung in the trees.

He made his way through the ruins. Singed wood everywhere—some black, some clear as though not burned at all. More evidence. The blast had shattered the structure and sent pieces soaring before it could catch fire.

Again, Mike saw Ryan, airborne, jetting in slow motion. Black smoke swallowing his body. Mike shook his head to clear the image.

He strode forward, moving a few pieces here and there with the toe of his boot. A far different scene than the one expected at the end of a training exercise. An answer needed to be found. An explanation, so this could never happen again.

After an hour of drifting in and out of the tree line and poking through the rubble, Mike was ready to give up.

"Hey! Over here!" Laredo stood at the section where Ryan had thrown the torch.

"You find something?"

"I'm not sure," he answered Jared. "Look at that."

"What did you find?" Cooper hurried over and stopped next to Mike.

"I don't see anything."

"Study this spot right here for a minute. It doesn't look right."

Hell, there was nothing there. Mike studied the ground and the burnt cinder blocks.

Wait a minute.

"Something has been moved." Jared took a step closer. "See here? Something was here and now it's gone."

Laredo nodded his head. "Yep. That's what I think."

"What do you figure it was?"

"No idea. But all these boot prints were after the fire was put out. Look at this. It's a different color. Heat got here but no flames."

"Hooley," Mike said. "Hooley must have found whatever and took it for his investigation."

"That means he found something," Jared said.

"Something important," Cooper agreed.

"Which means this was no accident."

"We don't know that," Mike quickly interjected.

"He took it. It's essential."

"Maybe."

"There's no maybe to it, Mike. You know that explosion was no accident."

"Calm down, Coop. We can't play guessing games. That's why we have investigators."

Cooper mumbled, but Mike couldn't distinguish what he said. He wasn't meant to hear anyway, so he ignored it.

"The rest of you find anything?"

"Not a damn thing," Jared grumbled.

"It took us an hour to find this, so we might as well leave."

Mike hated leaving empty handed. So did the rest of the team. What had he expected? To miraculously trip over evidence that a specialist might not discover?

Chapter 12

Cassie should settle down and concentrate on her lessons. That would be the sensible thing to do. But lately she'd been far from sensible. After a long day of working with active eight-year-olds, she was restless. Which had nothing at all to do with her students.

Mike.

She remembered the feel of his chest hair beneath her cheek. The way he smelled like a clean breeze and her own shampoo. The way he held her close and caressed her skin with amazing fingers, as if he couldn't stop touching her. She lowered her head in a deep sigh and placed her hands on her scalp.

If she could just get him out of her head she could finish her third-grade lesson plan. With her attention span this evening, it was a good thing she did not teach high school. There was no way she could focus on essays and difficult questions. Cassie could be tough when needed. A teacher had to be strong. If not, her elementary students would walk all over her.

There were times when she wanted to be soft and feminine. And allow a strong, compelling man to take care of her. She looked around her living room, taking in the large empty space—full of furniture, but empty because she lived alone. Mike had filled the room with his overpowering presence. Without Mike's company, the apartment appeared cold. The fireplace gave the impression of real flames and burning logs. She could turn on the heated lamp and live in the illusion of a warm and welcoming fire. But the temperature had nothing to do with the warmth she craved.

His accepting manner, his demeanor, the way he looked at her with those bone melting eyes, she could lose herself in a fantasy of Mike's affection and his welcoming arms. She could imagine them stretched out on her couch. His hand sliding up her thigh, sending delicious tingles—

Enough.

She rose from the table she used as a desk and arched her back, deciding if she was going to play make-believe, she would indulge herself with a glass of wine. Mike had taken center stage in her mind, so she might as well relax and enjoy the evening.

On a teacher's salary, she couldn't splurge often, but she did have a few bottles of wine in her cupboard. A Bordeaux Dry White wine, a Merlot red grape wine, and a Ménage a Trois Silk Soft Red Blend 2015.

Cassie remembered the first time she saw it. She'd been shopping with Tammy and they'd found a wine store with rare wines. They couldn't afford anything in the place and were just browsing. Then she'd spotted the label. Tammy had nearly gotten them thrown out with her jokes and sniggering laughter, but Cassie had purchased a bottle, which had calmed the owner down rather quickly. If for no other reason, she'd bought the wine for proof it existed—she would have the name *in print!* And it was a great conversation piece.

That's the one she chose tonight. She poured a generous amount into a wine glass and inhaled the berry fragrance.

Mmm. She wondered if this brand was supposed to beguile one into a night of passionate activity.

A night like the one she'd had with Mike.

She'd been perfectly content living alone in her apartment, her teaching job, her routine. Then the big firefighter had crossed her path and she'd found her perfect little world was no longer perfect. Even more disturbing, she discovered she liked this man disrupting her very ordinary life.

His job was dangerous and he'd scared the life out of her the night of the accident. But that was Mike. Saving people was his life. She wondered what obstacles had shaped him and made him choose the career of a firefighter. She took a sip of wine and settled back into the cushions, thinking of Mike, naked, with only a towel to cover himself. Then a blanket and how quickly it had landed on the floor along with her own clothes. She took another sip and leaned her head on the back of the couch, feeling the tension dissolve at the back of her neck.

In her first twenty-two years, her life had been filled with school, hard work and surviving her sister. Cassie loved children, so the decision to be a teacher had been an easy one. As for relationships, men were more interested in her physical assets than anything she might say and she had no desire for male contact just for the sake of having sex. She had hoped to find a man who would be comfortable with her. Someone who would share the day with her, not just the night. But she'd spent most of the last seven years alone and not actively looking.

When she'd seen Mike, she hadn't thought about any of those things. One look into his alluring eyes and her brain scrambled. One touch and she'd melted. She closed her eyes and inhaled a deep breath, trying to recapture the scent of the man who filled her mind.

Men had come on to her before and she'd given in, wishing for contentment, a connection, a bond she'd never found. But Mike had scattered her senses and knocked her world upside down. She hadn't succumbed to him because of a dry spell. The choice of abstaining these past two years had been her own.

So why did she lay awake at night, craving the touch of this one man? She couldn't stop thinking about him. Now that she'd tasted bliss, she wanted him again, and again.

***

Another sleepless night.

Should he call her? Usually Mike dodged phone calls from women. Being on the initiating end was new to him. But Cassie had captured more than his interest.

The woman was educated, a teacher. Of little kids. He could only imagine the stamina needed to put up with a dozen or more pint-sized balls of energy on full throttle. She must be a saint. Not to mention gorgeous. And had a body men fantasized about.

Jesus. He gripped the coffee mug as he recalled the night he'd spent with her, visualizing naked limbs and plush curves and how much he'd like to see her again. The first step would be to call her. After losing the battle with his conscience, it only took a matter of minutes to bribe his buddy in the police department for Cassie's number.

Just as he reached into his pocket, his cell phone vibrated. He checked the screen.

Laredo.

"Yeah."

"Hey, Mike. It's my turn to cook."

"What are you fixing?"

"That's the thing. What are you in the mood for?"

Loaded question. At the moment, he had his mind set on more of Cassie.

"Why are you asking me?"

"Thought I'd fix one of your favorite dishes."

It occurred to him that Laredo was up to something. "Again. Why?"

Laredo laughed. "Can't put anything past you. Thought maybe you'd like to go to the grocery store with me. It's the best place to meet women."

Mike didn't want to meet anyone other than Cassie.

"I'll pass," Mike said with her image in his mind.

"Well, thing is, I need a ride."

"What's wrong with your truck?"

"It's due for inspection and tire rotation. I thought I'd leave it at the dealership for the afternoon. Can you pick me up at the Dodge place?"

"Now I get it. You're trying to bribe me with food."

"You're a big man. I figured I'd appeal to your appetite."

Mike glanced at his watch. *Nine fifteen.* He still wanted to call Cassie. "What time?"

"Noon. That gives us plenty of time to decide what we want. How about filet mignon?"

His mouth watered. A little sizzle in the pan and a steak was perfect. Laredo made vegetables in the same spicy sauce he used to marinate the meat. Mike could almost taste it. *Noon.* That gave him plenty of time to work up the courage to contact Cassie.

Agreeing to pick up Laredo, Mike ended the call and braced his palms on the kitchen counter. He stared at his cell, his stomach in knots. What the hell was wrong with him?

He liked her. She touched a place inside him he'd never allowed anyone to get close enough to tap before. His track record had been a lot like Laredo—love 'em and leave 'em before they had a chance to get attached.

Attached? Wasn't he putting the cart before the damn horse? There was and would be no attached. He'd never had a long-term relationship and didn't want one. He knew better than to be emotionally vulnerable to a woman. That lesson had been drilled into him by watching his father.

***

Mike walked with Shep out of the open bay door. Sun glinted off red metal, so shiny he could see his reflection. If paint could be washed off a vehicle, the quint would be bare.

"Laredo!" Shep shouted to be heard over the radio.

Laredo turned around. Seeing the Captain, he tucked a rag into his back pocket. "What's up, Cap?"

"I think it's clean."

Laredo gave one of his sheepish grins.

"Got a new guy coming early before the next shift. Need you to show him around."

"Sure thing, Cap." Laredo climbed into the quint with a bounce in his step.

"You'd think that truck was his pride and joy," Shep said and shook his head.

"It is," Mike answered.

"Got the report back on the Wimer property."

"The house we used for training? Took them long enough."

The quint's engine roared and Shep waited for Laredo to back it into its spot in the bay before he continued.

"You were right. Signs of gas and explosives were found."

Mike whistled through his teeth. "I knew it had to be something like that. Damn thing went up the second Ryan tossed the torch."

"Heard you went with Jared to see him. How's he doing?"

"Pretty banged up. Did you know he has staples from his knee to his groin? He could have lost his leg. The force of the blast broke his arm and a few ribs. He's still on pain medication, but he seemed comfortable. The suit protected his body, but his face is burned. Backlash."

"Sounds like he's lucky to be alive."

"Ryan said the same thing. His attitude is great. Still has his sense of humor. Can't say I'd be as chipper if I were in his situation."

"A good woman will do that to you. His wife is one of the good ones."

Mike couldn't help but wonder if she'd stick around after what had happened. She seemed nice enough. Ryan looked happy. They had both been smiling when he and Jared left.

"There's too many questions on this one. Why would someone want to blow up that house?"

Mike drifted back to the conversation with Shep. "Especially when we were going to burn it down. Do you think the person responsible knew the fire department would be there?"

"I had that area cleared and posted. By all means, whoever did this knew about the training exercise. If they didn't know anything else, they sure as hell saw the *keep out* signs."

The idea had Mike clenching his fists. "Firefighters were hurt."

"Yes. And I want answers. Hooley will find them."

"Damn. It could have been a lot worse. If those guys had been standing any closer ..." Mike didn't want to think about the fact that the men he thought of as his brothers could have been seriously hurt or killed.

"You two look entirely too serious." Jared stepped from one of the bay doors behind them. "I came out here to tell you the new guy is here. Mike, you got that look."

"What look?"

"The one that says there's trouble. What's going on?" Jared shoved his thumbs in his front pockets. The smile he wore on a regular basis turned down in a worried frown.

"I got the report from the fire investigator," Shep answered. "Looks like someone was out there messing around."

"Some idiot turned on a gas line?"

Shep gave a nod. "Explosives."

"The Wimers wouldn't do that."

"Of course not," Mike agreed.

"I spoke to the old man," Shep added. "He told me he cleared out the place and made sure everyone knew to stay away from there."

"The posted signs were still up," Jared said. "I saw them."

"I confirmed with the gas company that Mr. Wimer did notify them about the department using the property, and the gas was turned off."

"Then what the hell—" Mike started but Shep interrupted him.

"Tanks. Three of them."

"What kind of son-of-a-bitch would plant those? And for what purpose?" He didn't expect an answer and was taken back when Jared spoke.

"You know, Cap, this means someone knew firefighters would be there. Someone knew *exactly* when we'd be there."

Mike spotted the moment Jared's words registered with Shep. "This was no chance occurrence. No ordinary man, either. It's beginning to sound like someone with a grudge."

"Or some nut job who has targeted the fire department."

Mike's anger boiled. "How the hell did the bastard get gas in the house without our men detecting it?"

"Open air. Outside," Jared said, holding his arms open toward the sky. "The crews had their masks on. Timing was everything."

An uneasy chill quivered down Mike's spine.

"Christ. Was the weasel wearing one of our uniforms? Our gear?"

"Either that or ... someone's gone rogue."

Mike locked eyes with Jared. "Not one of our guys."

"I prefer to think it's an outsider," Shep said, his voice full of uneasiness. "Keep this under wraps."

***

You need to die.

Seth followed the seam down the barrel of the gun, his target lined up perfectly in his sights.

But not yet. I will make you suffer, the way my brother suffered.

He slowed his breathing, knowing he needed a calm head if his plan was to work.

Did his target know he had been the one responsible for the explosion?

Bitterness wedged in Seth's throat.

The big business man. CEO of Accent Dynamics. His brother's partner. The one who had set up a major deal then stabbed Shawn in the back. Shawn had gone to prison while that cocksucker kept living his important life, with his big deal corporation.

The company owed Shawn.

Now owed him.

Shawn survived two years before those bastards finally killed him.

His brother.

His blood.

The saying went *revenge is a dish best served cold*. But Seth liked things hot.

Fire.

A corner of Seth's mouth lifted in a grin.

A brother in the Staunton Fire Department. A fireman. Another fucking hero. How convenient that bit of knowledge fit perfectly into Seth's plans.

Didn't men die in fires every day?

You will suffer, you bastard. The way my brother suffered.

It's your turn. See how you like knowing your brother is in danger.

Seth lowered the rifle, thinking of the man he despised.

"You need to die. A little bit at a time."

CHAPTER 13

"You're in a foul mood." Cassie stood at the classroom door and watched Tammy scurry around in a tizzy. She chewed on her bottom lip, her face was flushed and she jerked at the things on her desk. It had to be her ex. He was the only one who could put Tammy in a bad mood.

"Oh, I'm just peachy," Tammy said as she grabbed some papers from her desk and stuffed them into her bag with force. From the crinkling sounds, the papers were scrunched. If Tammy shoved any more in there, they'd be unsalvageable.

"Do you plan on grading those and giving them back tomorrow? Your students will think you threw them in the trash and then dug them back out."

Tammy froze. When she turned around, her eyes clouded with defeat. Abruptly, she braced her hands on the cluttered desk, as if seeking the sturdy structure to hold her up. Red thick hair covered her face as she hung her head.

Instantly concerned, Cassie hurried forward and clasped Tammy's shoulders. "Breathe, deep. Count to ten."

"I'm okay." Tammy straightened and began stuffing papers again. "The jerk."

Ahh. Just as Cassie expected.

"Now what did he do?"

"He's taking me to court," Tammy said, flicking the latch on her case.

"What?" Cassie asked in a stupor. She could not have heard right.

"He thinks because he now has a new wife, he should have the boys."

"After two years of being an absentee father, now he wants the boys?"

"Of course, he doesn't want them," Tammy spouted in anger. "The boys would make him look better if they lived with him. Prestige and all that crap. And he wouldn't have to pay child support." She flung her bag across the room. Papers scattered and floated to the floor.

Cassie retraced her steps and closed the classroom door. When she turned back, tears slid unheedingly down her friend's face. She wrapped her arms around Tammy's shaking body and held her.

"He's a son-of-a-bitch. A rotten bastard." Tammy jerked her head back, her eyes flashing with anguish. "What am I going to do?"

"Take one breath at a time," Cassie soothed.

"I'm pissed. Really pissed." Tammy tilted her tear streaked face up. "But I'm scared, too."

The fact that Steve planned a custody suit was too much. He was an absolute shithead. "When did all this happen?"

Stepping back, Tammy took a deep breath, attempting to calm herself. She snatched a tissue from the box on her desk and blew her nose.

"Principal Marsh called me to his office at lunch. He received a phone call from Steve." She hesitated, twisting the tissue in her hands. "He wanted the boys' records. Since they would be coming to live with him, he would make the decision whether or not they stayed in *this* school."

"Good Lord." How had Tammy been able to teach her class after receiving that shock? "He's not serious."

Tammy whirled in fury. "I thought he was bluffing and told Clayton as much. Then I called Steve. The SOB wouldn't answer."

Clayton Marsh was a good man. The teachers liked him because he was fair and went to bat for them. He would be on Tammy's side and do everything in his power to help her keep her boys in this school.

"What did Clayton tell you?"

"I'm glad he told me what Steve was up to. But since Steve has shared legal custody, Clayton had to give him the boys' records."

"That's normal. As teachers, we see things like this all the time. That doesn't give him permission to take the boys from this school. You have sole physical custody."

"For now." Tammy collapsed in the chair behind her desk and covered her face with her hands. "What am I going to do?"

"Don't worry. We'll figure this out."

"He's taking me to court. I know him. He's painfully systematic. And thorough. What if he manages to get full custody?"

A tightness settled in Cassie's chest. "Where are the boys?"

"I asked Carmella to keep them in her classroom." She lowered her trembling hands. "I'm afraid to let them see me like this. They'll know. They're so smart. They will sense something."

An idea struck. Cassie pulled her cell phone from her purse.

"What are you doing?"

"My sister can be a real bitch, but she'll come through in a pinch." When her sister answered, Cassie made arrangements for Jennifer to pick up the boys and keep them overnight. When she ended the call, Tammy stared at her with regret.

"Jennifer is taking the boys? I'm sorry, Cassie. Now you owe her your soul."

"Don't worry about it. She's good for some things, although I'm not sure what." Cassie slid her phone back into her purse.

"That girl has two faces," Tammy said as she cocked her head. "If I didn't see how she treated you, I'd think she was one of the sweetest people around."

"That's her front. The face she shows the rest of the world. She wants everyone to believe she's sugar and honey. She's an angel, blah, blah."

"Why do you let her get to you?"

"Believe me, before I became a teacher, it was ten times worse." Cassie remembered how Jennifer thrived being in the spotlight. As long as Cassie had remained in the background, they mostly got along fine. She'd learned at an early age that she had to toughen up and ignore her sister's digs.

"I learned to cope. She still gets my hackles up, but I'm used to it."

"I have three sisters and none of them ever treated me the way your sister treats you. Though, we do have our share of fights. With four of us, usually one of my siblings takes my side."

"I'm glad Jennifer is my only sister. I have my hands full dealing with her. Just because she's older she thinks she can boss me around."

Tammy stood, propped a hand on her hip and said in a comical voice, "You ain't the boss of me."

Cassie laughed at the childish pose.

"Didn't you ever tell your sister that? We did it all the time."

"I remember kids at school doing that. Didn't work with Jennifer."

"You're one of the strongest people I know," Tammy said. "But when your sister is around, you shrivel up."

Shrivel?

"I do not." As soon as the words left her mouth, she knew they weren't true. Her sister always made her feel inadequate.

"Well, your defense mechanism turns on, anyway. You go all stiff, your jaw does that clench thing, and it literally looks like you could kill someone." Tammy tightened her arms by her sides as though demonstrating. "And when you're around men, humph."

Cassie narrowed her eyes as her anger surfaced. "Just what do you mean by that remark?"

"Okay. Example." Tammy shoved out of her chair. "The night we met the fire guys in El Puerto's."

Cassie wasn't sure where this was going, but where men were concerned, Tammy was constantly pushing Cassie out of her comfort zone. "What about it?"

"You're a beautiful woman, Cassie. Striking. You have the looks, the hair, my God, a fabulous figure. You could be on the cover of *Vogue*. Yet you act like you're unattractive." Tammy leaned in her personal space and glared. "Mike was hot for you."

Yeah. He was. She'd found out just how hot Friday night.

"I saw your insecurity," Tammy continued as she stepped back. "I saw you slink into your protective cloak of armor.

"I don't know what you're talking about."

"I know you," Tammy said leaning closer. "I saw all sorts of questions running through your mind. You questioned his motives. If he really thought you were pretty. Why would he pick you?"

Cassie felt her face flame.

"Am I wrong?"

No. You're not wrong.

Cassie being four years younger than her sister had been a lot like growing up alone. She was never allowed to go anywhere with Jennifer. When her friends came over, Jennifer would tell Cassie to get lost. The constant rejection and derogatory remarks had left some pretty deep scars

"I'm not beautiful and I hate when men tell me I am," Cassie declared. "They only say things they think I want to hear because of my big boobs."

But Mike had been different.

Clearly frustrated, Tammy flung her arms about. "My God, Cassie. What do you see when you look in the mirror? You're a knock-out. Men tell you that because it's true!"

"Stop. You have no reason to flatter me. I'm already your friend." Cassie tried joking. She couldn't believe the nonsense Tammy spouted. But she wanted to believe Mike liked her looks. After all, he'd seen every part of her body.

"I give up," Tammy said as she whirled around. "Your sister has done her work. Or those high school boys, college guys, whatever idiots ridiculed you."

Yep, they did. All of them. And what did she know?

Only what her sister had told her.

When Cassie left home, she'd learned from experience that guys' brains were controlled by their dicks. She'd been so stupid. At the age of eighteen, she'd quickly discovered just how little she did know. But she'd learned. The hard way. Life had taught harsh lessons.

All guys wanted sex. If the woman was willing, plain or pretty, a man scored. Cassie had allowed herself to believe they cared. A quick roll in the hay did not mean adoration or devotion. Cassie had been seduced. Like so many others, she'd fallen for a college boy's charms. She'd felt love and then heartbreak. But she could not deny the passion. Or the fierce longing right up until the guy was done with her. Then all she'd felt was empty and unfulfilled.

She put a halt on her wandering emotions before they could rein free, and forced her mind back to the situation at hand.

"You've got a sitter for the evening. I think we both could use a drink."

Tammy crossed her arms over her chest. "What do you have in mind?"

Cassie gestured to the floor. "First, we're going to clean up these papers. Then we're getting you out of here."

***

Jared wore a button-down shirt with the sleeves rolled to his forearms. His cologne told the entire team he had a date. Jared never wore the scent to work. By the smile lifting the corners of his mouth, Jared's date must be a hottie.

"What are you doing here? Don't you have a date?" Mike asked.

"Who said I had a date?"

Mike gave an exaggerated sniff. "Did you get all sweet smelling for us?"

"Nope. I'm headed over to Roanoke coliseum. Chippendales are performing tonight."

Cooper hooted. "You got off early, flying solo, to go see the Chippendales?"

"*Pretty Boy* couldn't score a date? Come on man. The Chippendales are dudes!"

"Very funny, Laredo."

"Your idol has lost his *chinga'* mind, Coop."

"I'll have you know the women will be crawling all over me tonight." Jared tugged at the collar of his shirt with flare.

"At Chippendales?" Mike asked, joining in the fun.

"Christ. Can't a guy get a break. Not *at*. Because *of*." Jared placed his hands on his hips, clearly aggravated. "Women flock to those shows. They drink, they get horny. All a guy has to do is wait. When the chicks hit the bars, they're looking for any guy available."

"Sounds like a plan." Cooper snorted.

Jared made a show of looking at his watch. "It takes two hours to get there. I'm leaving now."

"My shift ends at eight," Cooper stated, rising to his feet. "Hang on. I'll be your wingman."

"I'm not waiting."

"Come on, Jared. Give your groupie a break."

Cooper glared at Laredo.

Mike thought he'd help the kid out. "Women won't hit the bars until ten."

"Yeah. Don't the shows run about two hours? If it begins at eight—"

"By the time your shift ends, I'll be casing out the best bars."

Cooper took a step forward. "I can meet you in Roanoke. Just tell me where."

It pained Mike to watch. The anxious expression on Coop's face was pitiful.

Jared released a sigh that clearly indicated he'd given up. "All right. I guess I can wait."

Mike's shoulders shook as he tried not to laugh. Looked like the kid would be shadowing his idol.

CHAPTER 14

The Pitt Stop sign glowed above the brightly-lit building centered in the middle of a huge parking lot filled with cars. Cassie had been here a few times. The bar had great food, but was better known for music and dancing. By the time she followed Tammy to her house, waited while she changed and then drove home to get ready, darkness had settled. The news that Tammy's ex wanted custody had thrown them both for a loop. They needed a night out. Cassie decided to be the designated driver and if her friend needed to get roaring drunk, so be it.

A young couple hurried up the steps and bolted inside, letting the door slam behind them. Manners were a thing of the past.

"Prick," Tammy muttered.

"Look at the bright side." Cassie opened the door and aimed for an ear-splitting grin. "You don't have to say thank you."

"I like the way you think." Tammy winked and marched through the doorway.

Loud voices and laughter greeted them. A country "somebody-done-somebody-wrong-song" blared from the jute-box. Most of the tables were already full. One waitress sauntered over with a tray balanced above her head. "Hey, ladies. There's a booth back on that wall."

"Thanks," Tammy said. "Are you our waitress, 'cause I'm ready to order a drink."

The girl laughed. "Gotta be a man. Sure. I'll be right there."

Cassie swerved her way around bodies, following Tammy, and slid into the empty booth. "Thank God it's Friday."

"Do you think Jennifer will keep the boys overnight?"

"I already asked her. She's got this big ta-do planned. Movie night, where the boys can dress the part. *Ninja Turtle*. She even has costumes for them. They'll love it."

"That's really great of her. She likes kids. Why doesn't she like you?"

"I stole her glory of being an only child." Cassie shook herself. "We're here to forget our woes."

"Okay, ladies. What'll you have?" True to her word, the waitress stood there ready to take their order.

"B52 Bombers," Tammy said without hesitation. "And keep them coming."

The waitress popped her gum and replied. "You got somebody to carry you outta here tonight?"

Cassie spoke up. "I'm the designated driver."

"Oh, no you don't," Tammy quickly corrected. "You are joining me, shot for shot."

"Oh, great. I can see the headlines now. Elementary teachers sprawled on the bar floor. And a snapshot I'd rather my students did not see."

The waitress chuckled. "Don't worry, girls. There's always plenty of men willin' to take a lady home."

"That's what I'm afraid of," Cassie mumbled.

"Bring a couple of Ultra Lights, too," Tammy added.

Cassie flung her hair over her shoulder. "If I carry you home, who's going to carry me?"

"Didn't you say we're here to forget our woes? How else are we going to do that? I plan to drink my mind numb." Tammy glanced around the dim room. "At least I won't have to worry about running into my ex. He's too good for this place." A shadow of sorrow covered her face.

Cassie swallowed the worry she couldn't express. Her friend had gotten a real shock today. How hateful could the man be? Threatening a custody suit. Those boys belonged with Tammy. She had taken care of them when Steve couldn't keep his dick in his pants. This second marriage probably wouldn't last, either.

"Okay. You talked me into it," she said. What the hell. "We can call a cab."

"'Atta girl." Relief mingled with Tammy's expression of joy.

The waitress returned in no time carrying beers and two small glasses of dark brown syrup. The grin on Tammy's face matched the sparkle in her eyes. "Bottoms up."

They were really going to do this. Oh, well. Cassie hadn't been drunk since ... college? She raised her glass. "Bottom's up."

Good thing she'd consumed it in one gulp, because the fire in her throat and belly would not allow her to do it again. "Oh ... my ... God," she wheezed when she could get her breath. Tears threatened.

Tammy sucked in air as if she couldn't get any. When they glanced at each other, they both broke into laughter. "Aren't we a pair?"

Cassie grabbed her bottle of beer and gulped a large swallow. It helped. "Maybe we should sip the next one."

"I agree." Tammy giggled. "And get some food."

By the time the food arrived, Cassie felt no pain. And Tammy had forgotten all about her ex. "Yum. Over the lips and straight to the hips. I'm going to enjoy every bite of this sinful burger."

"Speaking of sinful, looked what just walked in the door." Tammy gave a nod.

With her mouth full, Cassie turned and squinted, trying to decipher who ... Her eyes flew wide.

Mike.

"Am I mistaken or are there two of him?"

"If you're seeing double, then so am I." She recognized the guy with Mike as one of the firefighters that had been at the Mexican restaurant. Same height, a touch of gray at the temples, distinguished looking. Cassie chewed faster, watching them as they stopped at the bar.

"Invite them over," Tammy urged.

"What?"

"Close your mouth. You look like a deer caught in headlights. Ask them to join us."

Cassie glanced at her burger. Her melt-in-your-mouth burger. "Do you know how long it's been since I've had a burger this good? *And* fries?"

"So. Eat. *And* ask them over."

"How can I eat this monstrosity in front of a man?"

"Easy. Watch."

Tammy grasped her burger with both hands and shoved the thing in her face. When she pulled the juicy bun away, both of her cheeks were poofed out. Cassie couldn't help it. She busted out in laughter.

"Like that." Bits of mayo drooled down the side of Tammy's lip.

"Don't talk with your mouth full. You're not going to outdo me." Cassie grabbed her burger and did the same. Her mouth was so full she could barely chew. She took a gulp of beer to wash down her food and Tammy made a face. They busted out laughing again. Then, before she knew it, Tammy shouted across the packed room.

"Over here. Hey guys. Look. We're over here."

Thank God, the noise kept Mike and his friend from hearing her.

A few other guys turned in their direction. Cassie wanted to crawl under the table. "Stop that. People will think you're an idiot."

"You're an idiot if you let that man get away."

"You're making a scene."

"Huh?" Tammy followed Cassie's gaze and noticed two men heading their way. "No. No. Not you." She pointed and waved her finger. The confused expressions on the guys' faces was priceless. Cassie busted out laughing again.

The waitress showed up with two more shots. "All right, ladies. Is this the limit?"

"Hell, no," Tammy said and swiped up the glass. "Let's have a toast."

"You mean, *the* toast?" Cassie raised an eyebrow.

"Is there any other?" Tammy cleared her throat and waited for Cassie to pick up her shot. Together, they recited a poem from her college days.

"Here's to you. Here's to me. Friends we shall always be. But if we should ever disagree ..." Tammy winked and they clinked glasses. "Fuck you. Here's to me."

Cassie tossed back the fiery liquid and shook her head as a warm shiver flowed down her chest and arms. *Damn, that stuff tastes good.*

"Well, I can honestly say I've never heard that one. You gals rock." With a spin, the waitress went to the next table.

"We should give her a good tip," Tammy said.

"Definitely."

"What are you going to do about your fire guy?"

After the night she'd shared with Mike, she knew exactly what she'd like to do. But she was sloshed. And her friend was playing matchmaker.

"You think he wants a drunk?"

"You're not drunk. Just happy." Tammy nodded her head, reminding Cassie of a bobble-head.

She couldn't help it. She laughed. "At least I'm a happy drunk."

"*At least* there are two of them. They just got here, so they'll probably stay for a while. That gives you time to make a glutton of yourself."

For some reason, that seemed funny too. Cassie couldn't remember the last time she'd laughed this much. She took a huge bite of her burger and closed her eyes. "Mmm mmm." Rich beefy flavor smacked her taste buds. Tangy mustard blended with crunchy lettuce, spiking her senses. She chewed slowly and swallowed, savoring each zing. "Heaven." She opened her eyes to take another bite and froze—with her mouth open.

Standing there with an indecent grin, Mike leaned against the wooden post connected to the back of Tammy's seat, his eyes fastened on *her*.

"Heaven?" His voice rumbled in a sexy drawl.

Damn if he didn't look like a dark angel.

Breathtakingly gorgeous. Tall—dark—the devil's own sinful smile—delicious.

She was in soooo much trouble.

"Hi, Mike. Introduce your friend." Tammy was staring at the man beside Mike.

"This is Shep. Shep, this is Tammy. And this"—he angled his beer at her—"is Cassie."

The low hum of his voice sent shivers down her spine. But when their gazes locked, her breath caught in her throat and a slow burn hummed in her belly, one that had absolutely nothing to do with liquor. She barely heard his friend's response.

"It's a pleasure, ladies."

Cassie looked scared to death. Had he made a mistake in coming over? She didn't seem too happy to see him. Although, the dreamy look on her face, a moment ago, reminded him of the pleasure he'd given her the other night—a look of pure contentment, while her long slender legs had held him captive. Who would have guessed this elementary teacher could purr like a fine-tuned engine?

Damn. She'd jolted him. Then and now. Long blonde hair, gold lashes dusting her cheeks. Creamy skin as smooth as silk, all over. He willed his body to control the erection already forming.

"Hello Shep. You a big, strong firefighter, too?" Tammy asked with a hint of innuendo, which most likely had been prompted by the empty shot glass in front of her.

Quieter than the rest of their team, Shep kept to himself a lot. He certainly wasn't a lady's man like Jared. Mike had cautioned Shep about Tammy's playfulness before they'd approached the girls' table. By the ear-splitting grin on Shep's face, he didn't care. Interesting.

"Why, yes ma'am. I am."

"Well, come on over here, fire-hero, and tell me all about yourself."

Chuckling, Shep slipped into the booth beside Tammy. Mike stared at Cassie, waiting for an invitation. When she didn't say a word, he motioned with his beer for her to slide over. She blinked as if coming out of a daze. Then she gave him a smile that melted his insides.

He slid into the booth beside her, intentionally brushing his thigh against hers, sending a bolt of heat straight to his gut. She felt it, too. Her heart shaped face jerked up and her tempting lips parted as a silent gasp escaped her sexy mouth. Mike swallowed hard. She had an absurd physical effect on him.

"When Mike mentioned coming to this place, I almost suggested another bar. At the time, it didn't make a difference to me. Now, I'm glad we came here."

"Is that so?" Tammy's glassy eyes were glued on Shep. Mike half expected her to bat her eyelashes.

"Yes, ma'am."

"Please don't call me ma'am."

Half-teasing, half-serious, Shep replied in that low drawl of his. "My mother taught me manners."

"I appreciate a boy that listens to his mama."

Shep showed his pearly whites. "The evening had promised to be another boring one for me. Not so, now."

"Really? How come?" she purred.

Mike watched the exchange with a bit of awe. Shep would never fall for such brazenness, but he probably thought Tammy was harmless. Whatever the reason, Shep played along. Mike had fun watching. It was all he could do not to laugh or stare with his mouth hanging open.

"Because we met you," Shep answered.

"I have met you before," Tammy said with a little pat to Shep's arm. "Well, not actually met. But I remember you from El Puerto's. The whole fire department showed up there."

"We had training that week. Several County units gathered for drills and preparation exercises. Later that evening, we went out for some dinner and that's when you saw us."

"I'm glad you chose the Mexican restaurant."

"One of my favorite places. So, you like Mexican food?"

"Oh yes. Cassie and I go there often. You men in your blue uniforms caused quite a stir." Tammy leaned closer to him and Shep never moved. He just grinned as if he liked her attention.

"We get that a lot."

"I love a man in uniform."

Oh brother. She's bombed.

Mike glanced at Cassie, wondering how much they'd had to drink. Just then the waitress placed two shot glasses on their table. Dark liquid with a layer of brown foam on top.

"Here ya go, gals. You said keep them coming." The lively waitress propped one hand on a shapely hip. "What can I get for you boys?"

"What's that?" Mike pointed to the shot glasses.

"B52 bombers."

He'd hit the nail dead on. They were bombed.

"Sounds good to me. Two more," Shep said.

Mike raised his brows. Shep did not drink hard liquor. Hell, he rarely drank beer.

Shep turned back to Tammy. "Are you ladies celebrating?"

A cloud of darkness screwed up Tammy's face. Cassie quickly filled the silence.

"We, uh, received some troubling news."

"And we're here to forget." Tammy lifted one of the glasses. "Bottoms up." She stared at Cassie as if daring her.

"Why don't you take mine?" Cassie slid her glass across the table to Shep.

"Oh, no. I couldn't take yours," he said in a long drawl as he shoved it back. "That wouldn't be gentlemanly."

The two girls glared at each other with an undercurrent of meaningful communication. Mike sure as hell couldn't figure out the message they'd exchanged. Seconds ticked by.

"Bottoms up," Shep repeated, coaxing the girls to drink.

A gleam sparked in his eyes, like a troublemaker instigating mischief. He seemed eager, keen on seeing if they would drink the B52s in one gulp. Mike had not seen this side of Shep.

"We agreed ..." Cassie started talking, then stopped as Tammy flung back her head and the contents of the shot-glass disappeared.

Shep propped his arm on the booth behind her and offered his beer. She grabbed it like someone dying of thirst.

"What the hell," Cassie mumbled just before she tilted the glass and drained it. When she slammed the glass on the table, her hair hid her face. Even though Mike couldn't see her eyes, her quick raspy breaths indicated the B52 had burned going down.

His shoulders shook with mirth. What a woman. He was glad he and Shep showed up. These girls would definitely need help getting home. If luck came Mike's way, he would spend the night with his sensual teacher. Even though sex was off the table, he'd still consider himself lucky.

The waitress placed two more drinks on their table. Shep held up two fingers. "Two more."

"How you doing on beers?"

"Another round, please. And two more burgers."

Burgers sounded good to Mike. *The Pitt Stop* served man-sized burgers. As if suddenly seeing the food in front of her, Cassie said, "Oh, yeah." She picked up her burger and took an unladylike bite.

"I love a woman with a good appetite," Mike said watching her.

"See? I told you." Tammy shouted.

"Told her what?" Shep leaned closer to Tammy.

"She was worried about eating a juicy burger in front of a hunk like him." Tammy pointed at Mike.

Cassie made choking sounds. He patted her on the back, grinning like a fool.

Shep clasped Tammy's arm. "Can you two-step?"

Her eyes flew wide as he tugged her from the booth and led her to the dance floor.

Mike caught Cassie's gaze. "Hunk, huh?"

Cassie shoved him with her shoulder. "You know you're hot."

"I know I'm glad I came in this bar tonight and found you."

"Shoving a burger in my face like a ... hog?"

"A very pretty—" Mike hesitated when he saw Cassie's scowl. "Uh ... like a hungry female."

"Nice save."

"Honey, you ain't seen nothing. Wait till I get mine."

He turned up his bottle for a swallow of beer completely aware she watched. He loved having her hungry eyes on him. Jade gemstones, filled with yearning. He wouldn't mind a repeat performance of the other night.

"You looked well satisfied when I walked up. If a burger can do that ..." He stared at her lips and leaned in for a taste. "Reminds me of another time I saw a similar expression, with your hair spread out over your pillow."

Her eyes begged him to kiss her. To make love to her here and now. The very idea of kissing those pouting lips, of tasting her sweet honey, triggered a surge to his beating pulse. Only the sheerest willpower held him immobile.

"Okay, kids. Burgers for one hungry appetite."

Mike jerked back.

The waitress gave a wink aimed at Cassie. "Don't think you'll need a cab."

That's when he realized Cassie had nearly crawled into his lap. Her stimulating curves were still pressed against his side. He struggled to speak.

"A cab?"

"I was supposed to be the designated driver," she said moving away.

"The distressing news was Tammy's?"

"Yeah. Her ex." Cassie picked at the label on her beer. "She needs a good lawyer. But I don't want to talk about it now. She needs this."

"A diversion."

Cassie faced him. "She deserves to have some fun. Some enjoyment in her life. She has two kids and ..." Her voice trailed off as she turned back to her beer.

"And what?" he asked softly.

"This guy knows how to dance." Tammy skidded into the booth with a grinning Shep behind her.

"I grew up in a house with four brothers. My mom believed we were made for dancing and took great pleasure in torturing us." Shep lowered his voice and directed his words to Tammy. "Which is the way we thought of dancing, until we found out girls liked boys who danced. A girl will pick a guy that can dance over the best-looking guy in any place."

"Like you have anything to worry about." Tammy's fingers walked up Shep's chest. He grinned. Tammy was getting awfully familiar. And Shep seemed to enjoy it.

Which was damn puzzling, since Shep stayed out of the limelight. Flattery never mattered to him. A person's goodness carried more weight. He was usually quiet around women, too.

More drinks and a few dances later, Shep offered to take one of the tanked females home. Food had helped, but neither woman could walk on their own. Mike settled Cassie in the passenger side of her car while Shep poured Tammy into his SUV.

Still puzzling over Shep's unusual behavior, Mike had to rag on him a bit. He pointed a finger and spoke in an accusing tone. "You aided and abetted."

"Don't worry. They won't remember a thing in the morning. I'll take her home"—Shep nodded his head to Tammy—"put her in bed and leave. I won't even undress her." Shep slapped him on the back. "You've landed a school teacher. She has to be something special."

"So is her friend."

"I saw that right away. I figured if the girls wanted to cut loose, let them. Better with us than some other guys that could have happened along. At least with us, they were safe. I'll take care of Tammy."

CHAPTER 15

Cassie wished someone would just shoot her. Put her out of her self-induced misery. Her temples pounded. Her eyes hurt. She didn't dare move.

"Is Sleeping Beauty awake?"

She flinched, and wished she hadn't. Pain exploded in her brain.

Mike?

The evening might have been a blur, but she knew Mike had brought her home. She was too miserable to worry about her actions. And now she must surely look like death warmed over.

She took slow even breaths.

"Don't you dare laugh," she struggled to say, which only set off the drums to pounding again.

"Come on. Sit up. I brought you some aspirin. And a little special tonic for the morning after."

She cracked one eye open. He looked so devastatingly handsome, she hated him.

"Come on. I'll help you."

Mike arranged pillows against the headboard and gathered her in his strong arms, helping her up. Within a millisecond, she felt better. Soothed, comforted, and then he opened his palm revealing two aspirin. She hoped the tablets didn't upset her stomach. Thank God, she hadn't gotten sick.

At least she didn't remember getting sick. Just how bad had she humiliated herself?

"Bottoms up." Then the rat chuckled.

"You're partly responsible for this," she told him.

"Me? How am I at fault?" His brows arched but his expression was not so innocent.

"You kept giving me drinks."

His face relaxed with a mocking grin. "Oh, and I guess I poured them down your throat."

She scrunched up her face in a hateful glare, but the pain in her head made her quickly regret her action.

Mike eased onto the bed beside her. "Here. Drink this." How could he sound so sexy when she felt so bad?

Good grief, what was in that glass? It looked a little like tomato juice, only more brown in color. She took a sniff and tried not to gag. It smelled a little sweet. But how was she going to get it down? Squinting her eyes, she asked, "What is it?"

"Trust me. It will help."

Never trust a man who says "trust me".

She took a sip. Not so bad. She held her nose and drank the rest.

Mike eased her back against the pillows.

"I'll never drink again," she groaned.

"Until the next time." He laughed.

"I hate you."

He chuckled again. "In my own defense, Shep kept ordering the drinks."

That's right. Shep was there too. He and Tammy had sure hit it off.

Tammy.

Cassie struggled once again to sit. "Where's Tammy?"

Mike shrugged those immaculate shoulders. "I guess at her house."

"What do you mean *you guess*?" Cassie quickly took in her surroundings. Yep. This was her bedroom. "Did you bring me here? Did you take Tammy home? What happened?" Her voice rose with each question, which didn't help her headache at all.

"Slow down." His gentle hands stroked her arms, stimulating each nerve cell. "Everything is okay. Shep took Tammy home and I took advantage of you." He said it so matter-of-factly she knew he was lying.

"Hmm. Must not have been worth remembering," she managed to tease.

"Ouch." His expression turned sour. "I see you're feeling better."

With extreme effort, she achieved a smile. "Then come clean. Why did Shep take Tammy?"

"So, I could have my way with you." Mike wiggled his brows, reminding her of Groucho Marks.

"Are you sure he took her home?"

"Set your mind at ease. Shep is a good man. He probably helped Tammy inside, settled her on her bed—*fully clothed*—and left."

She hoped so. Tammy had really been out of it last night, and Mike's friends were strangers. Cassie studied Mike's face. He lifted her hand and laced his fingers with hers, creating a fuzzy warmth in her tummy.

"He's that kind of guy. He's not a creep."

"Well I'm glad to hear that," she said guardedly, wondering if Mike had read her mind. She hadn't actually accused Shep or anything, but what did she know about the guy?

"You were thinking something similar."

A flush rose up her neck. Maybe Mike was clairvoyant.

Some of the tension eased from her shoulders and her headache had lessened to a dull thud. Maybe his concoction was working. The way he looked at her triggered a different kind of tension. His intense gaze and his warm fingers laced with hers sent prickles racing over her skin.

She shoved her hair out of her face, thinking she must look absolutely dreadful. Then she realized she wore her nightgown. Mike had to have undressed her. *Oh Lord.* She shivered at the thought of him rummaging through her under things.

What else could she not remember?

"Now what are you thinking?" His deep voice, evocative.

"Um. Nothing."

He shifted on the bed, bracing one arm close to her hip. "Um, yes, something."

She chewed on her bottom lip. When she didn't answer, he took pity on her.

"I put on coffee," he said. "Why don't you rest and I'll bring you a cup?"

"A man after my own heart." She looked away. "I need to take a shower."

He rose, and once again, she admired his physique.

He stretched to his full height. "What do you need? I'll help—"

"No." Her voice came out a tad breathless, thinking of him naked in the shower with her. Even though she could not remember the details, she figured he had helped enough last night. "I'll be fine. I'm not completely helpless."

He gave her a two-finger salute. "Yes, ma'am."

She watched his backside as he walked from the room. *Mmm mmm.*

Hot. And he was taking care of *her*. There was more to her handsome firefighter than she'd originally thought and she fully hoped he hung around long enough for her to learn all the good stuff.

Tammy.

Cassie reached for her phone. Quickly, her fingers flew over the numbers. One ring, two.

"Hello." Tammy's groggy voice sounded like she was still in bed.

"You sound as bad as I feel."

"Oh, Cassie. I've died and gone to hell."

"Tell me about it." She leaned back against the fluffy pillows. "When I woke, I wanted someone to shoot me."

"My head feels like Spartacus raced his chariots from one temple to the other." Tammy grumbled. "Now Thor is swinging his mighty hammer."

"Tammy, are you okay?" Cassie had been worried ever since Mike's evasive answer. She was supposed to take care of her friend. Be the designated driver and make sure nothing bad happened. At least nothing that Tammy hadn't wanted to occur. Cassie could barely remember getting home herself.

"Are you deaf?" Tammy groaned as if it pained her to speak. "I just told you—"

"Are you alone?" Cassie interrupted.

Silence.

Shit. He's still there.

"What? Oh ... your sister still has the boys. I don't think I'm up to getting them just yet."

Crap. Cassie had forgotten about them. "Don't worry about the boys. There're fine." At least they should be. "So, um ... you're not alone?"

She heard shuffling noises and rustling linen sheets. "Hold on a minute."

What should she do? Hang up? Apologize?

Cassie threw back the covers and swung her feet to the floor. She felt too ill to pace. Finally, Tammy came back on the line.

"Okay. What's up? Why did you call?" Tammy was back in control. She must have gotten her second wind.

"Took you long enough," Cassie said crisply. "Did you forget I was on the phone?"

"I took some aspirin. With two boys, you learn to bounce back quickly. Even after a night of spontaneous drunkenness. What was I thinking?"

"Is anyone with you?"

"No, I'm by myself. Who would be with me? What's with the questions?"

Cassie released a huge sigh. "Neither one of us were thinking. I just wanted to make sure you got home okay."

"Didn't you bring me home last night?"

"Um, about that ..."

"Please don't tell me something I don't want to hear," Tammy groaned with regret. "Good Lord. What happened?"

Might as well take the bull by the horns. Cassie sucked in a breath. "Mike brought me home. Shep took you home?"

Again ... silence.

"Did you hear me? Tammy?"

"I heard you. Shep brought me home? Were you with us?"

"No. I don't think so."

"You don't think? What the hell do you mean, you don't think?" She shrilled. Cassie flinched. Tammy sounded ready to go off the deep end. And Cassie couldn't reassure her.

"I don't remember," she said miserably. "We both were out of it. Mike told me."

"Mike? When did … Is he there now?"

Cassie scooted back and planted her feet on the bed. "Yes."

"Damn. Why couldn't I get that lucky? And you're on the phone with me?"

Cassie nodded, not even thinking that Tammy couldn't see her.

"Now I understand. You called me to see if Shep was still here. Well, I'll be damned. A chance at a fireman and I blew it. Drunk. Just my luck. How will I ever live that one down?"

She sounded so disappointed Cassie wanted to cheer her. But had no idea how. Especially not knowing what had happened between Shep and Tammy. It sounded like Tammy didn't even know.

"Oh, noooo," Tammy wailed. "What if I got sick? Oh God, Cassie."

She'd had those same thoughts earlier. "Don't beat yourself up. It's over now. We did what we did." It was easier to calm her friend than to appease her own anxiety. "You really don't remember?"

"Do you?" Tammy countered.

"If Mike hadn't been here, I'd be at a total loss. I have no memory of leaving the place or how we got home."

"Shep didn't bother to hang around, so I must have repelled him." Tammy sounded so down, Cassie's heart went out to her.

"Don't even think that. Mike said Shep was a gentleman. The kind of guy who would take you home and leave without taking advantage."

"Just what I need. A good Samaritan."

What Tammy needed—and deserved—was a good man. "You've got more spirit than that. Once you feel better, things will be more clear. You'll bounce right back to your bubbly self."

"You're right. I don't like pity parties. Thanks for the info dump. I'm going to take a shower and rejoin the living. I'll call later when my head is clear. Or you can call me after your man leaves."

"He's not my—"

The line went dead. Tammy had hung up. Cassie stared at the screen, then tossed the phone on the night table.

She needed a shower.

She padded to the bathroom and avoided the mirror. She turned on the water and stepped inside the tiled-shower stall. Warm water sluiced over her body, revitalizing the lax nerves under her skin, but when she stuck her face under the spray, the streaming beads felt like needles poking her sore head. She hoped the concoction Mike gave her worked, although she shouldn't really complain—it hadn't tasted that bad.

A strong cup of coffee. That's what she needed.

She picked up a bar of soap and inhaled the crisp, clean scent. It helped to clear her head and stimulate some energy. Maybe by the time she washed her body, her headache would be mild enough for her to try washing her hair.

Fifteen minutes later, she opened the bathroom door, allowing steam to escape into her bedroom, and noticed a mug sitting on her night stand. You had to love a guy that brought you coffee. She padded to the bed and sat down before picking up the cup. She slowly inhaled. The scent of fresh Columbian beans floated through her nose to her formerly fuzzy mind. Her taste buds anticipated the pleasure of a good cup of brewed java. She took a sip. A little milk, just the way she liked it.

He remembered.

Feeling much better, she tugged on her clothes and checked her appearance in the mirror. The pink top brought out the pink in her cheeks. Turning sideways, she ran a hand down the seam of her jeans. What she wore didn't matter, but she did want to look her best. She banded her wet hair in a ponytail and went in search of Mike, trying not to dwell on the eagerness in her step or the flurry in her chest.

What was a girl to do? The man was hot, hot, hot.

Mike stood looking out her kitchen window, sipping his coffee. His shoulder muscles bunched as he lowered his cup. Cassie couldn't help but sigh. He must have heard her for he turned and braced one hip against the counter.

"Feeling better?" His lips lifted in a slight curve on one side, sending a pool of heat to her belly.

"Much."

"Let me warm that up." He took her cup, poured hot coffee into it, and then handed it back to her, grazing her fingers.

She caressed her mug, wistful of the warmth of his touch on her skin. She pulled a chair out from the kitchen table and sat down. Taking a sip of her coffee, she savored the taste while contemplating long, muscular legs covered in washed-out denim. Her gaze slid upward over a shirt tucked into low riding jeans. She swallowed, thinking of the sculpted abs she knew lay underneath his shirt, the cuffs rolled a few turns back showed a sprinkling of dark hair that matched the blanket covering his wide, masculine chest. A sigh escaped her lips as she remembered the night she had caressed those very abs, his skin soft and warm beneath her hand. She glanced at the opening at his neck and the tuffs of black exposed. She swallowed. She could almost—

A sound much like a groan escaped Mike drawing her eyes to his searing gaze.

A slow grin spread over his mouth and her heart took a giant leap. One smile. Just one. And she turned to liquid.

She felt the heat in her face as she flushed with embarrassment. He'd watched her ogle him and knew what she'd been thinking.

"Like what you see?"

She took a gulp of her coffee and nearly choked.

He laughed, soft and deep.

She changed the subject. "What was in that stuff you gave me?"

"Trust me. You'll feel better not knowing."

There again with the *trust me*. She didn't trust lightly.

"I seem to remember there being no end to drinks last night. Did you deliberately try getting us drunk?"

"You girls were well on your way to getting snonkered before Shep and I found you. I'm glad we did." He gave her scowl to drive his point home.

Yeah, that wasn't exactly fair of her. She and Tammy had been lucky. Needless to say, if it hadn't been Mike, she would never have lost control. Too much alcohol gave courage to the shyest individual, making them lose their inhibitions. For a control freak, she didn't welcome the idea of lost minutes, or hours of time.

"I don't normally do that." She wiggled in the chair, uncomfortable under his scrutiny.

"Shep said you were nice girls."

"Nice?"

"He figured you didn't normally drink yourselves stupid."

"Stupid?" Silently she agreed.

"Do you own a parrot?"

Cassie covered her forehead with the palm of her hand, wishing she could clear the fog in her brain. "I don't drink a lot. I never get drunk."

"No harm done. Shep said we should let you have your fun. You were pretty funny."

"Shep said," she mocked. "You were there, too." She groaned in mortification. "If I did something I shouldn't have, would you tell me?"

"Nope."

"I'd rather find out now than be totally humiliated meeting someone who witnessed me making a jackass out of myself."

"Okay." Mike shoved from the counter and placed his mug on the table. Then he spun a chair around and sat with his arms crossed over the back. "You didn't do anything out of character. Or, that is, anything you'd be embarrassed about. You let your hair down. And I get the idea you don't do that too often."

"Never."

"Everyone needs to let loose once in a while."

"Letting loose for me was drinking the shots I already had before you arrived."

He leaned forward, his eyes as big as her saucers. "You mean climbing on top of the table and doing a strip tease was out of line for you?"

"Oh my God," Cassie shrieked. When he belted out in laughter, she knew he'd been lying. The stinker.

"Enjoying yourself at my expense?"

"Couldn't help it. You're too easy when you're hung over."

"Well, get your jollies now, because you will never see me like this again."

"Come on. Let me see a smile." A corner of his sexy mouth lifted as he coaxed. Then he leaned his head to one side and peered into her face, delving into her eyes.

She'd never seen a man with such beautiful, blue eyes. Oh sure, she'd seen plenty of blue, but his were a hint darker that sapphires, closer to Persian blue. And when he looked at her the way he was looking at her now, she wanted to dive into them, dive into *him*, and ...

He lifted his mug and leaned back, breaking their contact. As he stared into his cup, a puzzled expression crossed his face. The moment broken, she wondered if maybe he too, had been a little lost in her.

Who was she kidding? He'd brought her home and made sure she, nor Tammy, had gotten into trouble. End of story.

She should be more appreciative. Another man would have taken advantage.

"Thank you," she said. At his raised brow, she explained. "For looking out for us."

"My pleasure." Again, he gave her a smile, hot enough to melt her bones.

Trust me.

Cassie studied Mike, probing beneath his good looks, penetrating his gentle eyes. There's a saying—*the eyes are the mirror to the soul*.

If she could trust any man, it would be Mike.

CHAPTER 16

Mike drove up the two-mile road and pulled his Ford pickup to a stop in front of Shep's A-frame log house. Every time he journeyed up the tree-lined lane, the sight of Shep's home took his breath. Huge logs defined every section, from the A-structured ends with oak framed windows large enough to walk through to the A-designed middle, which centered another window showing the upstairs foyer. Slated rock with cement housed the wood pillars on the front porch. Trees surrounded the structure, completing the rustic, cozy home. Someday Mike hoped to have an eighty-acre farm and a house as nice as this.

Knowing Cap would probably be on the back deck, Mike made his way around the side, heading for the garden path and found Shep right where he knew the man would be. Hutch, his Alaskan Malamute, ears at attention, came loping to Mike's side with his tail wagging. Mike scratched behind the big dog's head.

"Figured you'd be along." Bare feet propped on the wooden railing, Shep leaned back with a steaming mug in one hand.

"Oh yeah? Why's that?"

"Checking up on your girlfriend's cohort."

"That's one way to put it." Mike chuckled as he climbed the steps. Hutch padded over to curl up beside Shep.

"Want a cup of coffee? Help yourself."

"Nah. Had mine already. You sleep in?"

Shep took a sip of his brew before he answered. "That your subtle way of asking what time I got home?"

"The thought crossed my mind."

"Hmm."

"You're deliberately being evasive." Mike crossed his arms and leaned against a sturdy post. A twelve-inch pillar matching the ones in front.

"I took her home, put her to bed and left."

Mike glanced at Shep, then looked toward the mountains. "Didn't think otherwise. Short and simple."

Shep dropped his feet and placed his mug on a small table to the side of his chair. "Nothing simple about it."

Curious, Mike raised his brow. Silence stretched and he thought Shep wouldn't say any more. The man stared out into the pasture beside the barn.

"Tammy is something else."

Mike smiled. So, the redhead had kindled Shep's interest? About time someone did. "Think I'll get that cup of coffee."

He shoved from the post and went inside. When he came back out to the deck, Shep had his feet resting on the railing again. Mike took the empty chair. "Looks like Tammy got your attention."

"She's pretty. And fun." Shep shook his head. "When she forgets about that asshole husband of hers."

"Ex," Mike corrected.

"I'd like to make him an ex. As in *extinct*."

"Cassie said he's been giving Tammy some trouble. The latest is why they were in the bar last night."

"Trying to take her kids," Shep added then took another gulp of coffee. "I don't cotton with a man trying to take kids away from their mother. Especially when the dad is a parasite."

"You know him?"

"Nope."

"She must have been pretty shaken up. She tell you about it?"

"Yeah. She talked a lot on the way to her place. A regular chatter box."

"Alcohol will do that." Mike snickered.

"She talked about her boys, too. Sounds like a great mom. You can tell how a woman is with her kids by the way she talks."

Mike nodded, but had no idea since his mom had left when he was just a boy. He stared down his long legs at the toe of his boot. "Cassie said those boys were her life."

"I got that impression."

After another long silence, Mike asked, "Are you going to tell me or not?"

Shep knew exactly what he was asking. Hell, if Mike had to admit it, he was damn curious of the answer. Shep hadn't dated in a long time. If he did, he'd never mentioned anyone special. Maybe Tammy could change all that.

"Not."

Mike gawked at Shep while he stared out toward the field. "So that's the way it's going to be?"

"Are you asking for your girlfriend?"

Mike thought about that. *Girlfriend.* The idea pleased him. *Relationship.* Could he have a relationship with Cassie? He wanted one. Guess Cassie could be his girlfriend.

"One of the first things Cassie asked when she woke up was how Tammy got home."

"No need asking you the same question you asked me."

Mike glanced over to find Shep studying him. "Yes, I stayed the night. I slept on her couch. I gave her a tonic when she woke up."

Shep laughed. The first sign of emotion since Mike arrived. "Your hellish hangover cure?"

"Don't knock it. It works."

"I'll take your word for it. Did she drink it?"

"Yep."

"Without any coercion?"

"No strong-arm tactics. Just told her it would cure what ailed her."

"Pretty bad?"

Mike chuckled remembering Cassie's reaction when he'd said *bottoms up*. "Yeah, she was kind of green. She didn't care much for the smell of the stuff, but she drank it."

"I'm sure Cassie has called Tammy by now. If I know women, she called the first chance she got. Either you were asleep or the minute you gave her some space."

Thinking back, Cassie had asked a lot of questions and had seemed a tad anxious when he'd mentioned Shep had taken Tammy home. Then in the kitchen, she'd been much calmer. Bet Shep was right.

"Wonder if Tammy remembered last night? Cassie didn't remember much."

"Those girls were pretty bombed."

"It didn't help you kept ordering more drinks."

Shep shrugged. "Looked like they needed it. Besides, we were there to keep an eye on them."

"Thank God."

Shep took another gulp and let out a long heavy sigh. "I will admit I kind of liked the way Tammy clung to me. Felt good."

Mike's jaw dropped. He turned in his seat giving Shep an I-knew-it stare.

Shep ignored him. "Didn't have to help with her clothes much. Not sure she was aware of what she was doing. When she started pulling off her clothes, I put her in bed and pulled the covers to her chin." A chuckle escaped.

The sound surprised Mike. Shep kept his personal life private. Mike was pretty sure there had been no woman in Shep's life for a long time. Not since Mike had known him, anyway. It was nice to see Shep interested in someone.

"And then, like the gentleman you are, you left." Mike teased in a droll tone and waited for Shep to confirm it.

"Naturally. Don't need a remorseful mamma out for blood."

The smell of country air filled Mike's lungs as he watched leaves dancing in the breeze. As far as the eye could see, lush green trees. Acres of it. Once again, a longing for pastures and a wooded area of his own invaded his thoughts. Away from the city's noise and flashing lights. Away from smoke filling his lungs every time he entered a burning building.

Peace.

Contentment.

Thoughts to dwell on another day.

"So, what do you think?" Mike raised his mug and watched Shep over the rim.

"Of what?"

"Haven't seen you show much interest in a woman."

A long time passed before Shep answered. "She's got something. A zest for life. A kind nature. I hate to think of her menacing hus—*ex* ... bullying her."

"Cassie tried to get Tammy's mind off the custody threat. That's why the girls got hammered." Mike crossed his boots over at his ankles.

"I might be able to help her with that."

Mike choked down his mouthful of coffee. His attention caught, he asked, "How?"

"My brother."

Oh yeah. One of Shep's brothers was a lawyer.

"I think I'll give Eddie a call. Maybe do some checking into this ... ex of hers." His salt and pepper brows drew together in a frown.

"That's a good idea. I don't think Tammy has a lawyer. Cassie didn't mention one."

"I'll call Eddie anyway," Shep said and tilted up his mug.

"You know, if you help get her a lawyer, it might get you in her good graces," Mike jabbed. "Especially if she gets pissed about last night."

Shep cringed. "Women. And their damn sensibilities. She doesn't have anything to get upset about. She didn't molest me, no matter how much I wished she had."

Mike smiled. Yep. His buddy was most definitely interested. And he'd bet Tammy was, too. "The woman doesn't give me the impression she is timid."

The sound of hearty laughter flowed from Shep. "No. She's bold, no mistake about that. Brazen even. I haven't had that much fun, real fun, since I can remember."

Hutch raised his head as if he too, enjoyed the sound of his master's laughter. Shep ruffled the dog's fur and stroked his back. The image sent another emotion through Mike. One that he couldn't ignore.

Damn. He was too emotionally drawn in. Cassie threatened his very existence. Made him think of what he wanted in his future. In a perfect world, he could feed his need and she would never leave. She would surrender herself to him and they both could be happy.

In his dreams.

That was a guarantee in which he had no control. Women were fickle. Yet Cassie was one temptation he'd willingly contemplate making permanent in his life.

"Do you know her ex's name? Any other information you can give me."

Who?

Lost in his own deliberation, Mike tried to focus on Shep's question and recall his last conscious thought before falling into the chasm of Cassie. *Oh yeah. Tammy.* "I'll ask Cassie."

"Enough data to make sure I have the right guy. Eddie will get any dirt the man has to hide."

"Sure thing. Cassie will give me the lowdown." And maybe they would get down to a little business of their own.

God, the woman had a body and she knew how to use it. Sex with no emotion? Not anymore. Not since he'd tangled with Cassie.

He was in deep shit, and he knew it.

***

Mike finished his coffee and grabbed a bottle of water out of the fridge. He liked his caffeine, but he needed water to keep his body hydrated. Between the workouts, lack of sleep and fighting fires, he drank several bottles a day.

He took in the rigs as he headed down the steps. Usually, Laredo had the bay doors open and at least one truck parked outside. Mike glanced at his watch and realized it was early yet.

Cooper had already checked the air tanks, but Mike had a habit of striding down the line, making sure the hoses and connections were in their designed locations. The kid did a pretty good job.

"Hey Hoss." At the top of the steps, Cooper waved his arm toward Shep's office. "Cap's looking for you."

Wonder what that's about?

Mike gave a nod and grabbed the water bottle he'd sat on a bench. He made short work of getting upstairs.

"Cap doesn't look too happy," Cooper said with a straight face.

"I don't get excited when the Captain calls me to his office." Mike gave the kid a mock glare.

"Just saying." Cooper shrugged.

"Give it up, pup." All the guys goaded each other now and again. Being the newest, not to mention the youngest member of their squad, Cooper caught most of the taunts. So, he tried every chance he got to pay them back. Couldn't blame the kid for trying.

Mike gave two raps, then opened the door to Shep's office. "You looking for me, Cap?"

"Come in and close the door."

Shit. Maybe Shep did have a bone to pick.

He took the chair in front of Shep's desk, right in the line of fire.

"I just got a call from a Mr. Williams."

Mike racked his brain and couldn't remember a man by that name. "Who's he?"

"Apparently the father of a boy you met at the hospital."

"Todd?"

"Todd Williams. The boy who fell on a saw in his back yard."

"Well, yeah," Mike rubbed a hand over the back of his neck. "The boy was waiting in ER. Blood oozing down his leg. He hadn't been seen and I asked Tracey to look at him."

"Tracey," Shep repeated.

"Yeah. I know most of the nurses there. She recognized me and took him into the examining room." Actually, he'd carried the boy. "Is this because I carried the boy to the examining room?"

"Why'd you do that?"

"Hell, Cap. He hadn't been seen yet. The place was full. He was bleeding."

"Doesn't explain why you carried him. How old is he?"

"Ten, I guess. And it was faster. By the time Tracey had to go looking for a wheelchair, I had him on the table."

"I see." Shep gave a nod. His voice remained steady, but it always did. Unless Cap wanted to hand you your ass.

"His father mad 'cause I touched his kid?"

"No. Evidently the boy is singing your praises."

"He's a sharp kid." Seeing the look on Shep's face, Mike quickly explained, "What I meant was, the kid is intelligent. He talks like an adult. He's tough. Not squeamish. Hell, he had a gash in his leg. Didn't even cry. His mom said he came walking in the house with blood running down his leg. I think she was about to have a heart attack."

"His mother the one who brought him to the hospital?"

"Yeah. And I remember her telling the kid her father wouldn't be happy."

"Would you like to hear why Mr. Williams called?"

Mike knew that tone of voice. Time for him to shut up. "Yes, sir."

"Like I said, it appears the boy, Todd, has been pestering his dad to come to the firehouse. Station eight. He was very specific about that."

Shep took a breather and Mike figured he better remain quiet until the Captain was done.

"Mr. Williams wanted to make sure it was all right for his son to pay us a visit. He said his son doesn't lie. But since Mr. Williams was not part of the conversation, he wanted to know our policy on children coming to the fire station, or if it was even allowed."

"That's it?"

"What did you think? He was suing you for manhandling his son?"

"Well, you never know."

"Seems you made an impression on the kid. His father's work takes him out of town a lot. He can bring the boy by next week. I explained we might get a call, or if there was an emergency you'd be gone. Mr. Williams said they'd work that out."

"That's great, Cap. Wait till you meet this kid. You'll see what I mean."

"I've got to handle something else, so that's all for now."

"Sure thing, Cap." Taking his cue, Mike closed the door as he left.

Shit. He left his water in Shep's office. He went to the main room to get another one.

"Cooper made a grand gesture of looking at Mike's ass."

"I don't fly that way, pup."

"Just checking to see how much the Cap chewed off."

"What?" Laredo called from the corner. "Mike get an ass chewing? What'd you do?"

Leave it to Laredo to pick up a dead ball and run with it.

"No, I didn't get my ass chewed. I'm going to have to teach pup here some manners."

"I didn't do nothing," Cooper said, throwing up his hands in defense.

"Wait till Jared—"

Mike interrupted Laredo. "You yahoos better straighten up. We got a kid coming to the station."

"A kid? Whose? Yours?"

Mike glared at Cooper.

"When did you have a kid?" Laredo chimed in.

"Why do I bother?" Mike said, rolling his eyes.

"All right. All right." Laredo got serious. "Who's the kid?"

"A boy I met in ER. About ten years old."

"Is he okay?" Cooper asked.

"You wouldn't believe this kid. Fell out of a tree onto a saw. Put a gash in his leg and walked into his house calm as a cucumber."

"That's the way my kid will be." Cooper beamed.

"Your kid? Better have someone else raise him then."

Mike walked off while Laredo and Cooper went at each other. He had other things on his mind.

Like a sexy blonde with a great body.

Cassie might have behaved pretty funny last night, but thinking back, she looked like the answer to all his fantasies. Limp in his arms, she'd teased him, tempted him, and if she hadn't been drunk, he might have had one hell of a night. But he didn't take advantage of helpless women. Even if Cassie struck him as one of the strongest women he'd ever met.

She'd needed him.

That gave him pause. He'd never been *needed* before. Plenty of women had come on to him and he'd gladly taken them up on their offer. But that was only sex. What he experienced with Cassie surpassed anything he'd encountered with other women. He'd liked watching out for her, protecting her, without sex being on the agenda.

He wanted to see her again. Go out with her. Talk to her. Just be with her.

He snatched the phone and punched the numbers before he had a chance to change his mind.

"Hello?" Her soft voice greeted him, causing a stiffening behind the zipper of his jeans.

"Uh, hi Cassie." A gasp and the sound of scuffle made him wonder what the hell she'd been doing. "Are you okay?"

"Yes, I'm fine." He heard water running. "I spilled my coffee."

"I'm sorry."

"Just me being clumsy. How are you?"

"I'm fine." What the hell? Would they discuss the weather next?

"I wanted to check up and see if my special potion helped."

"You should bottle and sell that stuff. I bounced right back."

"How about Tammy? She okay?"

"With two kids, she's doesn't have time to suffer. She hides it well."

Shit. Here goes.

"Was she mad about Shep taking her home? I promise you, she had nothing to worry about. Shep is a real gentleman."

"That was the problem." He thought he heard her mumble, but it was so low, he couldn't be right. "No, she's not mad."

"The thing is, Shep wondered." Christ, Mike felt like a damned kid passing notes in school. "Shep wondered if he should call her."

"That would be great. Tammy would welcome a call from Shep."

I'll be damned.

"Uh, look." He shoved a hand through his short-cropped hair. "I'd like to see you again. Maybe you'd like to go out or something." Christ. He was bad at this. How long since he'd asked a girl on a date? Picking up women at bars didn't count.

"I'd love to."

That was fast. Some of the anxiety drifted from his stomach.

"Or maybe you could come to my place for dinner," she added.

That sounded just fine and dandy to him. More make out sessions on her couch. And more sex in her bed. He put the reins on his testosterone. Cassie was worth more than a roll in the sac. He wondered at his need to impress her.

"I'm at the station. I'll be here until late this evening. How about tomorrow? I'm not the fine dining type, but I would like to take you to dinner. Maybe we could take a drive over the Blue Ridge Parkway."

"I'd like that."

Hot damn. He'd see her tomorrow.

***

The bartender lined up two shot glasses and poured a generous amount into each. He placed one in front of Seth and the other in front of the man sitting at his side. *Poor shmuck.* Had that long face look. The kind a man had after a woman took him for a ride.

Not Seth. He was too smart for women who thought they could get their hooks into him. Nodding a thank you to the bartender, he picked up the glass and swallowed the contents with a quick toss of his head, then relished the burn in his gut.

He turned his attention to the crowd filtering into the bar. He thought back to other Saturday nights, long ago, when he'd sneak out of the house to follow his brother. If their dad had caught either one of them, there would have been hell to pay.

His brother had caught him once and that was the end of that. He'd preached a sermon about how Seth should follow the rules, but never paid any attention to them himself. Trouble trailed Shawn like the whirl of a tornado. Seth often wondered if Shawn had carried a demon on his shoulder. Pushing him. Driving him. Seth hadn't seen his brother in years. If Shawn had lived, if they met today, would he be as crazy as he'd been back then? Would he raise as much hell now as he had at seventeen?

Didn't matter anymore. Besides, Shawn hadn't been crazy. He'd just liked to let loose. Anything was fair game. Shawn had managed to make it in the big corporate world, but Seth doubted his brother would have changed. Shawn always did what he wanted. Took what he wanted.

Until the day a cocksucker put a blade in him.

Shawn would never have been in that hellhole if it weren't for that rat bastard.

Seth's grief fueled his anger.

Revenge.

It would be sweet.

With a circle of his finger, he signaled the bartender for another round.

CHAPTER 17

A low rumble sounded outside Cassie's condo. She peeked out the front window and caught her breath. A shiny, black, convertible Mustang roared into a parking space. She couldn't tear her eyes away from what was obviously a collector's car. A 1969, if she had her guess.

She watched Mike's large frame as he crawled from the low car, thinking of the major difference between it and his big four-wheel-drive truck. He pulled his phone from his pocket.

Cassie ran to the bathroom to check her appearance and her cell phone rang. Retracing her steps, she grabbed it and gave an out-of-breath hello.

"Hi yourself. Are you ready? I don't want to leave my car unattended for long."

"What year is it?"

"You see me?"

"I heard you first." His laugh sizzled her insides. "Give me two minutes." She ended the call before he could say another word. She gathered her hair up in a ponytail, snatched her purse, made sure she had her keys, and slammed the door behind her.

Mike leaned against the rear fender, a big smile and a pair of sunglass on his face.

"Hello, beautiful."

"Hello, handsome. Think I can catch a ride?"

"Your wish is my command."

He opened the passenger door and waited for her to get inside. While he sauntered to the driver's door, Cassie ran her fingers over the smooth, red leather interior.

"It's beautiful, Mike."

"1969," he said, and she realized he'd answered the question she'd asked on the phone.

"428 or 390?"

"You know cars?"

"I know Mustangs. A sixty-nine fastback is my favorite body style."

"428 Cobra jet with a four-speed transmission."

"Smooth. There have been a lot of changes in body styles over the years. I'm glad Ford brought back the 1969 design for the newer models. Where did you get your love for Mustangs?"

"My dad. He liked hot cars. How about you?"

"My uncle. He had a sixty-four and a half, a 1969 Mach I and a 1970 302 Boss."

Mike whistled through his teeth. "You do know your cars." He turned the key and the engine cranked right over, purring like a lion.

"Buckle up."

She quickly obeyed, then leaned back, enjoying the wind blowing a few wisps of hair about her face.

The blue sky held few clouds and the sun's rays flickered through the trees as Mike maneuvered down the open road. A glorious day for a ride in a convertible. He followed Route 250 up Skyline Drive and turned onto the Blue Ridge Parkway. He shifted the gears with precision, very different from her days of driving a stick shift. She remembered her first time, learning to drive a standard transmission on her friend's car. In a mall parking lot. After a few jumps and leaps, Cassie had gotten the hang of it.

No communication was necessary. Every now and then Mike would turn to her and give her one of his sensual grins. He popped in a CD and turned up the volume so the music could be heard over the engine and the roaring wind. Rock and roll from the eighties blasted from the speakers. Another thing they had in common. She loved the oldies music.

Cassie leaned her head against the headrest, listening to the songs, appreciating the scenery, relishing not having a care in the world. Ahh, the freedom of just being. No restraints, no conditions, no thought, no obstacles, no worries.

Mike pointed out a few landmarks and when they hit a straight stretch, he hit the gas. The engine revved, and her excitement right along with it. Mike smiled with pride. His handsome mouth tilted up at the corners, making her heart flip and triggering flickers of desire dancing in her belly. Could a man be more perfect?

An hour later, he pulled into Pecks BBQ.

"I don't know when I've enjoyed anything more." She took his hand as he helped her from the car. She'd been excited to ride in a collector's car, but the tingles that swept up her arm just from his touch had her electrified.

"I get the same feeling every time I take her out."

"Lucky you."

"Don't worry. If you're a good girl, I'll take you for another ride."

Cassie immediately presumed a different kind of ride. One involving her on Mike's lap. By the sparkle in his eyes, the double meaning had been exactly what he'd intended. Her belly quivered.

Although it was spring, the temperature had reached eighty-three degrees. Mike opened the door of the restaurant and motioned for her to enter. When she stepped inside, cool air hit her face along with the scrumptious smell of Peck's barbeque sauce. He placed his hand on her lower back, guiding her to a table in the corner where he could keep an eye on his car. A rush of warm tingles raced up her spine. She immediately felt the loss when he removed his hand.

After the waitress took their order, Cassie glanced out the window admiring Mike's Mustang. "How long have you had it?"

"Longer than I've been able to drive it. It hasn't always looked like that."

"I can tell a lot of work went into it."

"Dad taught me everything he knew about cars. He had a 1966 Mustang. When he wasn't fighting fires, he was working on it. Then, when I was old enough to drive, he let me take it out once in a while. Showed me how to take care of—what he called—a muscle car."

"She looks like she has plenty of muscle." *Just like its owner.*

"She?"

"You used the word she earlier. I believe you said you get the same feeling when you take *her* out. Do all men think of their cars as females?"

Mike laughed. "Cars are a slight easier to handle."

"Hmm." She propped her elbow on the table and braced her chin on her palm. "Tell me you didn't name your car."

"I did not name my car."

Cassie jerked up in surprise. "You're kidding. I thought all guys named their cars."

"Not this guy."

The waitress brought their food and they dove in.

"Mmm, this is good." Cassie licked a drop of sauce from her lip. When she met Mike's gaze, his eyes were fastened on her mouth and the heated look in them caused a flurry in her belly.

He gave a slight groan and took a big bite of his barbeque. The sexual tension broken, she chewed her food.

"You were telling me about your muscle car."

"When I was a teenager, I got a part time job working in a mechanic shop. The owner had a Mustang and I wanted to buy it. My dad said I could get the car or go to college. And I better make the right choice. Which was his way of telling me to forget the car."

"So, you went to college?"

"Yep. But I never forgot about that car. After I graduated from Penn State, I went back to that garage looking for that car."

She dropped her bun in its basket and leaned forward, bracing her forearms on the table. "What a great story. You bought it after all those years?"

"No. It was gone. He sold it."

Her smile turned down to a frown. *That sucks.* "That is not a good story. I expected a happy ending."

He gazed at her under heavy lids. "There's a happy part. The shop owner offered to hire me right away."

"Oh. Well, that's good. I guess." She'd expected him to be upset, but his shrug told her he was okay with the car being gone. She would have been devastated.

"I wasn't sure what I wanted to do with my life and I hadn't gotten a job yet, but I knew I wanted my own Mustang. I went to work for him, saved my money and one day this guy pulled in with a flat bed and guess what was sitting on the back."

"Your Mustang."

"The very same. The guy was hauling it off to auction."

"To auction? Why?"

"Turns out, right after the man bought the car all those years ago, he got a divorce. Said his wife sucked him dry. Lost his house, his wife thought the car was a piece of junk so she let him have it, but he no longer had a garage to keep it in. Friends covered it up and kept it behind their barn. He didn't have the money to restore it, so finally decided to get rid of it. Wouldn't start, needed work, so he was taking it to auction. I bought it right then and there."

"What a stroke of luck."

"Never put much stock in luck."

"You have to admit the timing was extraordinary. Tell me. What did it look like?" Cassie asked, then stuffed some fries in her mouth.

"Not like that." He nodded toward the window.

"I didn't think so." She shook her head. Cassie knew from her uncle that it took a good deal of money and a lot of work to make a car look like that.

"A rust bucket with a torn cloth for a roof. I had to replace just about everything. Starting with the engine."

"You buy one or build it?" she asked, popping another fry into her mouth. His brows rose in disbelief.

"A mechanic in a mechanic shop. What do you think?"

She'd suspected the answer before she asked. Still, she had to laugh at his expression. "From scratch?"

Mike nodded with his mouth full. He took a gulp of his drink to wash down his food.

"I sanded down the engine block and rebuilt the engine piece by piece."

Cassie thought back to an image she remembered of her uncle standing in the middle of a Mustang frame where the engine should have been. At the time, she'd been stunned. She couldn't get over seeing the empty space. Since her dad never took an interest in older cars or restoration, she'd spent a lot of time with her uncle.

"I bet it took you a long time."

"Years. I still had my job. I lived with my dad so I decided to build a big garage in the back yard. Dad was all for it and I could take my time with the car. Worked on it nights and weekends. Saved my money for parts. When I made up my mind to join the fire department, I had even less time to devote to the car."

A flicker of interest crossed her mind, making her wonder what made him join the fire department. But it disappeared as she stared at the shining car.

"You did a wonderful job. I know restoring cars is expensive."

"Especially if you want to use original parts. Body work isn't cheap either."

"I love the black."

"It had to be just right. It was originally white with a red top."

"You're kidding," she said in surprise.

"I found a body shop that did excellent work." He talked as he dug in his fries. "The shop did repair work for insurance companies, too. Those jobs came first since they had a deadline, working on mine in between. They had the mustang body for six months."

"The body?"

"I had the engine on a hoist in my garage."

Suddenly Cassie wanted to see his garage. She imagined a huge building with every sort of mechanical tool in existence. A huge open space with lots of room to work. Maybe even a few cars parked inside.

"What made you choose black?" It occurred to Cassie his truck was also black.

"Have you ever noticed there's not a prettier car than black when it's all shined up?"

"Black cars are pretty, but hard to keep clean."

"That's true." Mike leaned back and Cassie noticed he'd polished off two of Peck's barbeques while she'd eaten one.

"I'm glad you stopped here. I haven't had Peck's in a long time."

"He serves the best barbeque."

She picked up a fry and thought of how Mike spoke of his dad but never mentioned his mom. She wondered if his mother was still in the picture. Maybe Cassie should leave that topic alone.

"Does your dad live around here?"

"No. After his retirement, his sister bugged him until he finally gave in and moved to North Carolina. She thought he couldn't take care of himself. Although, I think there was an ulterior motive. She said she wanted him close so she could keep an eye on him. But I think she was playing matchmaker, or whatever you call it. She told Dad I needed my space. She hinted that I needed to find a woman and needed the house for when I got married."

"Sly woman."

"I love my relatives, but I don't need them running my life. Still, Dad moved. He's happy."

"He lives with her?"

"God, no. Those two would kill each other if they lived under the same roof. But she's a great cook and carries food to his house every day."

"And you stayed here."

"I had a career with Station Eight. Dad sold me the house, dirt cheap. Wouldn't have made me pay anything, but he needed money for a place in North Carolina."

"Why did you become a firefighter?"

A flicker of sadness entered his eyes and was quickly extinguished.

"It's in the genes."

"In the genes?"

"I've been around firefighters all my life. My dad took me with him to the firehouse a lot. Guess it grew on me."

"I think there's more. You're good at your job. I've seen you in action, remember?"

"Can't deny that. I like helping people, putting out fires." His eyes bore into hers. "It's what I do."

She wasn't sure what she was supposed to make of his expression. Okay, change of subject. The question of his mom nagged at the back of her mind. She bit her tongue. What could be so bad? She took a plunge.

"What about your mom?"

A cloud covered Mike's face making Cassie wish she'd kept her mouth shut. "I'm sorry. I didn't mean to bring up a painful memory."

"I don't usually talk about her because she walked out."

Way to go, Cass. Here was a wound that obviously had not healed.

"What about your family? Are you from around here?" He smoothly steered the subject to her.

"Born and raised in Staunton. My parents are from Highland County. Both grew up on farms. Moved to the big city when they got married. I have one sister, thank God. If I had another one like her I would not have made it to adulthood."

"That bad?"

"You have no idea." Discussing her sister would put her in a bad mood. She had no desire to waste time chatting about Jennifer. "Do you have any brothers or sisters?"

"None. I'm it. Just me and my dad since I was little."

"He never remarried?"

"Nope." Mike flipped the check over, glancing at the amount. Cassie took his short answer as meaning *end of discussion*.

"You ready?"

"Are you kidding? I can't wait to get back in your *muscle* car."

***

Mike had hoped to spend the evening with Cassie, but she received a phone call from her sister and it upset her. She didn't want to talk about it and suddenly the pleasant harmony of the afternoon changed to a dark cloud hanging over their day. Listening to her end of the conversation, he gathered the sister had called Cassie to come pick up their mother. That wasn't the part she'd been upset about. The sister was supposed to take care of her mom and changed her mind. She wanted to go out and told Cassie she had to come get their mother. There was more to it, but he could tell she didn't want to argue over the phone. That put an end to their evening.

It wasn't all bad. He had one hell of a goodbye kiss. If she hadn't been in a hurry, he might have had more. Their quick, passionate embrace gave him something to look forward to.

His phone beeped. He didn't text when he drove, but being a firefighter, he kept up with alerts in case he was needed at the station.

Jared.

He called the station. Jared answered on the first ring.

"What's up?"

"Hey, man. Shep is calling the team in for a special meeting."

"Why?"

"Don't know. Hooley's here. They had a powwow and Shep told me to get you guys in here."

"Be there in ten."

Mike took the next right and headed to Station Eight.

Ten minutes later, he strode into the firehouse and found Jared reclined on one of the sofas with his boots propped on a low table. Laredo and a new volunteer were trying to kill each other on the big TV screen via video game. Two teenagers, regular hangouts who had dreams of becoming firefighters, urged the players on with shouts of instructions and cheers. When Jared saw Mike, he dropped his feet to the floor and stood.

"What were you doing at the station?" Mike asked him.

"Edgar got a new Harley. Drove over to check it out. Cap saw me. Told me to get the rest of the team. Pronto." Jared gave a toss of his head toward Shep's office. "Hooley's in there. Been holed up ever since I came inside. Cap stuck his head out a few minutes ago. I told him you were on your way."

"What's going on?"

"Didn't say. With the investigator here, I figure it's about the explosion at the training sight. Maybe Hooley found something."

Mike hoped so. The damn incident had been chafing his brain for weeks. If Hooley didn't have any news, Mike would grab Jared and Laredo and head back out to the Wimer property. Have another look.

A door slammed with a bang. Cooper stomped into the day room, complaining.

"A guy finally gets a night off. I don't see no fire. There better be a good reason you called me back in here."

"Cap said call, I called." Jared gave a shrug.

"Get over it, pup. You're not the only one who had to end a hot date."

Jared smiled at Mike, obviously deducing he'd been out with Cassie. "Only Cooper's hot date was with Halo Reach."

Mike raised his brows. "A video game?"

"I'll have you know I was winning."

Mike glanced over to the side of the room at the group playing with handheld controls. He'd never gotten into the gaming scene, but his coworkers sure were involved. One of the teens grabbed Laredo's control.

"My turn."

The door to Shep's office opened, drawing everyone's attention.

"Good. You're all here. Come on in."

This felt a lot like Mike's school days, getting called to the principal's office. Hooley, the fire inspector, stood to the left, leaning against the wall. Mike nodded to him and took one of the empty chairs in front of Shep's desk. Jared took the other one while Laredo and Cooper filed in along the back wall.

"I know you all have been waiting, so Hooley is here to give us an update."

"You find out what happened at the training site?" Jared directed his question to Hooley.

Hooley pushed away from the wall and pursed his lips. "I found several things. For one, the explosion was most definitely arson. We gathered quite a bit of evidence. Gas tanks that an individual had to place and open at just the right time."

"How the hell was that possible?" Mike burst out. "I was there. Chief Wilson follows procedures by the book. He would not be so careless."

"We agree on that," Hooley replied. "I spent a lot of time with the firefighters at Station Nine this past week. I have the film of that day loaded on my computer and I want each of you to take a look at it."

"Hell, I forgot about the camera," Laredo said, shoving a hand through his hair. "Is there something on there?"

"I've gone over it, but I want you guys to see if you notice anything out of the routine. Anything that might be off."

"You were a firefighter before you became an investigator. You'd know if something didn't look right," Mike told Hooley.

"More eyes, more opportunity that each man might see something different," Hooley replied.

"Sure thing. Let's see this film." Cooper leaned forward, staring at the computer monitor.

Hooley hit a button and the screen came to life. The horrific explosion blew up on screen just as Mike remembered it. He watched every gruesome detail as men shouted and ran. He focused on the team, the instructor, Ryan as he threw the torch. When the footage ended, Hooley started the tape again.

"I didn't see anything," Cooper said with noticeable disappointment.

"It was a clusterfuck." Jared fisted his hands.

"After the explosion, every man went into action. Looks to me like they did exactly what they were supposed to do," Shep said.

"Take another look," Hooley slowed down the feed. "Anything. Anything at all."

There was too much going on at a rushed speed to catch everything. When the clip stopped, Hooley hit the feed again. And again. By the fourth time—

"Stop. Right there." Mike pointed. "Back it up."

Hooley backed up the action.

"There." Mike stared at the man in a flame-retardant suit.

"What is it?" Shep asked.

"That guy. He was right at the heart of the explosion just a few minutes back. Watch. Back it up."

Hooley rewound the clip a few frames and froze the image.

"Would you look at that?" Cooper whistled through his teeth.

"If I hadn't seen it, I wouldn't believe it. He's a member of Station Nine."

Hooley gave Laredo a puzzled look. "Chief says this isn't one of his guys."

Mike jerked his head in amazement. Between the film and Hooley's statement, it was just too much to absorb. Bad enough suspecting a firefighter. But who the hell was this guy if he didn't belong to Station Nine? He squinted at the image on the screen.

"Got too much gear on to see who he is. The number on his helmet is definitely Station Nine."

"Every Captain at each of the five stations that were on sight that day has seen this film. Every firefighter has been identified but one. Him." Hooley pointed to the same man Mike had indicated. "I've been calling in every member of each firehouse to see if we can figure out who this guy is. No one has recognized him."

"At least we know where he got his uniform." Cooper stepped around Mike's chair. "Some guy just waltzed into Station Nine and took their gear?"

"It's only five miles from Station Eight," Mike muttered out loud. Someone could just as easily have filched a suit from any of the firehouses. Who the hell would do that?

"And why?" Laredo uttered.

"This guy could be anyone," Hooley explained. "We have no idea of motive. He could have chosen a firehouse randomly or he could have a beef with a certain individual."

"Maybe we better keep an eye out since we leave our doors open most of the time." Shep made eye contact with each member of the team.

"This guy is good," Hooley warned. "He left no trace or clue of his identity. This is our only lead and you guys can see for yourself, it's not much."

Not much? It was worthless. Some guy in a fire-suit.

Mike's gut twisted with unease. It didn't sit well with him that some nut-job was out there targeting firefighters.

CHAPTER 18

The color blue is a safe colour - the most universally liked colour of all.

Blue is not impulsive or spontaneous and it doesn't like to be rushed - blue needs to analyze and think things through and work to a plan.

Blue needs to have direction & order- untidiness and unpredictability overwhelms it.

Blue likes familiarity. It doesn't like change and will stubbornly do things its own way, even if there is a better way.

– the colour of truth

Cassie closed the book with a heavy sigh. Not only her favorite color, but the color of Mike's eyes. *Safe?* She did feel safe with him. He'd given her more security than anyone she'd ever known. How could that be, when she'd only just met him? Even her confidence had received a boost.

Doesn't like to be rushed. That sounded like him. Mike had that easygoing, reserved manner. There were times when she thought he held back. Maybe that was the *analyze and think things through* part. She did a lot of analyzing, herself. To the point where she scrutinized and dissected every practical thought.

Thinking about Mike was a twenty-four-hour occurrence. She'd brought her students to the library for story time with the librarian and slipped to the corner for a few minutes of quiet time for herself. Even though she taught in an elementary school, the library had one secluded corner with shelves housing books for those over the age of twelve. Walking along the aisle, she'd slowly traced her fingers across the spines as she read their titles. One of particular interest had caught her eye.

Fire's Blue Blaze. Blue was her favorite color. And her firefighter had the rarest hue of blue irises she'd ever seen. Mike's eyes fascinated her, along with several other qualities he possessed. Interesting, what she'd just read. It made perfect sense. Blue could calm the mind and soothe the soul. But it could also be perceived as cold, unemotional and unfriendly. Like Mike's moods. Just when she thought she understood him, when she thought he felt the same as she, he'd pull back. Something bothered him and she was determined to find out what.

Admittedly, their relationship—if you wanted to call it that—was still new. Maybe he needed time. His allure might have hit her like a lightning bolt out of the sky, but guys were different. Maybe it would take longer for him. Although, whenever they'd shared a moment of intimacy, he'd been just as involved as she. The way he sighed when he held her, the times when his touch seemed almost possessive. Little things he did that she noticed expressed his feelings more than he knew.

Romance filled her head with believable dreams. To have a man want her. To have him touch her the way Mike did. To have him tell her she was beautiful, even when she knew she wasn't, although her body had all the right curves in the proper places.

She longed for a man to want *her*. To see the inner beauty. Could Mike be the one to give her these things?

Damn insecurities. Her sister's taunts came back.

What did she have to offer a man?

More than her body? More than lust?

When are you going to learn?

"Miss Peters?"

Cassie jumped.

"I'm sorry. I didn't mean to startle you. I've finished with your class."

"Oh. Uh. I was involved in this book." She held it out as if that explained her jumpiness. She quickly returned the book to its shelf, gave the librarian a nod and hurried to gather her students.

The children kept her busy until the school fire alarm went off.

"All right, children. Line up and remember, no talking in the halls. This is our fire drill. Philip, will you please turn off the lights and close the door?"

Once in the hall, she led her students out of the building, making sure she counted each one as they exited the double doors. Her class knew the procedure and also knew she tolerated no monkey-business during a fire drill. Just like they'd practiced, her students walked in an orderly fashion across the bus parking lot to the edge and stopped, along with the upper grade classes. Each teacher stood with their students waiting for the 'code green, all clear'.

Even the fates were against her.

Fire drill.

Mike.

His job was a dangerous one. Putting his life on the line for those in need. She gave a slight shudder. Praying for his safety had become another daily ritual.

The principal's voice on the intercom announced the code green. "Philip, you may lead us back inside."

Reading a book usually calmed the children after a drill, so she let them choose one and they gathered in a circle on the floor.

She made it through the next hour without further distractions and finally the bell rang at three o'clock. Excited children fled down the hall. Good Lord, she couldn't handle another day like today.

"Hey girlfriend. You look awful." Tammy blew into the room like a summer breeze.

"Hey. Heavy thoughts. I'm glad the day is over."

"How's this for heavy? I've got an idea. Let's get one of those hunky firemen to come to the school for a show and tell?"

"I'm doomed," Cassie groaned, raising her head to the ceiling. *The fates are definitely against me.*

"What's with you?"

Cassie shook her head in response.

"Think about it. It's a great idea." Tammy waved her hands, as if proving her point. "If you don't want Mike here in your little sphere, we'll get one of his buddies."

Don't want Mike?

That's the problem. She wanted him all the time.

"Oooh. You do have a glum face. What's bothering you?" Tammy propped her hip on the corner of Cassie's desk. "Is it time to go Mexican?"

"I could use a drink right now, but my stomach is not up to spicy food."

"What's up?" Tammy's brows lifted, creasing her forehead into a frown. Since the day the principal told Tammy about Steve's meddling, she'd been full of piss and vinegar. Her mood had improved greatly this week. Seeing a scowl on her face almost looked out of place.

Cassie turned and gathered papers she'd need to grade this evening. After what had been thrown at Tammy, if she could be brave, Cassie had no business sulking. She gave her friend a smile. "Everything's good. I'm ready to leave. Why don't you get your things and walk me out?"

"Sure thing. Be right back." Tammy left the room with the same speed she'd entered.

Cassie picked up markers, replaced some books, and straightened the students' desks. Before long, Tammy was back.

"Ready?"

"I'm ready." Cassie snapped her briefcase closed and placed it in her carry case. With the amount of supplies teachers had to carry, a tote on wheels saved a lot of back pain.

"You seem a little down." Tammy's expression was one of concern.

"No. Just thinking."

"About Mr. Muscles, no doubt." Tammy's smile was infectious. Who could be disheartened with a friend like Tammy around?

"Who else? Mike has taken permanent residence in my mind."

"They why so glum? Unless he hasn't been spending enough time in your bedroom."

Cassie stumbled, causing one of the purse straps to fall down. She heaved it back on her shoulder with a jerk. "Is that all you think about?"

"Come on. You know I'm teasing. Besides, you're the only one getting any action." Tammy quickened her steps matching Cassie's stride.

"We've had this discussion before."

"Then you already know the answers. So, don't ask the same questions."

Cassie laughed.

"That's my girl. Tell me. What had your brain working overtime?"

"That I'm already involved with a man I barely know."

Tammy grabbed her arm and brought them both to a dead halt. "Uh, oh. That fast?"

Cassie swiveled around in discomfort and continued walking toward her car. "Appalling, isn't it?"

"No, it isn't." Tammy called and then hurried to catch up. "It's great. Why would you say such a thing?"

"Don't you see?" Cassie unlocked her car. "He's in it for the fun. I really like this guy."

"Maybe he is and *maybe* your bad-ass fireman feels the same way."

For a moment, Cassie's pulse sped up. A pleasing thrill of delight warmed her chest. Then, just as quickly, her rational side squashed the sensation. "Be serious."

"I am serious." When Cassie opened her car door, Tammy shoved it closed. "All right. What gives?"

Anger and embarrassment at her earlier twinkling of hope, Cassie spoke in irritation. "Mike is hot. H.O.T. He can have any girl he wants."

"He wants you."

"For now. He wants an easy lay." She regretted the words as soon as they left her mouth. Saying them hurt. Made her aware of their accuracy.

"You're not easy," Tammy said with force. "Mike does not appear shallow to me. Have some faith in yourself."

"As gorgeous as Mike is, he could have any woman. What have I got to offer him?"

Tammy's expression registered shock. Rage took its place. "I get it. It's that sister of yours again. I should kick her ass from here to China." Tammy raised her arms flexing her fists. She sucked air in and huffed it out. "Ooooh. It's a wonder you survived your childhood. We've also had *this* discussion before. When are you going to believe in yourself? You give so much and expect so little. I've seen you tear into kids who bully others. I've heard the praise you give to all students whether they are pretty, plain or downright ugly."

"I'm a teacher." Cassie shrugged.

"Bull crap. If you two were raised in the same house, how come you turned into two very different people?"

"I've wondered the same thing myself. Maybe we were switched at the hospital."

"You are not dense. What about Mike? Hasn't he told you you're pretty or beautiful? The man swallows his tongue when he looks at you. It's pretty obvious how he feels. My God, Cassie, if you don't believe the mirror and you won't believe me, then believe Mike."

***

Fatigue encumbered every muscle in Cassie's body, making the burden on her shoulders more stressful. Her mother had been in pain for too long and the doctors finally performed the surgery they should have done months ago. No thanks to her sister. Jennifer had let their mother lie on the couch and suffer for weeks. After a phone call from one of Jennifer's friends alerted Cassie that her mother had been crying, she went to her mom and took her to the doctor. Cassie was the one who hounded the doctors until they developed a treatment plan. And then surgery.

It had been a long two days. Mom came through the procedure fine—one less thing to worry about. Family joined them in the waiting room and Jennifer held court like always. Cassie couldn't take any more of her sister's eye rolling, so she'd slipped down to the cafeteria for a coffee.

Enclosed in the elevator, she inhaled the aroma of fresh caffeine, willing away some of the tension that swamped her after spending too much time in her sister's company. When Cassie noticed the lift had not moved, it dawned on her that she'd never pushed the button. With a shake of her head, she quickly pressed the number to her mother's floor, wondering how she'd managed to get to the cafeteria and pour her coffee without burning herself. This time, she had not been preoccupied with Mike.

Her sister would be waiting. Who knew what nonsense she'd spouted to their cousins after Cassie left the waiting room? Some days Jennifer was tolerable. Even friendly. Other days, Cassie wanted to choke her. At the age of twenty-nine, Cassie supposed she should be used to her sister's degrading insults. They bounced off her quicker now than they had in the past. Still, the constant jibes wore her down. That's why she avoided Jennifer as much as she could.

Jennifer was four years older. They'd been raised in the same house, taught the same rules, morals, and mannerisms, but they were as different in their beliefs as two people could be. Jennifer had married for money. Twice. She'd received a handsome settlement from her first husband, and if she wasn't careful, she'd be repeating the divorce experience a second time.

Thirty minutes later, the family was allowed to see her mother. Groggy from the anesthesia, Mom fluttered her eyelids and then slipped back to unconsciousness. Another hour and she was moved to a private room. Once she was settled comfortably, the cousins said their goodbyes.

Cassie stared at the pale woman. Asleep she looked peaceful. Last night she'd been so scared. After Jennifer had left, Cassie talked with her mom, discussing the surgery and trying her best to alleviate her mother's fears. She'd sat with her through the night, dozing when she could. Mom woke once, but after seeing Cassie, she'd calmed. They held hands, shared a prayer, and blessedly, she had no trouble going back to sleep. Watching her now, seeing her even breathing, Cassie hoped her mother felt no pain.

"They're gone now. You don't have to pretend anymore."

Cassie glanced to her sister in confusion. "Pardon me?"

"Acting like you do so much for our mother."

"What?" The word came out in a half-confused, half-disbelieving voice.

Not now.

"She's going to need care. Don't think you're going to waltz off and leave me to do everything."

Resentment flared like shooting flames after throwing gas on a smoldering fire. Cassie's shoulders tensed and the hair stood on the back of her neck. Cassie had been the one to take their mother to the doctor. Cassie had spent hours at the hospital during x-rays and blood work and every test to prepare their mother for surgery. And now, Cassie was in no mood to put up with her sister's bullshit.

"You're going to do this *now*?" Cassie seethed. "While our mother lies unconscious in a hospital bed?"

"She's asleep," Jennifer said.

"I'm not doing this here." Cassie sprang from her seat, madder than she'd been in a long time. "Come on." How dare her sister start an argument only moments after their mother had left the recovery room?

"Where are you going?" Jennifer asked, following Cassie out into the corridor.

"Down the hall where we can talk." Outrage fueled her steps. Livid, she kept her eyes straight ahead. At the end of the hallway, she saw a little alcove with three chairs and a small table. She threw her purse on a chair and spun around. "Why did you wait until now to do this?"

"I wasn't about to have you put on a show in front of the rest of the family."

"Like you? Pretend you're so wonderful around our cousins and anyone else who will listen, acting like you were the only one who cared for Mom? Then, when it's just you and me, you're back to your nasty self."

"I did no such thing," Jennifer said with her usual air of haughtiness. "They know who is better."

"Better? All you care about is how people see you. You've always put me down. You've always thought you were better than me. As for Mom, I know what I've done for her. And she knows. That's all I care about."

Jennifer looked at her manicured nails, diamonds ringed on each finger. "I took care of Mom."

"For a few weeks while she lay in agony on your couch. And only because I have a job while you stay at home living off your rich husband. You have the room. You can be with her during the day. What do you want me to do? Quit my job to take care of her while she's recuperating? If I have to, I will."

"Don't be silly. She will stay with me, again." Her air of dominance made Cassie cringe.

Frustration cramped Cassie's stomach. She took in her surroundings, remembering they were in a hospital. She needed to keep her voice down. She had to think of Mom. She rubbed her temple, a throbbing headache coming on.

"Mother feels the tension between us," she tried reasoning in a calmer voice. "It isn't good for her."

"Tension." Jennifer gave a harsh laugh. "Try hostility. You're jealous of me."

Jealous? Was she serious?

"All you care about is money," Cassie shot back. "If this is what money does to you, I want none of it." Cassie loved her sister, but she was tired of being treated unfairly. "What have I done to make you so resentful? What do I have that you want?"

"You?" Jennifer eyed Cassie up and down, as if dissecting a bug.

Cassie couldn't believe her sister was so ungrateful. "Everything you have was given to you. Your house and your cars were given to you by your rich ex-husband. The new one dotes on you. Giving you diamonds for every finger. You don't appreciate anything. I wouldn't blame him if he leaves you, too."

Jennifer sprang from her chair in such a fury Cassie thought her sister was going to slap her. "How dare you mention my first husband! You wanted him for yourself. You stuck your big boobs in his face every chance you got.

Cassie was flabbergasted. "I did no such thing. You know how self-conscious I am of my size."

Jennifer laughed, an unpleasant sound. "Flaunting your chest is not what I call being unsure of yourself. You're just a bitch. You want everything I have. I've hated you since the day you were born."

Cassie gasped like she'd been sucker punched. And she had.

All Cassie remembered of her childhood was criticism, chastisement, and blame. Jennifer's bitterness had destroyed any sibling affection between them. She'd even taken their father's belt to Cassie when their parents were not at home. Never praise. Never kindness, or being allowed to join in with her sister or her friends. Never welcomed, never included in outings. When they got older, Cassie foolishly thought adulthood would make things better. But her sister married a man who had money and still continued to play her games.

"I don't want you back here when you've been drinking. The way you were with dad."

"What?"

"Dad called me the night before he died. He said you were drunk when you came to his hospital room."

It took a moment for Cassie to gather her scattered wits. Dad hadn't known how to call from the hospital bed. He'd been so strung out on pain medication, he could barely tell the difference between the phone and the TV remote.

"You upset him. He was out of breath."

"His lungs were black with tar. That's why he was in the hospital. He was on oxygen." This was just one of Jennifer's attempts to catch Cassie off guard. And it was working.

"He said you were loud and obnoxious. He was ashamed. I asked him if you'd been drinking and he said, 'You know your sister'."

That specific evening arose in her mind crystal clear. She'd kidded with her father and tried to make him laugh.

Cassie refused to permit her oppressive sister to bully her any more. Growing up was bad enough. Mom loved them both. Cassie couldn't figure out why her sibling felt insecure. She could not allow Jennifer to continue hurting her. She had to believe in herself. This was a discussion for another day and not while their mother lay in a hospital bed. She grabbed her purse and stomped away. Her sister quickly followed.

"Where do you think you're going? I'm not finished."

Cassie spun on the balls of her feet. "Well, I am. I am finished with you."

The shock on Jennifer's face should have given Cassie some relief. It didn't. She headed to her mother's room. Coming to a halt, she peeked in and found her mom sound asleep. By her slow, steady breathing, Mom appeared to be resting and not in pain.

Jennifer closed in, blocking the doorway.

"Do not say another word, Jennifer. Not one word." Cassie brushed past her and practically ran from the hospital. By the time she slumped in her car, tears flowed freely down her cheeks. Unable to see, let alone drive, she broke down and allowed sobs to rack her body.

Anguish crushed her core. With every tear, she battled the heavy burdens weighing on her soul.

Grief for her dad, worry for her mom, heartache for the wasted years she'd tried to please her family.

CHAPTER 19

Cassie made it home without crashing her car. Having Mike and his team respond to a car wreck and find her would be a hoot, wouldn't it? Between her tears and the buzzing in her ears, she could barely see. She unlocked her apartment door and dragged herself inside, the darkened room a relief to her pounding head. All she wanted was a shower. The blinking light on her answering machine caught her notice. She decided to ignore it.

Drained of energy, she kicked off her shoes and padded down the hall, more than a little weary. A soothing shower and then some coffee. No. Coffee would only make her more wired. Wine would do the trick. And some aspirin. With wine? She shrugged. What difference did it make?

When she reached the bathroom, she stood in the darkened doorway without turning on the light. In her mind, she could see her father on his last day in this world. To her knowledge, he'd never said a word against any member of his family. In his drug induced state, she supposed he could have spoken some sort of nonsense. Why did her sister have to be so spiteful?

Cassie flicked on the light, stepped to the tub and turned on the water faucets. When the temperature felt right, she removed her top, then the rest of her clothes and slipped under the spray.

Water rushed over her head, massaging her scalp. She wished it could wash away the pain. The headache and the stinging memory of the scene with her sister. She rotated her shoulders, the power of the nozzle kneading her muscles while she willed the stream to relieve the tension in her body. Her chest rose as she took a breath, inhaling as deep as her lungs would allow.

A long time passed before her body began to chill. How long she'd stood there, she didn't know. She'd lost all track of time.

She dried off and wrapped a towel around her, folding one end just above her breasts. She picked up her brush and ambled to the bed. Unable to ignore the blinking light, she plopped down on the comforter and punched the button on her answering machine. Hoping she would not hear her sister's voice, she brushed her hair as she listened to her messages. The hot shower had helped, but her black mood had not improved. On the third beep, she heard Mike.

Good Lord, the man's voice was lethal. His vibrant tone penetrated every nerve in her body. Her need for him overwhelmed her senses. After the confrontation with her sister, she was vulnerable. She began to tremble. A delayed reaction, she supposed, from the encounter. Tammy's words rang in Cassie's head.

If you don't believe the mirror and you won't believe me, then believe Mike.

Could she believe Mike? When he told her she was beautiful? When he made her feel like he truly desired her and not just a woman to warm his bed?

Right now, she needed Mike. She needed his strength. She needed him to restore her confidence as a woman. To heal her bleeding heart.

Mike.

I need him.

Cassie lifted the phone and tapped in the number before she could change her mind. On the first ring, she panicked. What would she say? What if she started crying? What if he didn't answer? What if he had another girl there? What if …

"Mike here."

Oh God.

Silence.

"Hello." His irritated voice came across the line. "If you're there, you better speak."

"Mike?" Her voice cracked.

"Cassie?" He sounded unsure.

"Yes, it's me."

"Are you okay?" His voice softened and filled with concern.

"Mike …" Her voice broke. *Oh hell.* "I need you."

"I'm on my way."

No words had ever given her more security. He didn't hesitate. He didn't ask what was wrong. He simply told her what she needed to hear.

I'm on my way.

A man of fortitude, his words were spoken with grit, guaranteeing his strength and protection. Giving her the assurance he was there for her. He was coming to her.

She stared at the phone in her hand. She should get up. She should get dressed. Her limbs were too heavy. She had no energy, no will to move. *Mike.* She'd wait for Mike. Vague thoughts rolled around in her head until abruptly, she heard a loud pounding on her front door.

"Cassie. Are you in there? Open up?"

Jerked out of her fog, she flinched at the racket.

"Cassie. It's Mike. Open up!"

Good Lord, the neighbors. She jumped from the bed and nearly lost her towel. Grabbing it with both hands, she ran down the hallway and stubbed her toe on a corner table. She shrieked.

"Dammit, Cassie. What's going on in there?" He pounded harder.

Her toe throbbed, tears threatened and she worried her neighbors would call the cops. She half-stumbled, half-hopped to the door and threw it open.

If she didn't already know Mike, the ferocious scowl on his face would have scared ten years off her life. With his arm in the air, he looked ready to break down her apartment door. She reached, got a fist full of shirt and hauled his butt inside. Which was no easy feat, since the man was rock solid. Refusing to stick her head out to see if her neighbors lined the hall, she slammed the door.

"Cassie. Are you alright?"

Mike's face softened, but his chest heaved like he'd just run a marathon.

"My neighbors may call the cops. What were you thinking, pounding on my door like that?"

His brows drew together in a confused frown as his gaze slid slowly down and back up her body. "I thought you were in trouble."

Realizing she stood practically naked with only a towel wrapped between them, she felt a rush of heat. Instead of desire, she saw his concern. Then his words sank in. She closed her eyes and shook her head.

"Did something happen?" he asked in a gentle voice, resting his hands on her shoulders.

"Yes. No. Oh, damn." Her head fell to the side, longing to melt into him.

"Cassie. Look at me."

She took a deep breath, inhaling tangy soap and musk cologne. When she lifted her gaze, pools of cobalt gleamed at her. She wanted to lose herself in their brilliance. Maybe he didn't offer his love, but something fierce shone in their amazing depths. Caring, compassion, and desire ... God, how she needed this man.

"Mike. Make love to me." The towel forgotten, she slowly raised her arms.

When Cassie dropped her towel, lust slammed Mike's gut and his dick hardened to steel. His heart cracked at the anguish he'd seen just before she'd fallen into his arms.

"Cassie," he whispered, his voice like sandpaper.

"Kiss me," she whispered.

He groaned and dragged her against his chest. Something crucial had happened; he'd find out what later. Right now, this was what she needed. He understood the signs. Something drove her. She needed to lose herself and she'd chosen him. God help him, he hungered for her. He was more than willing to give her whatever she needed.

He'd give her this moment.

He'd give her oblivion.

She kissed him with urgency, as if her life depended on it. Her naked body tempted him beyond all reason. Sinking his hands into her hair, he slid his tongue inside her open mouth, licking every crevice he could find. Her body melted into his and he moaned her name.

Impatient lust surged with raw need. He cradled her in his arms, reassuring her with his body. "Cassie, I'm here. I've got you."

He nibbled at the corner of her mouth, then licked the spot where he'd nipped. She dug her fingers into his shoulders and captured his lips again. His heart thudded as she opened her mouth eagerly, desperately. He groaned low in his throat, a deep hum of pleasure as hot desire ripped through him.

Moving slowly, he slid both hands down the sides of her body, kneading every inch. She jerked at his shirt, pulling it from the band of his jeans and slid her hands underneath, her hot, urgent fingers driving him crazy with need. She made him so hard so fast, he wanted to take her the same way—hard and fast. Her movements frantic, there was no slowing down, no foreplay. This woman was fired up. He'd be insane to deny her.

He cupped each breast, testing their weight, stroking his thumbs over her nipples until both stood proud and erect. Lowering his head to one breast, he kissed lavishly while rolling the bud of the other between his thumb and forefinger. She grabbed his hair and squirmed until all he felt was her desire. With a groan, he tore his lips from her flesh, his breathing ragged.

"Tell me what you want. Anything, and I'll do it."

"I want you. I need you. Now."

She found his zipper and then slid her hand inside. Hunger tore at him.

"You're magnificent. And silken," she whispered.

Christ, she fisted him in her hand. He threw his head back and relished the feel of her gripping him, stroking him up and down.

He bit her earlobe as he glided one hand over her smooth skin to the valley between her legs. He raked his teeth over her shoulder as his fingers drifted lower, finding her sensitive nub, slick with desire. He inserted a finger and heard her gasp, then her hips were lifting toward him. He stroked and rocked while the fingers of his other hand massaged her belly, inciting her arousal to fever pitch.

"I need you, Mike." She shoved at his pants, pushing them down his hips.

His cock strained and his pulse pounded. He fought to maintain control, but she was having none of that. When she positioned his tip at her entrance, he couldn't hold back. He lifted her and she locked her legs around his waist. Watching her face, he staggered forward, pressing her back against the wall and entered her with a long, hard thrust.

She moaned and clutched and arched into him. Swelling heat took over his aroused body and consumed his mind. He kissed her hot and hard. He meant to excite her, scorch her. Burn the image of him into her brain, and banish whatever unpleasant thoughts or events that had upset her.

Her grip tightened, her nails raked his back. He plunged again, filling her, burying himself to his balls. Her whimpering cries filled his ears, making him growl and thrust again, each lunge more powerful than the last. A black hole swallowed him, where the only thing he felt was need. Pure and raw.

"Harder. Faster," Cassie panted out between breaths, sending him into a mindless trance. He slammed into her roughly, sinking as deep as he could possibly go.

"Yes, Oh God, yes." She cried out as her muscles spasmed.

He could hold back no longer. He roared out her name and spilled himself into her, ecstasy ripping through his blood.

For a long time, he stood there, his legs trembling where his muscles clenched, waiting for his breathing to return to normal. Completely spent, he cupped the back of her head, his eyes holding hers. Emotion swarmed in her turquoise depths, engulfing his already raw nerves in overwhelming sensation. He couldn't breathe, couldn't move, for fear of the spell being broken. Cassie was right where he wanted her—in his arms.

"Stay with me," she whispered. "Don't leave me."

Never.

Her words stabbed his gut. Melted his bones and seized every cell in his body. He drew her up to meet his lips and kissed her with all the tenderness erupting inside him.

He'd never felt such strong sentiment before. His innards twisted in knots and a sting smarted in his belly so fierce, he ached. Slowly, reality intruded as their position slowly crept to awareness.

And the fact that he'd taken her without protection. He'd never been so careless. He dropped his forehead against hers.

"Cassie. I, I didn't use a condom."

"I'm on the pill. I haven't been with anyone in two years."

Two years?

"Believe it or not, I haven't been with anyone in a while. And I always use protection." So, they should be safe.

With tender care, he lowered her and removed the rest of his clothing. Then he swept her up into his arms, loving the feel of her cradled against his chest, wondering how he might keep her forever. Her arms secure around his neck, she skirted kisses over his collarbone.

After padding to the bedroom, he stepped to the bed and gently placed her on the edge, where she quickly scooted up and pulled down the covers. She crawled in and patted the space beside her. With a satisfied grin, he released a pleasured sigh and slipped under the comforter with her. Curling up with Cassie in his arms was the closest thing to heaven he could imagine. They lay entwined as the evening's light disappeared into shadows.

Sweet pleasure swirled through Mike's chest at having Cassie snuggled up against him. Mike was afraid to close his eyes for fear the one good thing in his life would disappear. Cassie's breath felt warm on his shoulder. Her even breathing created a sense of contentment. The slow rise and fall of her chest told him she was asleep.

What had possessed her to behave like a wild creature? He wasn't complaining, although he couldn't help but worry. All the signs were there.

Desperation. Agony. Distress.

The concept of something, or someone, doing anything to hurt Cassie ... he couldn't wrap his mind around what might have happened to make her react in such a way. The idea of her being hurt brought out the beast in him. He wanted to crush anyone who dared to harm her.

He did not want to delve into the reasons why.

The back of his mind niggled him. *What if?*

Was it too farfetched for him to want a life with Cassie?

What they had shared was deeper than anything he'd experience before. It could be the beginning of something real.

But it was doomed before it began. Even if he faced the truth that his attraction was more than physical, he knew in his heart to hope for a relationship would be wrong. He wasn't a fool. He knew she would leave him. He had no reason to think otherwise and every reason to believe his time with her would end.

Cassie was beautiful, smart and had a big heart. She loved children. But what woman would take a risk on him? He could never put her through the worry and torment. He never wanted to see the look on her face that he'd seen on his mother's. And he sure as hell never wanted to go through the pain he'd experienced with his mother's desertion.

If he took a chance and lost Cassie, it would be much worse.

Someone would surely get hurt in the end.
He feared it just might be him.

CHAPTER 20

Mike lay panting, Cassie's heart pounding crazily against his. She'd kill him if they kept this pace. She still hadn't told him what had happened to make her call, but he wasn't going anywhere until she did.

"Coffee or shower?" If she chose shower, they'd be at it again—which would suit him just fine.

"Definitely coffee. I suppose I owe you an explanation."

Seeing her vulnerability made his heart sting. "You don't owe me anything. But I'd like to know what happened. You were damn near frantic."

She chewed on her bottom lip.

"Why don't I make coffee?" he said, taking pity on her. "Then we can talk."

Relief flashed in her eyes, he gave her a kiss on her forehead.

He threw the covers back and looked for his pants. Realizing they were in the living room, he stood, uncaring of his nudity, and strode down the hall.

Until she told him what bothered her, he was at a loss. Last night had alarmed him. He'd thought she'd been hurt. When she'd said *I need you*, everything had gone out of his head but the desire to rush to her side.

Now that it was morning, would she change her mind? What if she no longer needed him? What if she'd just wanted to use him for sex, to get over her distress? Her hesitation this morning made him nervous. She couldn't just push him away—use him and then send him out the door without an explanation. He wouldn't allow it.

Besides, the anguish he'd seen on her face last night had nearly brought him to his knees. He wanted to crush the person who'd put it there.

He stepped into his jeans and pulled on his shirt, leaving it hanging open, then started the coffee. He stood staring at the dripping brew, listening to the hissing sound. He poured two cups of coffee and added milk to hers when the hair tingled on the back of his neck. Cassie had slipped into the kitchen. He turned and handed a mug to her.

"Thank you."

She wore a T-shirt that fell to her knees and had her hair tucked behind one ear. The urge to press his lips to her neck surged in his gut. But he and Cassie needed to talk.

"Feeling better?" he asked after she'd taken a sip.

"You always make me feel better, Mike." She turned and padded to the living room. She took a seat on the sofa and he sat beside her.

"Cassie, whatever it is, just say it."

Her gaze jerked to his. "It's nothing bad. I mean, it's nothing to do with you and me."

He released the breath that had been squeezing his lungs and lifted her hand, lacing his fingers with hers. The connection solid, grounding him. Linking her to him.

"You can tell me anything."

She fidgeted with the hem of her shirt. He had little patience when kept in the dark. The only way to take charge of a situation was head on. If she would just tell him, he could deal with it. Now he really started to worry.

"Would it be better if I held you?"

Again, her head jerked to him, her eyes filled with indecision.

"Come here." He pulled her into his arms, pressing her head to his shoulder. She slid her hand under the flap of his shirt and rested it lightly on the center of his chest. He began to relax as her fingers played with his wisps of hair.

Contented to stay just like this, he massaged her back. Having Cassie in his arms brought peace and a feeling of belonging. He'd never allowed a woman to get close, but Cassie had already gotten under his skin. She made him hope for what he knew he couldn't have. She fit perfectly into his life—until he remembered she would leave.

Yet he had allowed her in. Allowed her to be important. This woman could break his heart.

Lost in his thoughts, he scarcely realized she'd spoken.

"Hmmm?"

"My sister."

"Is something wrong with your sister?" His hands stilled.

Cassie gave a little sound very much like a snort. "You could say that."

"You want to tell me what happened?" He rested his chin on the top of her head.

"You know my mom had surgery."

"Was that yesterday?" He'd been so focused with her distress on the phone last night, he'd completely forgotten.

"Yes. My sister, two of my cousins, Mom's preacher and her best friend were there."

"She get along all right?" If something had gone wrong, sure-ly she'd have told him before now.

"Mom did fine. When she came back from recovery, everyone left but me and my sister."

When Cassie paused, he rubbed her back, offering comfort, letting her know she was safe in his arms.

"My sister attacked me."

He forced himself not to flinch. Cassie spoke as though it was a normal occurrence. No change in her voice, no agitation in her body. Attacked as in how? He hadn't seen any evidence of a fight.

"She said some horrible things. With Mom lying in a hospital bed not three feet away. Mom could have heard us. I was so mad I said some pretty mean things too."

He hugged her tighter. "I can't imagine you saying anything mean. I bet this will blow over after you both have had time to think about things. Your mom just had surgery. I'm sure your nerves, and your sister's, played a factor in the argument."

Sitting back, Cassie pushed against his side, bringing her eyes level with his. "I don't think so. The things we said ... this has been building up for some time. What made me so mad, she picked the day of Mom's surgery of all days to pick a fight?"

"She must have some insecurities."

"I'm the one with the insecurities. She's a barrel of attitude."

Cassie? Insecurities?

"Maybe she has a problem you don't know about."

"She's got problems, all right." Cassie settled back against him, her unique scent invading his senses. He closed his eyes and basked in her essence.

After a few moments, he noticed she still seemed anxious. "Is there something else?"

"Yes."

He waited.

When she buried her face in his shoulder, he tightened his embrace. "Honey. It's okay. I'm right here and I'm not going anywhere." He meant it. He wanted her and, God help him, he wanted to keep her.

"We were arguing about Mom and ... money and stuff, and she ... Out of the blue, she brought up our dad. He died seven years ago."

Mike slid his arms around her waist and lifted her onto his lap. Long strands of hair hung in her face. He shoved them out of the way.

"She went on to gloat and tell me that Dad called her the night before he died. He said I was drunk and came to his hospital room and upset him."

If he had her sister here, he'd ring her spiteful neck.

Cassie swiped the tears on her cheek. Mike pulled a handkerchief out of his pocket and handed it to her.

"I remember that night. I went with some of the teachers to dinner. I had one glass of wine."

"Your sister made that up. For whatever small-minded reason, she wanted to hurt you."

Cassie burrowed into him. God, he wished he could take away her pain. Undo the confrontation. She unburdened her soul, ripping his guts right along with hers. "I loved my father. We didn't agree on everything, but I respected him. I joked with him, no one else did. My sister is picking at anything she can to upset me."

Her lips quivered into his neck as she spoke. The woman had no idea what her fingers toying with his chest hair did to him. Yes, he desired her, but he cherished her. Cassie owned his heart. He was damn thankful he was the one holding her. Thankful he was the one comforting her.

"Keep your good memories of him, Cassie. Put what your sister said out of your mind." Mike could only assume Cassie and her sister were strung out over their mom's surgery. Stress made people behave irrationally. He'd seen it firsthand after responding to many 911 calls.

If it wasn't worry or release of built up tension, then her sister was one real piece of work. He couldn't imagine anyone attacking Cassie. She was the most sensible woman he'd ever met. A lot of fun, too.

He never had a sibling. Still, it didn't seem right to fight in your mother's hospital room. Sounded like Cassie's sister had some real issues.

"Thank you," she said cuddling deeper into his chest. "Thank you for being here. Thank you for coming when I called."

Holding her tight, he tried showing her without words how he felt. Her clinging was sending some serious signals prompting urges of desire. Triggering the impulse to turn her on his lap and drive himself into her heat. Like he had last night.

But for now, he'd hold her.

"Anytime."

Every time.

All the time.

It amazed him how much he meant those words—with a passion bordering insanity. Fierce possessiveness, violent protectiveness, savage yearning—feelings beyond any he'd imagined.

He was in way over his head.

***

Mike figured he spent so much time thinking about Cassie he might as well be with her. And he wanted to do something nice. She deserved nice after the scene with her sister. He'd asked Cassie on another date and she'd accepted.

He'd been doing a lot of thinking about what he wanted lately. What did he want?

A woman who'd accept him. Accept his job. Accept the fact that he would never quit. Fighting fires was in his blood. Whether the adrenaline rush or the need to protect and save, when the siren went off, his instincts kicked in. His training took over and he did what needed to be done. Second thoughts could get a man killed. When Mike charged into a burning building, the only thing on his mind was search and protect.

Wishes and fantasies were not for him. He lived in the real world. A world where his profession presented risk. Women wanted their man safe and be a good provider. A three-piece suit would choke him. He loved what he did and he wouldn't give it up for any woman.

But he couldn't resist Cassie. The woman drew him, grabbed him by the gut. Maybe this thing would blow up in his face, but he planned to enjoy her for as long as he could.

Fresh from the shower, Mike lathered his face with shaving cream. Before he picked up his razor, the phone rang. He grabbed a cloth, slung the linen around his neck and tightened the towel dangling around his hips while he strode into his room.

"Mike here."

"Hello, Mike."

"Hey, Dad." Mike dropped onto the rumpled covers of his bed.

"How are you, boy?"

"Doing good. How about you?" Mike lifted one end of the towel from his neck and rubbed the shaving cream off his face.

"Some days are good. And some days are even better." His dad laughed. An everyday comment since his dad had quit working. Shame his mom hadn't stuck around to share Dad's retirement.

"You must have been fishing," Mike said.

"Fish don't talk much. Not like your Aunt Lucy. She darn near pecks my ear right off."

"But she feeds you good, huh?" Aunt Lucy was the best cook in the state. Everything she made was from scratch, no box fare for her family. She thought it her duty to fuss over her little brother, since he didn't have a woman to look after him.

"Let's see now," his dad began. Mike could imagine his dad scratching his head. "This is Thursday. She'll be bringing spaghetti over tonight. She always makes her homemade sauce on Thursday. When you coming down, boy?"

Same question, same evasive answer. "Soon, Dad."

He stayed on the phone another ten minutes, solving the world's problems before telling his dad bye. The old man sounded good. With his aunt's cuisine, no need to worry about him starving.

Mike scrubbed a hand down his face. His shift didn't begin for another forty-eight hours. If he didn't have a date with Cassie, he'd be tempted to leave his brush of whiskers. He shoved from the bed and he padded to the bathroom. Half of his face was covered in lather when the phone rang again. Cursing under his breath, he grabbed the towel and mopped his face again. Calming his irritation, he answered in a reasonable tone. It wouldn't do to yell when the person on the other end might be Cassie.

"Hello."

"Mike."

He ran a frustrated hand through his spiky hair. Not Cassie. Then his alert system kicked in. "What's up, Shep?"

"There's no emergency and we're not on call, so relax."

"Habit." Mike rolled the tension from his shoulders and set-tled back on the bed.

"I just talked to my brother."

Shep has four brothers. Then Mike remembered their last conversation where Shep had mentioned the possibility of his brother helping Tammy with her ex-husband. "The lawyer?"

Mike glanced at his watch. Hope Cassie wouldn't mind his dark shadow.

"Yes. I mentioned Tammy's ex and he's going to look into it."

"That's great." Tammy was a sweetheart. She didn't deserve her asshole husband giving her shit.

"Thought you should know, so you can tell her."

Mike frowned in confusion. "What do you mean?"

"Thought you could tell Tammy about Eddie and she could give him a call at his office."

Mike's fingers tensed on the phone. Sounds like going around the barn to get to the barn doors. "Why don't you tell her?"

"Well, I'm not too sure of the reception I might get." Shep let out a sigh.

"Did something happen? Or is there something you didn't tell me about when you took her home last week?"

"No."

Just no? Nothing else.

"Then what's the problem?"

"You know how women are. They get these things in their head."

Yeah. He knew. "What things?"

"How's Cassie?"

"What's she got to do with it? And don't change the subjec t.".

"Not changing the subject," Shep drawled. "Just saying, maybe she said something."

"Who, Cassie? What would she have to say?"

"Whether or not her friend freaked when she found out I'm the one who took her home."

"You haven't talked to Tammy?"

"Nope."

"You're usually not so dense. Or chicken. Give the woman a call."

"If she's embarrassed, she won't want to talk to me. But if she wants me to call, and I don't ... see what I mean? You never know with a female."

Laughter erupted in Mike's chest. "I don't believe this."

Shep feared nothing. But he shied away from a conversation with a woman?

"Believe what? That I'm considering her reaction before I put my neck in a noose? Save a lot of trouble if Tammy doesn't want to see me again."

"I doubt she feels that way. According to Cassie, Tammy wants you to call her."

"When did she tell you that?"

"I didn't tell you?"

"No, you did not."

"I guess I had other things on my mind."

"She say anything else?"

"Wait till the guys get a load of this." This was too good an opportunity to pass up.

"If you know what's good for you, you'll keep your mouth shut."

"Come on, Cap. All's fair, you know?"

The guys picked on each other all the time. Shep did his fair share of jokes and teasing, although he did have to keep his crew in line. Seemed only fair they should have a chance at the boss.

"Bad enough to have you poking at me. I don't need the team sticking their nose where it don't belong."

"Why don't you give the woman a call and put an end to your misery?"

"Misery? No hardship thinking about her. She gets a man distracted."

Whether or not Shep meant to, he'd just confirmed what Mike had guessed. His friend had the hots for Tammy.

"Distracted, huh? I call it good ole lust." Hell, Mike knew the feeling. He lusted after Cassie. Once he had a taste, he needed more.

Shep laughed. "Yep. That too. But I need to know which way the wind is blowing."

"Something did happen, didn't it?"

"Nope."

Shep drove Mike crazy with his short answers. The man kept his thoughts to himself, not one to blow his own horn. Getting information out of Shep was like pulling teeth.

"So, what's the deal?" Mike pried, hoping for more information.

"She's fun. Plain ole fun. Down to earth. When she laughs, she doesn't snicker or act coy or none of that snooty, high and mighty stuff. She's easy to talk with. Hard not to like her."

"Didn't mention her looks."

"Red hair means fire. Paid close attention," Shep said with certainty. "She has a zest for life."

"Fire as in passion?"

"Who's to say we'll be anything more than friends?"

"You aim to be friends with her?"

"At least that. If my brother takes her case, we have a reason to see each other."

I'll be damned.

"You sly dog."

"We'll cross that bridge when we come to it. She's a mom. With two boys, she has to present a proper image. Tammy is a lady and needs to be treated like one. But she's still a healthy young woman with needs of her own. Who knows? She may want a fling. Or she may want to get back at that dickhead husband of hers."

"Ex," Mike reminded.

"If I have my way, it will be ex-dad. Asshole doesn't deserve kids if he can't be faithful to his wife. Or at least civil. Filing for custody and not having the balls to notify her—he's asking for a boot up his ass. Eddie's the one to give it to him."

"You planning on giving a relationship a chance?"

"Well, now. There's different levels of involvement in relationships. You know that, Mike. You won't let a woman get but so close."

Shep was right. Cassie created a gnawing hunger in him he tried to ignore. When he lay between her thighs, he felt more than just satisfying his need—even if he didn't want to admit it.

Hell. Who was he kidding? He'd clung to her like his very existence would cease if he let go.

Avoiding that topic, Mike asked Shep, "What will you do?"

"Take it one day at a time, my friend. And ride the ride for as long as it lasts."

That sounded like good advice.

Chapter 21

Like a teenager waiting for her first kiss, Cassie had difficulty controlling her excitement. It took everything she had not to show her eagerness by bouncing on the truck seat. Mike was taking her to see his house and she couldn't wait.

"You're quiet."

Cassie faced Mike. His attention on his driving, she noticed his steady hands gripping the wheel. "I'm impatient."

"You don't show it."

"When I'm nervous, I chatter. It's annoying. I'm trying very hard to keep my mouth shut."

He laughed, that deep rich sound that sent tingles racing down her spine.

"Why are you nervous? It's just a house."

"I get to see where you live," she said, her enthusiasm coming through in her voice. His space. He'd invited her and she'd jumped at the chance.

Mike glanced at her with a serious expression. "It's nothing special. Just a normal place, like yours. A living room, kitchen, bedrooms."

"It must be big."

"Nooo." He drew out the word. "It's the house I grew up in. I lived with my dad."

"Yes, you said you bought it from him. But you built a big garage." Where he housed his Mustang. Where he'd spent many hours sweating, building, restoring. The more she thought about his personal space, the more enthusiastic she grew. It was almost arousing.

"It's nothing fancy either. Just a building." He cleared his throat. "I don't know what you're expecting, Cassie. I hope you won't be disappointed."

Disappointed?

She suddenly realized her mistake. In her excitement, she'd blundered and made him think ... what?

"Mike. You've talked about a garage you built for you Mustang. You mentioned an engine hoist and tools. I just imagined a lot of space for you to work or tinker, or play with your big boy toys. I'm excited because it's your space. It's you. Where you spend your time. Where you worked on your beautiful car."

When his face eased into a grin, the tension in her chest vanished. "Ah. It's really the car you want to see."

She answered him with a teasing smile of her own. "Of course."

He turned at the intersection, taking a road to the right. They'd gone about a mile and he turned into a sub-division, then pulled into a gravel driveway, leading to a small two-story house. She stared at the quaint home as the truck rolled to a stop.

"Here we are. Home sweet home." Mike shoved the gearshift into park.

The outside was a soft yellow with white shutters and three steps leading up to a porch that was enclosed with wooden rails.

The driveway extended around the side of the house, making Cassie wonder if the garage was back there.

"I guess I should take you in the front. The driveway goes around to the back of the house."

"Works for me." Breathless with anticipation, Cassie hopped out of the truck. Mike met her and placed his palm on her lower back. Heat surged through every part of her, the way it did every time he touched her. She almost leaned into his warmth, but she wanted to see his house.

He opened the front door and motioned for her to go in first. "This is the living room."

The walls and furniture were done in greens and browns. In the middle of the room were two recliners and a leather couch. Definitely a man's taste. Box shades at the windows, instead of curtains, gave it a clean-cut look. A large book shelf, handmade, lined one wall holding more movies than books. And, not surprisingly, the man size TV. She'd guess at least sixty inches. A lamp and coasters were the only items on the end table. Simple, neat and very cozy.

"Through here is the kitchen."

She stepped into a nice sized kitchen with plenty of space for a dining table and four chairs.

They must have eaten their meals in here. Homey.

"Do you cook?"

"Of course. Mostly at the station. All the guys cook. We take turns. Although, Shep is the best. He and Laredo compete. I'm happy to pull clean up." He turned. "This way to the bathroom." He strode toward a doorway that led to a hall circling back to the living room.

Cassie was surprised at the cleanliness of his home. No clutter. Evidently, Mike was a neat freak.

"Tell me. Did you clean up for me or hire someone to clean your house?"

Mike looked offended, but he over-killed pretending to be insulted. He was too darn cute.

"Do you think I can't clean a house? Growing up, it was just me and Dad. We did it all. Cook, clean—no one else was there to do it for us."

"You've done a magnificent job," she purred. She knew how to stroke a man's pride and she promised to make up for it later.

"Bedrooms are upstairs." He hesitated, watching her reaction.

Was Mike nervous? Naw. If he wanted to go upstairs, he'd just pick her up and carry her. Maybe he was waiting for a signal from her. He could be such a gentleman. No matter how appealing falling into bed seemed right now, she was dying to see his garage.

"Hmm. And outside?" she hinted.

He chuckled. A deep rumble in his chest that made her re-think her decision of going upstairs.

"Come on," he said, leading her back to the kitchen and a set of glass doors. "I don't like sliding glass doors, so I put in a hinged patio door for my dad."

Which basically looked like one French door, only bigger. Stained and polished to a beautiful shine.

Wood porch, wood table that looked better than the quality found in furniture stores—a talented carpenter?

She stepped onto a huge deck the length of the house, stained in a beautiful shade of caramel. Sun glinted off a stainless-steel grill sitting at one corner. An ironwork table and chairs sat to the right. Railing surrounded the entire deck and down three steps to the ground.

"Did you build this?"

"Yep. Used to be a screened in porch. I ripped it out and built this deck. Dad and I sat out here as often as we could. Now, it's just me."

Bingo.

"It's perfect," she said. He smiled with pride, giving her a fuzzy feeling in her tummy. She pointed to the barbeque. "You like to grill?"

"I do," he said, then gave a shrug. "Not home enough to do it. The guys go to Shep's for cookouts." He pointed to the houses lining his backyard. "The Berry Farm used to be there. I had hoped to save money and one day buy a section of land, but the old woman died and her son, who lives in Texas, sold it to a developer. Now I'm surrounded by a subdivision with neighbors backed right up to my garage."

Cassie noticed a building at the edge of his driveway, but she'd heard the wistfulness in Mike's voice. He didn't like having people on top of him. She imagined him in a country setting, maybe even a farm.

"Okay. I know you're anxious. Come on." Mike headed down the steps and toward a building that had to be the garage.

Her feet danced along the grass in anticipation. He threw open the door and she stepped from bright sunshine to a darkened room, slits of light gleaming through high windows. Mike flipped a switch and florescent bulbs flickered to life, illuminating the entire space.

She blinked. Then tried to take everything in at once.

"Told you. It isn't much."

Cassie took a quick scan of the interior. Lots of tools and equipment to the left, some type of machines, an engine hoist and metal racks. Two cars were parked right in the middle of the building, each covered with a canvas. A tall wooden work bench, probably built to suit Mike's height, lined the right wall from the door to the back of the room.

"Are you kidding? This is awesome." She took a step forward. "I want to see everything. But first, I want to know what's under those." She pointed directly to the canvas in front of her.

He rolled one of the covers back. The Mustang. "Is this what's had you acting like a jumping bean?"

"Wow." She breathed in awe, just like the first time she'd seen it. Under the ceiling lights, the black paint shined, luring her like a homing beacon. "It looks just as spectacular as the day you took me for a ride." She couldn't wait to see what hid under the other cloth. "Do you have another one?"

Mike's leering grin reminded her of the cliché about the cat that swallowed the canary. Damn the man was handsome. Hot with a capital H. Before he could remove the cloth, she slipped up behind him and slid her hands around his middle. He froze.

Then he slowly turned and wrapped her in his arms for a perfect hug.

It didn't take a genius to figure out what was on her mind. The same as him. Entirely too much time had passed without Cassie in his arms. From the moment he stepped into the house, he thought of taking her upstairs to his bedroom. For Christ's sake, he didn't want to pounce on her first thing. But now? All bets were off.

"You feel so good. I love being all snuggled up to you."

He loved the way her voice got all throaty. He slid his hand up the center of her back and welcomed the delicious surge of arousal. "I can't go five seconds without touching you."

He leaned back and tilted her face for his kiss. Warm lips pressed against his. He cradled the back of her head, buried his fingers in her hair and kissed her slow and deep. He couldn't touch her without wanting to possess her. She brought out every urge, every desire to own her. Before his passion took control, he slowed the hunger in his kiss.

When they broke apart, he ran his nose along her jaw and behind her ear, enjoying the feel of her skin. "I love the way you melt into me," he murmured.

Her ragged breathing matched his. Her fingers tugged at the waist of his jeans. "Are you going to show me what's under there?"

He groaned at her double entendre, then forced himself to let her go. Unable to resist, he brushed his lips across her cheek once more, then readjusted himself. He turned around and began folding back the car cover.

"I saw a for sale ad in The Bulletin Board for this." He scrutinized the old Mustang that looked like it had gone through hell and back.

Cassie's face puckered in a frown. "Who would do that to a car? What year is it?"

"1966 fastback. Some older woman had it in her barn. The chickens were living in it."

"Oh, no." She stuck her head inside and quickly drew back out. "It smells."

Mike laughed. "You should have seen it when I picked it up. I cleaned the thing out before I put it in here. The whole place would be rank if I hadn't."

"Looks like it was in a demolition derby. What color was it? It's so rusted."

"The famous green that was so popular that year. Needs a lot of body work. Haven't checked out the engine yet." He pointed to the 1969 black convertible. "That one over there looked a lot like this when I started. Except for the crushed fenders."

"I can't imagine the effort required to get this one in good shape."

"It will take a lot of work and time." The image of Cassie beside him, grease on her face popped in his head. A nice dream.

He spent the next thirty minutes showing Cassie the things in his shop. He'd never seen a woman so engrossed in the tools and apparatuses a man toyed with. Most women would consider a garage a dirty space. Not Cassie. She questioned every item and listened with interest.

One more thing to love about her.

Before he could travel down that forbidden path, he shook off the fantasy. Her curiosity fed, he turned off the lights and closed the shop. Yet he couldn't stop thinking of how the beautiful woman at his side would fit right in here. His space. His home.

His life.

He popped the tops on two beers and carried the bottles out to the deck. Cassie sat on a chaise, her long legs stretched out. He imagined them wrapped around him and an immediate stiffening hit his groin.

"Thank you," she said as he handed her a brew.

He took the chair next to her. With the sun directing its rays on the front of the house, the deck was in shadow, making the afternoon temperature comfortable where he and Cassie sat in the shade. His mind flooded with craving. How he'd like to have his way with her. Right here. Right now.

He scowled, staring at the border of his property.

"Not much privacy," he said aloud, damning the other houses' presence.

"In my apartment, sometimes I can hear through the walls."

He grunted in understanding.

"I don't have a yard to plant flowers, I can't see the mountains. The flip side is I feel safe. It's a big building, but I have people around me."

He was just the opposite. He hated people invading his living space. Everywhere he turned he saw more development. More houses cluttering up his view.

"I like wide open spaces and I'd rather have the woods and sky around me. I'd like to sit on my back deck and see the mountains, not the neighbor's roof or their junk in their back yard." Or have them witness an intimate moment. Damn, he felt suffocated.

"Why don't you move?"

"Believe me, I've thought about it." He wondered if Cassie might like living in the country. With wide open spaces, lots of grassland, trees, woods.

"I guess it would be difficult leaving the home you grew up in."

Was she kidding? What did he care about this old place?

"After all, you've built that wonderful garage."

"I can build a garage anywhere. I've been tempted to sell this place and buy land out in the country."

"What's holding you back?"

"Good question," he answered with a sigh. "I suppose I haven't had a reason to motivate me." Would Cassie be his motivation? Would she give up the security of her apartment to live with him?

Christ. There he went again. Thinking of a future. With her. Was it that farfetched?

"I've been saving. If I'm going to purchase land, I want a place big enough I won't need to worry about someone moving in right beside me." Or watching me from their window. He didn't want another house within thirty miles of his. Fat chance of that happening. "I haven't had the time or the inclination to actually purchase another property."

"Would you sell this house or keep it?"

"I'd sell it. Dad's happy in North Carolina. I have no attachment to the place. I'd use the money for a new house."

Cassie took a swig of her beer and propped up her knee. "Tell me about the home you'd like to have."

He stretched out his long legs and crossed them at his ankles. *A place like Shep's.*

"I don't need anything fancy or big." He remembered Cassie's anticipation on the ride to his house. Did she want a big house?

All women did.

"A lot of land. Enough where I can't see my neighbor."

"Hermit."

Mike angled his head and gestured with his bottle. "Would you like looking at that every day?"

"What do you imagine? Woods? Trees? Grass? Fences?"

"Haven't really thought too much about it."

"Why don't you talk to a real estate agent? Just get an idea of what's available."

He thought on that for a good few minutes. If he wanted space, and land, and trees, and not freakin' houses in his face, why didn't he do something about it?

CHAPTER 22

The dazzling lights from the chandeliers illuminated Cassie's beauty, exhibiting her soft features, her full lips.

Mike had worked himself up into a fine lather before he'd gotten to her door. Seeing her in a sexy blue top displaying her curvy breasts and a skin-tight skirt showing her long legs, he'd damn near swallowed his tongue. Now, here he sat across from her in the chic restaurant and he thought he might explode.

Not once this evening had his mind been on food. He couldn't take his eyes off Cassie. Not while his mind created images of the two of them naked, tangled together. He kept envisioning her reclined across silk sheets, her long, blonde hair spread over a pillow, draped over her shoulders, her luscious breasts ... He swallowed, jerking his attention back to the conversation. The crease on Cassie's brow clued him in that he'd missed something.

She leaned forward, her generous breasts grazing the white linen. His eyes glued to her cleavage, his restraint damn near crumbled. He couldn't wait to get the hell out of here.

"Mike. You look like a caged bear. Will you wipe that scowl off your face?"

"What do you expect? You looking like that is like pouring gasoline on an already flaming fire. I've got about as much resistance as a match stick right now."

She snatched her napkin to cover her lips, but not before he saw her smile.

"You're beautiful. The outfit you're wearing is sexy as hell. You'd tempt Satan himself."

"I only have one person I care to tempt."

God, he loved it when she smiled at him like that. He reached across the table for her hand and rubbed his thumb across her dainty knuckles, wishing he could haul her onto his lap.

"I can't put into words what you do to me," he told her.

She curled her fingers into his palm. "You do the same to me."

"Then what the hell are we doing here?" He made a move to get up. She tugged his hand.

"We haven't eaten our dinner."

He lowered his voice. "I'm not hungry for food and you know it."

"Hmm. Anticipation makes the appetite stronger." She hiked a brow, teasing, taunting him.

"It makes a man a caged beast when he can't touch the woman he wants."

She giggled, hiking his lust up a notch.

"If you're hungry, we can raid the refrigerator." He was bound to have something in it.

"You brought me to this nice restaurant and I'm staying for my risotto."

Every minute he spent with Cassie, he fell deeper and deeper under her spell.

"I bet I can change your mind." Somehow, his hope to leave the restaurant had turned into a game. Now that the idea had taken hold, he kicked back, seeing if he could convince her. He rubbed his thumb over the inside of Cassie's wrist and gazed at her with such intensity, flames should be shooting from his eyes.

She trembled. He smiled at the satisfying response. She ran her tongue across her bottom lip and, sure enough, she bit down with her teeth. Desire stabbed every cell in his body.

"Take it to go."

***

They barely made it through the door when Mike grabbed her. He pinned her against the wall and angled his mouth over hers, devouring her. Claiming her. She clutched the back of his head with one hand while the fingers of her other tangled in his shirt, tugging him, crawling into him. He tasted of wine and hunger, and a craving she gladly reciprocated. She opened her mouth wider, her tongue dancing and mating with his, her lower body imitating the same movements. She couldn't get enough of Mike. Of his kiss. Of his seeking hands roaming over her body.

When his mouth slid down her jaw to her neck, she moaned, tilting her head just a bit as he sucked greedily on the skin just below her ear. The air around her grew heavy. Closing in on her, taking her breath. All she knew was Mike. All she felt was Mike, driving her steadily higher and higher. One of his hands gently grasped her breast, gripping, squeezing, while his thigh rocked between her legs. Delicious vibrations cannonballed straight to her center. She worked the buttons on his shirt. With a growl, he tore it off and flung the material aside.

Firm, sculpted abs met her gaze. Sprigs of hair begged her to touch. And she did just that, running her hands over steel and slick fur, absorbing the riveting tingle on the tips of her fingers.

Slowly, he slid the thin straps of her top off of each shoulder, trickling wet kisses over her heated skin. She felt the release of her bra and her bare breasts spilled free. She barely had time to catch her breath before his mouth closed over one aching nipple. Her head fell back and she arched, her body begging for more. He pinched her other nipple, rolling it between his fingers, shooting heavenly shocks of pleasure to her belly. Unable to hold back her moan, she let out a purring sound, and slithered into him like a needy kitten.

Rock solid abs grazed her breasts as his mouth found hers again. He scorched her with his burning heat, melting away all her defenses. One hand slid over her hip and under her short skirt, sizzling every nerve ending in his path. She closed her eyes and marveled at the delicious sensation swamping her senses. When he slipped his fingers inside her panties, she whimpered.

His fingers teased, plucked, making her tremble and jerk. Wanting more. Needing more. He inserted a finger and it felt so good. He felt so good. Thrusting again and again, he slowly drove her crazy. He took her mouth thoroughly in a devastating kiss, spinning her mind in turmoil.

She writhed in earnest. Her world spiraled out of control, pitching her to another universe. Desperate for completion, her body spasmed and shuddered and came apart.

Such sweet, aching pleasure. Such mind-blowing ecstasy in the talented hands of her hot firefighter. Who continued to stroke and caress until she felt the stirrings of passion again. Her will was not her own. She ran her hands over his shoulders and down his chest, delighting in his muscled body.

At the same time she reached for the button on his trousers, he leaned back and yanked at her skirt, letting it fall to the floor. Then he hooked his thumbs in her panties and dragged them down.

"So fucking beautiful." Taking his time, he caressed the flesh of each leg, letting his hands roam higher and higher until he found the triangle between her thighs. "So wet."

She gasped, then bit her lip. When he glanced up, his blue eyes were hazed with desire.

"Spread your legs," he demanded.

She quivered at the idea his command suggested. She ached with anticipation, wanting his mouth on her so badly. While part of her wanted to savor every second, another part of her wanted to give him the same ecstasy he'd given her. Pleasure should be shared. And she so wanted to please him.

"Mike," she pleaded. "I need you."

"I know, babe. I'm giving you what you need."

Oh God yes. Please.

But instead she said, "I want to make you feel good, too."

"Shhh. Relax. And enjoy." He massaged her thighs while he spread butterfly kisses across her belly, each one lower than the last, blazing a trail to his intended destination. Easing her legs apart, he touched her with his thumbs, stroking in circles. Her tummy quivered with need. He slid his big hands to her butt cheeks and gripped. Then, urging her forward, he pressed his mouth to her.

The air seized in her lungs. The pain in her chest increased until he nuzzled her—there. Then the air escaped, one throbbing breath at a time. Her legs shaky, she grabbed his head for support, angling him just where she wanted him to be.

He lapped and stroked, parting her flesh while squeezing her behind, holding her prisoner to his thrusting tongue. It was too much, and not enough. Her legs buckled, but he held her tight. Her insides were a quaking mess. In a matter of seconds, he took her to another realm of pleasure. She shattered again. Wave after wave of intense ecstasy ripped through her. His kiss relentless, he fired her frenzied pulse pounding deep inside.

This man would kill her with bliss.

"My God, Mike," she panted.

He took her in his arms and swooped her in for a long drugging kiss. When she tasted herself on his tongue, the tang spiked her to desire, once again.

Breathless, he tore his mouth from hers, then cupped her butt and hoisted her up as though she weighed nothing.

"Wrap your legs around me, beautiful, and hang on."

Without taking his mouth from hers, Mike maneuvered them down the hall toward the bedroom. Walking wasn't easy with Cassie wrapped around him and their mouths fused together. The only thought in his mind was completing what they'd started. He was on fire.

Cassie belonged to him.

He made it to the bed and allowed her to slide down his body. His fingers fumbled with the zipper on his pants and her hands tangled with his. Together, they shoved downward. Then, he jerked his black boxers and his erection sprang free.

She stared up at him, causing him to harden to steel. When she touched him with the tip of her finger, he sucked in a breath. The strain unbearable, he waited, unable to move. And wanting to see what she'd do next. Needing her touch more than he needed his next breath. She circled him with the palm of her hand and he swore he saw stars.

Thunder pounded in his temples, blood roared in his ears. Her touch singed him, branded him. She stroked her fingers over him, caressing the ridge of his erection, all the way from the base to the head. Cassie, his incredible Cassie. He wanted no woman but her. She looked up with glowing, brilliant eyes, seeking his approval. How could she not know how much she delighted him? Thrilled him. Drove him crazy. He couldn't resist. He hauled her to him and kissed her with a fever that burned in his soul.

God, he needed her.

Now.

They fell to the bed together, him snuggled delectably between her thighs. Smooth skin, soft flesh, he burrowed into her warmth. She clutched him in haste, her need as great as his. His heart swelled with pride, knowing this woman wanted him with equal frenzy.

Positioning himself, he nudged her slick folds. "This what you want, babe?"

"Yes, Mike. Yes."

He thrust into her.

Fully inside, he locked his jaw, his chest squeezing with satisfaction. Bliss. He remained still, savoring the sensations flooding his mind. Her soft sigh rang like a rousing hum in his ears. Driving him forward. Compelling him to move. He eased out and thrust in again. She whimpered and wrapped her legs around him. He ground his teeth, angled his hips and thrust again.

Deep. So deep. "God, Cassie. That feels so good."

She whimpered and squirmed, trying to move her hips, but his weight pinned her to the mattress. Careful not to mash her, but Christ, she tempted his sanity.

"I can't hold back," he managed to growl.

"Don't." She tightened her arms and legs as her voice came out in a breathless pant. "I want it all."

The last shred of his control snapped. With long and sure strokes, he thrust again and again, harder and faster.

Arousal built to a fever pitch. His breathing grew labored. He jerked his hips, pounding harder, determined to have all of her, denying her to withhold anything from him.

Her little mews drove him, thrilled him. She ground against him, desperate for her own release.

"Mike!" Cassie's body tightened and he felt her walls spasm. She uttered a long, high-pitched wail, her climax sending him over the edge.

He gave a shout and his whole body stiffened. Unbridled ecstasy whirled in his mind. Reeling, he didn't move. Couldn't move. He rode the wave of pure rapture until the last throb faded and his breathing slowed to almost normal.

Cassie's face glowed. He'd never seen a more beautiful woman.

"I'm too heavy for you."

"I don't care. I love having you on me," she panted.

"Me too."

On you. In you.

"You can't breathe." He rolled to the side and pulled her snug in his embrace. "There. That's better."

"Mmm. I feel absolutely wonderful." She snuggled against him, skidding her breasts on his chest.

"Hmmm, wonderful," he said, feeling exactly the same way.

Damn, he loved the feel of this woman. He was finding, he loved everything about her. Way too much.

Heartache may lay ahead, but for now, that didn't bother him. He would snatch the precious moments they shared—however long it lasted.

Chapter 23

Slow days were appreciated at Station Eight. That meant there were no fires and, for the moment, people were safe. Jared and Laredo had the radio blaring while taking inventory of the gear. Cooper was taking his turn in the kitchen, showing off in front of the new recruit. Mike inhaled. Hmm, oven fried chicken. The kid was preparing one of Mike's favorites.

Shep had been closed up in his office. Mike tapped on the door.

"Come in."

He stepped inside and found Shep buried in paperwork. "Anything I can do to help?"

"I've been going over the updated manual. Nothing new. It outlines the same procedures we followed in training last month."

"But?" Mike asked as he settled himself in one of the two chairs in front of Shep's desk.

"I keep tracing our steps on this one."

"We did everything by the book," Mike interrupted.

"Wilson is a by the book guy. But I wonder how the perpetrator managed to get the gas open and get out of the way before anyone caught on. How?"

"The bastard was watching us, waiting for his opening."

"Still. Someone should have seen him. Smelled the gas, even if he'd planted the shit before the crew showed up that morning."

"What else can we do? Put guards at our training sites?"

"That's not a bad idea." Shep raked a hand through his cropped hair in frustration. "How did the son-of-a-bitch find out about the training site? The location, the time? How the hell did he get his information?"

"Following procedure and Wilson keeping the crew back is what kept the number of injuries down. For this to happen the way it did, this character had to be planning this strike for a while."

Shep stared out the window with an exasperated expression. "What pisses me off even more is the prick could have been there watching."

"The thing that scares the shit out of me is he wore a firefighter suit, walked around with the rest of us. Like he was one of us."

By the grim look on Shep's face, he didn't like the concept any better.

"Close enough to set it up, but at a distance where he wouldn't be in the fallout."

"The cocksucker planned for men to get hurt." That was one thing Mike could not ignore. If he got his hands on the guy, he'd snap the motherfucker's neck.

Shep released a sigh. "Hooley's on it. He's a good investigator and he won't stop until he gets his man."

"Does he have any leads?"

"You know Hooley. Closed mouth. He won't give up anything until he has all of his facts."

"What about the film?"

"After you guys had your say, he made the rounds, stopping at each fire station. The perp covered himself pretty well."

"*No one* recognized that guy?"

Shep shook his head.

"Jared, Coop, Laredo and me went back to the Wimer place. Took another look around."

Shep narrowed his eyes. Mike read the expression somewhere between disbelief and pissed the hell off. It was the look Shep gave when you didn't know if he was getting ready to let you off the hook or ream you a new asshole. Mike quickly threw up a hand in defense.

"Look, Shep. I know we were supposed to stay away from the site, but things like this just don't happen. Besides, it's been weeks. We just wanted to scout around. See if we could come up with some sort of explanation."

"And did you?"

"Well..." Mike hesitated as he rubbed the back of his neck. "There's no way a man could have gotten by us unless he was in full gear. I just hope that guy on the film was the only one."

Shep's mouth turned down as he studied the desk calendar in front of him. "I can't believe I didn't consider another conspirator. After Hooley's visit, I just thought it was the one guy."

"This guy knows too much. To fit right in, walk among us like he belongs there ... You think a firefighter might have had a hand in this?"

"I'm not ready to believe that, or the idea of an inside source. This guy could be working alone."

"Our arsonist has balls. He walked right in and helped himself to Station Nine's equipment. What's to keep this guy from entering any of the stations?" Mike didn't want to think of some criminal messing around the firehouse. Damn, what a staggering notion.

Shep seemed to consider Mike's words for several minutes, then he wrote some notes in a book. He tossed his pen down on the desk. "The bastard walks in here, he's going to get a nice surprise. I want every man on alert. I'll give Hooley our suspicions. We'll take a closer look at that film."

Mike gave a nod. He wanted the prick caught. Now that there was a woman in his life, he'd rather spend his time thinking about her. Being with her.

"Got something else on your mind?" Shep closed the binder he'd been writing in.

"Nothing," he answered a might too quickly. Cassie was always on his mind, but Shep didn't need to know that. "The guys are keeping themselves busy. Glad to have some free time without a crisis."

"You never know how long that will last."

"Yeah, I know. By the way, did you, uh, call Tammy and tell her about your brother?"

Shep leaned back in his chair, making the seat creak. "Yeah, I called her."

"Getting something out of you is like pulling teeth with a pair of pliers." Mike rested one ankle over the opposite knee.

"What do you want to know? I called her. Told her Eddie would to see her."

"What did she say?"

"Said she wanted me to go with her."

"Is that so?" Mike enjoyed seeing Shep squirm. Even if there were no obvious signs, he knew the man was uncomfortable. When Shep didn't offer anything more, Mike prodded him. "Was the woman civil to you?"

"Yep." Damn, the man was tight lipped.

"Was that before or after you told her about Eddie?"

Shep studied the ceiling and Mike grinded his teeth waiting for an answer.

"When I told her who I was, she did act kind of, out of breath."

Now that was interesting. Mike couldn't help himself. "As in heavy breathing? Over the phone? Like an obscene phone call."

Shep shot him a scowl. "You want to hear this or not?"

Mike held up his hands in surrender, but a chuckle escaped.

"Once I told her why I called, she talked my ear off. Kept thanking me. Took me by surprise when she asked me to go with her."

"You going?"

"Yep. Already made the appointment." Shep stretched his arms behind his head and propped his feet up on his desk. "How are things going with you and Cassie?"

Mike noticed how adeptly Shep changed the topic. Let's see how Shep liked one-word answers. "Fine."

Silence.

Sometimes Shep irritated the hell out of him with his calm, composed, unruffled demeanor.

"Well?" Mike asked.

"Well, what?"

Mike's booted foot hit the floor as he sat straight. "You want to know, so why don't you ask."

"Figure if there's anything you want to tell me, you will."

Irritating ass.

"She's getting too close," Mike blurted.

Shep passed him a look full of condemnation. "*She* is? Or *you* are?"

"I can't have a relationship."

"Seems you already do."

Yeah. He'd known spending the night with Cassie would be special. He didn't expect his time with her to be so spectacular that he couldn't stop wishing for more.

"I can't … I can't afford an attachment. You know that."

"I don't know any such thing. You've babbled such nonsense before. I don't see any reason you and Cassie can't have a future."

"Future? You forget my mom walked out on my dad because of his profession?"

"Don't mean Cassie will."

He wished that were true. Cassie was a special woman, but how could he be sure she wouldn't leave? "It takes a certain kind of woman to accept her husband being a firefighter."

"You think she wants some pencil pusher?"

He didn't know what Cassie wanted. Their relationship had not progressed far enough for him to find out. Hell, they just started dating. Even though they'd shared a hell of a lot more than *a date*. He wouldn't get his hopes up. She wouldn't stick around.

"My job is too dangerous."

Shep scooted his chair forward and braced his arms on the edge of his desk, locking his eyes with Mike's. "If a woman loves you, she'll accept your job."

Mike gave a harsh laugh. "You're one to talk."

"My being single has nothing to do with my job. I hope to marry the right woman someday. You and Cassie make a fine couple. From what I see, that woman loves you. Don't throw that away."

Mike scrubbed a hand over his clean-shaven face, and admitted what he'd been afraid to admit. "I want her in my life. I want her for keeps. But I can't let go of the fear that she'll leave."

"You'd be—"

Three loud tones came across the intercom. Shep shoved from his chair without finishing his sentence. Mike rushed out the door behind Shep and hustled toward the bay. He threw on his suit, jumped into his boots, and grabbed his gear. He climbed into the truck the same time as Jared.

"What we got?"

"Wreck downtown," Jared answered, buckling his seat belt.

"Shit. At this time of day, traffic will be a bitch."

Mike leaned back against the seat, letting the hum of the engine seep into his bones.

Within minutes, they were at the scene. Lights flashed from two police cars parked off to one side while one of the officers directed traffic away from the blocked intersection. Jared pulled up behind the police cars while Laredo drove the quint to the front of the wreckage.

When Jared jerked the Midi to a stop, Mike jumped out, rushing to the collided cars to see if there were injuries. He and Jared had just reached the front of their rig when a loud crack sounded. He must have flinched—something he normally did not do—for his helmet jerked to the side and something buzzed past his ear.

"Shots fired. Shots fired."

Before he knew what was happening, Jared knocked him back, behind a fender. Officers grabbed their guns and stood in a crouched position behind the mangled cars.

"Christ." Jared fell to the ground beside Mike.

"What the fuck?"

"Some asshole with a gun."

"Stay back," Shep's voice came over the radio. "Don't get out of the trucks. If you're already out, stay the hell on the ground. We're in the middle of gunfire."

"Right, Cap." He managed to radio back while keeping his head down. Crouched together, he and Jared didn't budge.

"I need to ask Cooper if *Hoss* stands for *horse*," Jared gasped. "I feel like I tried to tackle a wall, big guy.

"Check in," the radio barked.

Mike silently counted as each crew member replied to Shep. Thank God, no one on the team had been hit. What the hell had they run in to?

Mike peered around the bumper, keeping his head low. Sweat ran in his face, but he knew better than to remove his helmet. Flames rose from under the hood of one car.

"Cap. Better get those cops away from that car. It's going to blow if we don't get those flames out."

No sooner than he'd spoken, he heard Shep shouting to the policemen. No more shots had been fired—still the officers weren't taking any chances. And neither were he and Jared. Jared spun around and sat, leaning back against a wheel.

"I don't hear anything but I ain't going out there."

Minutes trickled by, seeming like an hour had passed.

Sirens sounded, coming their way in a hurry. Tires squealed while sliding to a stop as more police officers arrived. Mike raised his helmet and wiped at the sweat dripping into his eye. He took another glance at the burning car.

"Those flames aren't getting any smaller, Cap. Do you think the gunman is gone?" he spoke through his radio.

"Hold." A moment later the radio crackled. "The officers want to secure the scene before we move."

"They better fucking hurry or we'll be directly in line of the explosion."

"Uniforms entered the building where the shots came from. Hold your horses."

Waiting had never been Mike's strong suit.

"What about the drivers of those cars? Anyone still in them?" Jared asked.

"You mean you don't know?" Shep's voice came back.

"We never made it from the truck."

A curse and another moment of silence.

"All clear," Shep barked from the radio. "Get to it."

Mike and Jared leaped to action. Cooper and Laredo hosed the cars while Mike and Jared searched for survivors. The vehicles were empty.

An officer waved, signaling Mike over. Standing beside the cop, a man had his arm around a sobbing woman. As Mike drew closer, he saw a policeman sitting on the curb. He'd been shot. Mike removed his helmet and swiped again at the sweat on his forehead.

Crouching, he examined the wound, then ripped the pant leg to see the extent of damage. Blood trickled, but he could tell the bullet had shattered bone.

"Put pressure here until we can get him to the rescue squad," he told the officer standing behind him.

"Are you okay?"

Mike glanced at him in surprise. "I'm fine."

"Sorry to put you guys in harm's way. We had no idea a shooter was here until you guys showed up. We thought it was just a routine accident when we got the call."

"You guys have my respect," Mike told him. "You never know what you're walking into. At least we know there's a fire and we aren't usually surprised by anything else."

"Well, you got one this time."

Mike agreed just as another officer approached.

"Are you all right?"

Mike looked up and realized the policeman was speaking to him. The cop should be more concerned about his teammate who had been shot. Then Mike saw the stripes and figured this officer must be a Police Captain.

"Yes, sir. I'm okay. I'm taking this guy to the medic squad."

"What the hell happened here? We got a call that shots were fired at firefighters."

"That's what happened. When our trucks rolled in, the scene appeared like a normal traffic accident. We got out and all hell broke loose."

"The shooter got away. My men are still searching for him. No evidence of more than one."

"I better get this guy over to rescue. My captain is over there." Mike pointed to Shep.

After he secured the injured officer, Mike took stock of his surroundings and was pleased to find no other injuries. He wondered what the hell happened to the occupants of the vehicles. Steam hissed from the smashed cars, people huddled on sidewalks gawking at the incident. Even *TV3 News* had showed up. When a camera man headed in Mike's direction, a policeman blocked his path. The last thing they needed was someone to get hurt while the squad cleaned up their equipment.

"You hurt?"

"Naw, Cap. We stayed behind the truck while the shooting was going on."

"There a reason you're not wearing your helmet?" Shep's tone had Mike pausing in mid-stride.

"I took it off while I was checking out a wound," Mike answered.

"Whose blood on your face?"

Mmm. He must have smeared it on himself when he'd wiped his brow. "One of the officers got shot."

Shep acknowledged with a nod. "Damn, what a clusterfuck. I'd rather fight fires than bullets any day."

"You and me both."

"Let's wrap this up and head back to the station."

"You got it, Cap."

"You okay, Hoss?" Jared asked as he shoved the shifter into gear.

Why does everyone keep asking me that? "I'm good. You?"

"I'll feel better after I change my underwear. I nearly shit my damn pants."

Mike would laugh but he didn't feel much like laughing. He had been scared too.

"I tell you, I've never been shot at before."

"Sheds a whole new light on first response."

"I'd rather tackle a burning building any day."

Mike agreed, but at the moment his jaw ached and his temple throbbed like hell. He leaned his head back against the head rest.

Back at the firehouse, Mike was peeling off his gear when he heard a shrill whistle. He glanced over his shoulder and found Laredo holding Mike's helmet, clearly fascinated by it.

"Would you look at this?"

"Damn, Hoss. You lucky to be alive," Cooper said, staring at it.

"What are your dumbasses gabbing about?"

Laredo held out the helmet. "See for yourself."

Mike took the headgear and a knot caught in his throat.

A bullet hole.

"You sure you're okay? You've got blood on the side of your head."

Are you all right?

Whose blood on your face?

Mike touched his temple, remembering wiping what he'd thought was sweat.

"You're looking a mite pale there, Hoss." Cooper clasped him on the shoulder and proceeded to examine Mike's head. "You better thank the man upstairs. He had an angel watching out for you tonight."

Still in a haze of shock, Mike glared at the kid. "That is a bullet hole, right?"

"Sure looks like one to me. You've got a crease, right here." Cooper touched a spot above Mike's ear and drew back a spot of blood. "With your black hair, this blended right in."

"I thought it was sweat."

"Maybe you better get checked out, Mike," Laredo said, sticking his noggin right in Mike's face.

"Blood? Thought you said it was the officer's blood." Jared stepped next to Cooper.

"Looks like Mike's helmet caught a bullet," Laredo told Jared. "I better go tell the Cap."

"You sure you're all right?" Jared asked Mike.

"Hell, I was until I saw this." He handed Jared his helmet. Jared gave a whistle. Pain buzzed in Mike's temples to the drum of his speeding pulse. "Guess I am a lucky bastard."

"I'd say."

"So are you. You were right beside me." Like a building falling on his head, the impact of what could have happened crushed into his skull. Jared could have been shot, too. He'd knocked Mike out of the line of spraying bullets. Mike thought they'd missed. An inch or two over and the bullet could have entered Mike's brain.

Blood drained from his face to his toes. Nausea cramped his belly, nearly making him puke. "Thanks for shoving me out of the way."

"Are you kidding? I was trying to save my own ass."

Mike gave Jared a look that clearly stated he knew better.

Jared clapped Mike on the back. "All in a day's work, Hoss."

Heavy boots with a sharp stride clonked on the cement. "What's this I hear about a bullet hole?"

Jared handed Shep the offending object. His brows slanted down and the muscle in his cheek tightened, making Mike worry it might pop.

"Looks like the bullet went through here," Shep said, pointing to the shield.

"I remember hearing a hiss. As for the shield, I figured it got scraped."

"Laredo. Take him to the hospital."

"Now, wait a minute. I'm fine."

"He's got blood on his head."

At Cooper's words, Mike shot him a glare. "A scratch."

"Yours?" Shep asked, his piercing eyes intense. "*Not* the officer?"

Mike shrugged.

"Get your ass to the hospital and don't say another damn word." When Shep used that tone of voice, you moved your ass and kept your mouth shut. "The rest of you, get this gear stowed."

Mike gritted his teeth in annoyance. And dread.

He could have been shot in the head.

***

Damn tightlipped hospital nurses.

Wouldn't tell him a goddamned thing.

How was he supposed to get any information with half the fire department in the waiting room?

Seth crept back to his vehicle in the parking lot, his muscles tight with tension. Leaning against the back bumper of his SUV, he lit up a cigarette, tilted his head to the sky, then released smoke into the air.

He could hardly wait for the news to reach his enemy. "Your brother has been shot."

Feel that, motherfucker.

Now you'll know what it feels like to have your guts twisted when you hear that kind of news.

It would be dark soon. Although that wouldn't make much difference inside the hospital, it did mean shift change.

The staff always slacked off at night.

He'd get his chance.

CHAPTER 24

Traffic was horrible. Cassie had meant to leave school on time to go do her shopping, but the principal had called her to his office to discuss one of her students. The student wasn't the problem—the parents were. She'd never known people could behave so outrageously until she'd become a teacher. Some parents behaved like vipers. And the poor kids were the ones who suffered.

The office secretary had a saying, which she freely verbalized quite often. "You want to know why a child acts the way he does—look at the parents." Cassie had found that to be true on all occasions.

Her refrigerator was bare, so she had to go to the grocery store on her way home. Then she'd gotten stuck in five o'clock traffic and hadn't gotten home until six.

Her cell phone rang just as she placed her groceries on the kitchen counter.

"Cassie! Thank God, you're home. Where have you been?"

"The gro—"

"Never mind. Turn on the TV."

What had Tammy so riled up? Cassie picked up the remote and pointed it to the television. "What channel?"

"It's on every channel. The six o'clock news. A fireman has been shot."

A cement boulder slammed Cassie's chest. She couldn't get air. A voice screeched from somewhere on the floor. Realizing she'd dropped her phone, and the remote, she snatched them both.

"Tammy. Slow down," she gasped. "Stop. Let me catch my breath."

Cassie turned up the volume and listened.

"Local news involving one of our fire departments. An investigation is underway after a downtown shooting occurred this afternoon at the intersection of Liberty and Coalter Street. Police responded to a call of an accident. Station Eight fire department responded as well. Police on the scene called for backup with a report of gunshots fired at the same location. An armed gunman fired at a fire truck."

Cassie stood frozen, glaring at the newsman on the TV screen.

"An Augusta County Fire Department spokesman told TV3 News that firefighters arrived on the scene expecting to assist in a crash when shots were fired. One firefighter, Mike Armstrong, was struck by a bullet and was taken to the hospital. His condition is unknown."

A buzzing filled Cassie's head. The ringing in her ears grew louder in intensity.

Count. One, two, three ...

My God. Mike.

She grabbed her purse and was out the door in seconds. No sooner had she started the car than her Bluetooth activated her cell-phone. She pulled onto the highway and hit the off-hook button.

"Dammit, Cassie. Why wouldn't you answer your phone?"

"I'm too busy driving. Now that I'm on a highway—"

"Driving!" Tammy shouted loud enough for other passing cars to hear. "You should not be driving. I'll come get you."

"I'm half way there," she said as she drove up the ramp to I64.

"Well, for God's sake, don't take the interstate."

"Too late."

"Shit. All right. I'll meet you there."

Good. Cassie didn't like talking while driving and she had enough to distract her as it was.

Mike.

Struck by a bullet.

What had happened? She sped to the hospital like a demon.

She rolled into the ER parking lot on two wheels.

Her stomach rolled with nausea.

Keep calm.

She ran through the double doors and straight to the emergency counter.

"I'm here to see Mike Armstrong. The firefighter that was shot."

"You and every other reporter, honey. Get in line."

"What?" Horrified, Cassie stared at the woman on the other side of the desk.

"Are you family?"

"Uh, no. I—"

"Then don't waste my time."

Anger flushed her face. "Now, see here."

"Cassie?" She turned to the sound of a man's voice.

Jared.

Cold dread washed over her. Seeing Jared's worried expression suddenly made everything real. She fell into his hard chest and his arms clasped around her. She couldn't fall apart now. She had to be strong, whatever the news might be.

Oh God. Please let him live.

Tears filled her eyes and spilled down her cheeks. She couldn't stop them. The floodgates had burst. Her shoulders started to shake.

"There, now. Mike will be okay," Jared rumbled in a low voice. Sturdy hands rubbed her back, ringing out the pent-up tension. The last time she'd cried, Mike had held her. Mike had been the one to soothe her.

With her eyes closed, she stepped back and inhaled, filling her lungs. The potent smell of medicine filled the corridor. She dug in her pocket for a tissue. Finding none, she swiped her cheeks with the back of her hand.

"Do they know anything? Is it bad?"

"Mike's been in tougher spots than this." A man she didn't know stepped beside her. A slight smile lifted the corners of his mouth. "The bullet was just a scratch."

"Then he *was* shot?" Her eyes flew open with renewed terror.

"He's okay," Jared assured her.

"Tell me what happened."

"Mike had on his helmet. Like Cooper, here, said. It's just a scratch. We're waiting on the doctor now. I promise. He'll be right as rain."

"Hi. I'm Cooper. Why don't you come on over here with us?" the young man said, guiding her. "We're all waiting."

A rush of footsteps and a whirl of colors came hurtling toward her. "Cassie. Cassie. I'm here." Tammy rushed forward, arms open wide.

Cassie stumbled into her friend's jostling embrace.

"Shep called me," Tammy said as she released Cassie. "Are you okay?"

"I will be. As soon as I see Mike."

Tammy handed her a plastic pouch of tissues. "You haven't seen him?"

"Shep called you?" Cassie asked at the same time.

"A while ago. He wanted me to find you and be with you when you heard."

"Oh."

"Hi Tammy," Jared said. "We were about to sit down."

"He better be okay," Tammy growled at Jared as if it was his fault Mike had been shot. Jared just smiled and held out his arm in Cooper's direction, silently suggesting she join them.

Cassie followed Cooper to a corner where a dark, handsome man sat.

"Hello, *querida*. I'm Laredo." He might have a blinding grin that would turn any woman's head, but all Cassie could think about was Mike.

"I'm sorry. You know me?"

"Only your name. Everyone at the station knows your name."

She wasn't sure if she should be embarrassed, but she didn't care.

"Don't look so glum. Mike's as strong as an ox." Cooper directed her to sit down. "Shep's back there with him."

"He's probably giving the doctors a fit and that's why it's taking so long." Laredo grinned. She knew he was trying to cheer her up.

"How long have you been here?"

"A couple hours. Usually they take care of us pretty quick. But Mike was being impossible and Shep had to go calm him down."

She twisted her hands together to keep from shaking. If Mike was giving the doctors a hard time, then his injury might not be too severe. But until she saw Mike with her own eyes, she would not relax. At the moment, she wanted to scream. To run up and down the lighted hallway, venting, doing something. Anything but waiting, which drove her nuts.

A Styrofoam cup, steam rising from the top, entered her vision. She glanced up, seeing Jared's concerned expression. Coffee would make her heart pound faster. She couldn't risk it jumping out of her chest. *Shit.* She needed something to calm her.

Before she could say anything, Shep came strolling into the waiting area. Every member of the team stood and gathered around expectantly.

"He's fine. He's being an ass. The doctor wants to keep him overnight for observation, but he's determined to leave." Shep stared at Cassie. "Maybe you can make him listen to the doctor."

Knowing Mike was awake and impatient to leave the hospital sent a rush of relief through her veins. A strong arm came around her shoulders just as she wobbled. She leaned into Jared, glad for his strength and comfort. For without it, her legs might not have held her.

"Cassie?"

She lifted her gaze to Jared.

"Did you understand Shep? You can see him."

She squared her shoulders and took a deep breath.

Mess or not, Mike Armstrong, here I come. What you see is what you get.

***

No matter how hard he tried, Mike couldn't get up without nausea hitting his gut. Damn, he hated weakness. But he knew he was lucky to be alive. The ringing in his head was a damn nuisance. It had started on the way to the hospital and had gotten worse after the stitches.

"Mr. Armstrong. If you try to stand up again, I'm going to tie you down." The nurse was such a little thing.

"Don't worry. I don't plan to humiliate myself by falling on my face. How long before the dizziness will pass?"

"That's why we need to monitor you."

The curtain moved and the face he'd been longing for emerged.

Cassie.

Afraid he was dreaming, he stared, willing the angel not to disappear. Red-rimmed eyes, hair hanging in disarray, she was the most beautiful woman he'd ever seen. Even in her disheveled state, she was a stunner.

"He's all yours, honey," the nurse said. "He needs to stay off his feet."

"Mike." Cassie sniffed and her bottom lip trembled.

"I'm fine." He held his arms open.

She rushed to his side, and stopped within inches. "I was so scared."

"It's okay to touch me."

She threw herself at him, showering his face with kisses. He pulled her close and inhaled her sugary scent.

"They're keeping you in the hospital," she said on a hiccup.

"Not if I have anything to say about it."

"You don't." She pulled back and glared at him, anger evident in every muscle in her gorgeous body. "You're staying and that's that. Overnight. You can leave in the morning."

Bossy little thing. He'd leave now if he thought he could stand.

"I'm staying with you." Her fingers stroked his hair, which had to spike in every direction. Something else spiked too. All she had to do was touch him and he hungered for her.

I'm staying with you.

"In that case, come on up here, darlin'." He reached out, lifting her onto his lap and she squealed. Then calmed. Her glassy, green eyes took on a jade hue, expressing such love his mouth went dry.

"It's on the news. They said you were shot."

"A scratch."

"Where?" she asked struggling to get down. "Am I—"

"Hold still," he said at the same time. Then he tapped his temple. "Right back here."

Her eyes flew open in shock. "Oh Mike. You've got stitches." Then she swallowed as if a lump the size of Virginia had lodged in her throat. Tears pooled in her eyes.

"Hey, I'm okay."

"Your head. You've been shot in the head," she choked.

"Come here," he said enfolding her in his embrace. She snuggled right up. Right where she belonged. "Sweetheart, I'm okay. Don't think about anything else, but this. Me holding you. Your heartbeat next to mine." He held her, feeling the steady thump of her heart. He rubbed her back, aware of the change in her body. Her pulse slowing, her breath calming, tension gradually slipping away.

"The guys are here." She sniffed. "All of them. They let me come back first."

"They can go home. You're the only one I need."

She shifted, lifting her head to meet his face. Her smile lit up the room. She glowed like he'd just given her the world.

"They've been waiting. Your team is worried about you. I'll go get them."

When she moved to get down, he tightened his arms. She wasn't going anywhere.

"Let me down," she said with a delightful laugh. "I promise I'll come back. I'm not leaving you."

Her words pierced his soul. *I'm not leaving you.* Ever? Would she promise? Would she stay with him forever?

"*¡Oye.*" Laredo stepped around the curtain.

"Just what you'd expect," Jared said. "Secluded in here with a pretty woman." The guys filed into the small space, one by one.

"She doesn't look like a nurse," Cooper teased. "Some guys will do anything to hook up with a nurse. Even make up an excuse as stupid as *I got shot.*"

"Let go of your woman and tell us how you're doing."

"Can't you see for yourself, Jared? Looks to me like he's doing just fine," Laredo said and clapped Jared on the back.

"All right, you clowns. I am fine."

"I take it you've conceded to staying at the hospital overnight." Jared sent Cassie a cunning grin.

"Cap coaxed her into getting you to stay," Cooper said with a nod in Cassie's direction. "He also said you needed rest

Having Cassie in bed with him wasn't the best concept of him getting rest. All sorts of ideas popped into his head—and were immediately crushed. This was a hospital. That fact shot his lust-filled ideas all to hell. He hated hospitals. Although, he would definitely sleep better knowing she was with him.

The nurse came in chasing everyone out and moved him to a room on the fourth floor. Cassie had disappeared to the ladies' room and now he waited for her to return.

I'm not leaving you.

The statement was as alien to him as little green men.

How could he consider a life with her when he knew he'd cause her pain? He was a firefighter. His career choice would never change. How could he subject her to the terror and panic his job would trigger? Was it worth the heartache of knowing she might leave him?

Tonight, he'd found out his life could end in an instant. Every minute counted and he shouldn't waste a single one. His time with Cassie was precious. His gut told him to enjoy his moments with her. Life held no guarantees.

A soft rustle alerted him of Cassie's presence. He opened his eyes.

"Hi."

Long blonde hair, like silk in his fingers. Green sparkling eyes that smoldered warmth. A face he'd never tire of seeing.

"Hi, beautiful."

She pulled a chair close to the bed and hung her sweater and purse on the back. She seemed calmer, more in control.

Her tortured smile sliced his gut.

How could he squander one second on *might* and *if*? He'd gone too far, become too invested.

"I wish we were home," Mike said taking her hand. "I want to spend the night with you."

"I told you. I'm not going anywhere."

Those words again, scraping his already raw heart. His wall of self-preservation crumbled.

"In that case, why don't you crawl up here with me?"

She kicked off her shoes and climbed up beside him. With a contented sigh, she snuggled in the crook of his arm, resting her cheek on his chest.

Cassie already held his heart.

***

Son-of-a-bitch.

The man in the hospital was not his brother. Did the guy have a horseshoe up his ass?

Twice he'd schemed and twice he'd fumbled.

Maybe he needed some help.

Seth pulled his cell from his pocket and hit the keypad.

"Carl. It's me."

"Seth? Been a while, man."

"Yeah. Got anything goin' on?"

"Naw. I need a job. You got something?"

"Sure do. Taking a man out."

"No shit. You got a plan?"

"Got several plans, but the guy is a fireman. Got the eye of the public, you know what I mean?"

"That will bring some heavy heat."

"Yeah. I'll give you the details of why later. You in?"

"Sure, man. I owe ya."

"Good. When can we meet?"

Seth agreed to the place and time, then ended the call. He shoved his phone back in his pocket, turned around, and—

Froze.

One of the nurses stood glaring at him. Then she stuck her prissy-ass nose in the air and walked on down the hallway.

Fuck.

How much did she hear?

Seth thought back over his conversation, trying to remember the exact words he'd said. Was there anything to incriminate him?

Just what he needed. A nosy nurse. A loose mouth. Someone to finger him.

Could this night get any worse?

CHAPTER 25

Cassie went for coffee when the doctor came to examine Mike. He could use some alone-time and she needed to freshen up. She checked her appearance in the mirror and decided it was good enough. In the large waiting area downstairs, she grabbed a newspaper and scanned the headlines. Mike was ready to leave when she returned to his room. Mint soap wafted to her nostrils. Not the usual spicy musk, but still, he smelled nice. Stubble on his jaw, he looked good enough to eat.

Without warning, he grabbed her and planted his mouth on hers. Her hand slid to the back of his neck as she gave in to the desire his blistering kiss ignited. He wrapped his arms around her, pulling her flush against his arousal. Good Lord, she'd only been gone a short while. She wished they were anywhere but here.

When he finally released her, she sucked in air. "Hmmm. Did you miss me? I haven't been gone that long."

"Long enough. Come on. Let's get out of here." With his release papers in one hand and her fingers in the other, he pulled her down the corridor.

Mike remained quiet on the ride home. Driving him to her place reminded her of the last time she'd driven him to her apartment. The night he'd saved that woman from her car crash. But then, on that particular ride, he'd been asleep.

"Where are we going?" Mike asked.

"I thought I'd take you to my place."

"You don't need to be my nurse. I'm fine. Besides, I need a change of clothes."

"What makes you think you need them?" She glanced in his direction and heat flared in her belly from the fire she saw in his burning eyes. "Do you want me to wreck?"

"I didn't touch you." His voice was low enough to send tingling vibrations down her back.

"But you're looking at me like you want to devour me."

"Then keep your eyes on the road."

She tried. "Doesn't help."

"You're the one talking about not needing clothes," his deep voice rumbled.

The pressure in her belly rose to her chest. Damn, it was hot in here. He laughed and she glanced at him again.

"You think this is funny?"

"Damn right I do. You're horny and can't do a thing about it." He leaned his head back on the headrest, his knees bumping the dash. He completely filled the space in her car. "Don't worry, beautiful. I'll scratch that itch as soon as we get there.

Cassie almost stomped on the gas pedal. What kept her from it, she wasn't sure.

Another ten minutes and she pulled into a parking space at her apartment complex.

"We're here." Cassie had no idea why she felt the need to say that.

Mike snapped his seatbelt and was out of the car before she turned off the engine. Her nerves tingled on the back of her neck. When her car door opened, Mike stood there glaring down at her, his eyes blazing with intent. She gathered her keys and grabbed her purse. Anticipation jacked up her eagerness making her edgy. By the time they got to her door, anxiety had traveled to her fumbling fingers. Mike took her keys and opened the lock.

They barely made it inside when he grabbed her and pinned her to the door. He devoured her mouth with a passion bordering obsession and she clung to him with equal fervor. She arched toward him, wanting to crawl inside his skin, kissing him with all the urgency and anxiety she'd contained since hearing he'd been shot.

His mouth moved to her jaw, where he left a blazing trail of hot kisses down the side of her neck. Her eyes closed, she allowed her head to fall back on the wood. Mike was here. She could have lost him. She tightened her hold and sank into the warmth of his body. His lips grazing her skin, his hands holding her hips ...

"Is this what you want?" he whispered. "I want you, Cassie. All of you. You excite me beyond all reason." He nipped, then laved with his tongue.

"Yes. I want you so bad I'm shaking. Make love to me, Mike."

With a growl, he scooped her up into his powerful, strong arms. She pressed her cheek into the curve of his neck, giving him an open mouth kiss, then a little suction.

He jerked. "God, woman. I can't wait to get you naked. But this time, we're making it farther than the door."

She gave a little laugh, but never moved her lips from his delectable neck.

In her bedroom, he lowered her feet to the floor, then delved his tongue into her mouth and tore at her clothes. Breathing hard, he ripped each item away. When she stood completely naked, his eyes blazed, giving her no doubt to his hunger.

Unable to do anything else, she stared at him and watched as he removed every stitch of his own clothing down to the last piece. He had an impressive body, all bronze and solid muscle. She was fascinated by the size of his arousal. Standing at attention, pointing up in the air. Long, thick ... glorious.

She met his gaze. He wanted her with an intensity that took her breath.

His eyes darkened as his gaze roamed over her like a lover's caress, heating her blood from the tips of her breasts to her woman's core. She would always remember this moment. His proud stance, his adoration.

He stepped forward and with the gentlest of touches, scooped her up. He lowered her to the bed then crawled beside her. She trembled with eagerness. Slowly and ever so sensuously, he kissed her cheek, her jaw, the side of her mouth. Her eyes closed as she swam in breathtaking wonder. Enjoying this perfect man making love to her, and feeling like a woman being cherished more than she ever thought possible.

He laced his fingers with hers and raised her arms above her head. He did not rush, but blazed a fiery trail with his mouth and tongue. Sensations bombarded her, from the top of her head to the tip of her toes. He circled her breasts with his tongue and a series of open mouth kisses, carefully avoiding her nipples, prolonging her torture. She didn't think she could take anymore when he finally latched onto one pebble and suckled. The scalding heat of his mouth on her breast flooded her insides, scampered through her veins and settled in a sweltering pool in her womb. When he paid homage to her other breast, cool air tickled her skin where his lips and mouth had been.

His teeth scraped, sparking a rush of tingling hunger. She stretched and arched and silently begged for more. Her mind kept chanting *Mike, Mike, Mike*. His fingers slid down over her rib cage to her navel, caressing her belly. She held her breath. As his hand drifted lower, she bit her lip, but could no longer hold back a moan.

He whispered in her ear. "You're mine." At the same time, he pushed his finger inside, as if staking his claim. Her shriek turned into a gasp as his hungry mouth covered hers in a hot, fierce kiss.

He inserted another finger, stroking her core, melting her bones, bringing her to erotic heights. She opened her legs wider and writhed under his ministrations. He rubbed her harder and increased the rhythm until a tidal wave stormed her, roaring through her veins. Every nerve she had exploded, shattering her wits. Reeling her into mindless ecstasy.

Abruptly, Mike's erection replaced his fingers. Gripping her bottom, he thrust, filling her completely. Giving her exactly what she needed. He threw back his head, the veins protruding in his neck, and gave a hoarse shout.

"Don't move. Just let me feel myself inside you for a moment."

Overwhelming pleasure engulfed her. She couldn't help it. She squeezed.

"Holy hell, woman." He shifted his hips and plunged deeper. His groan of satisfaction pricked her heart.

He caught her mouth with crazed urgency. Then he took her with a passion bordering on madness. She wrapped her legs around his waist, meeting his every thrust.

Her body tightened and quivered and she could do nothing but hold on.

Hold him.

Forever.

His nostrils flared and he released a guttural groan. He annihilated her, crushed her heart with a love so fierce she wondered if he felt it. She clung to him, love filling her to bursting.

Joy pierced her soul. This strong, colossal, powerful, gentle, tender, sensual man had robbed her of her senses. Made her body a pool of Jello and had given her the most sensational experience of her life.

She loved him.

***

Cassie's heart beat steady against his. Reminding Mike he still lived and breathed. In the blink of an eye, one's life could be over. And his life would be over if he lost Cassie.

He still couldn't believe how close he'd come to death. If the bullet had been a fraction of an inch over ... He didn't need to think about what might have been.

Cassie all nestled up to him made life perfect. It didn't get any better than this.

He closed his eyes in exhaustion, which was to be expected since the meds were probably kicking in. He could use this to his advantage. Confess his feelings in his groggy state and deny everything tomorrow.

Shit.

If yesterday had taught him anything, he would not let another day, or night, go by without telling Cassie of his love. The idea of life without her brought reality crushing down on him.

I love you.

Say it. Just say it.

"Mike?"

"Hmmm?" His voice thick with his thoughts.

She snuggled deeper into his embrace.

"God, you feel good." His hand drifted to her rump and squeezed.

"I love you."

His hand stilled. Had he heard her correctly? He placed his fingers under her chin and lifted her gaze to his. "Did you just say you love me?"

Her eyes glassed over and she looked so scared he felt her pain. Had she meant it?

"Cassie. You have no idea how that makes me feel. I love you, too."

Tears pooled in her eyes and one slipped down her cheek. "Oh, Mike. You do?"

"Is that so hard to believe?" He caressed her cheek, his thumb following the track of her tear.

"I love you so much. I was afraid you didn't feel the same."

"I do," he whispered. "I do." He lowered his lips to hers.

The moment his tongue slipped into her mouth, the kiss turned hot. He licked and stroked and lost himself in it. She returned his passion, pouring every ounce of love she'd just confessed into their kiss.

After a long heart-shaking moment, they drew apart gasping. He pressed his forehead against hers. With one finger, he traced her lips. "I can't believe what you've done to me. What I'm feeling. Cassie, I love you. With everything in me, I love you."

"Promise you'll never let me go."

All his doubts and fears. All his worry over risking his heart and having a woman leave him. And here she was asking him not to leave her. He hugged her tighter.

"You're not going anywhere. Not without me."

"Good." She burrowed deeper.

"Cassie? I have to ask you something."

The tightening of her body cautioned him. But then, she half crawled onto his chest, propped her chin on her fingers and gave him a curious look. He had to address the elephant. The one that had plagued him most of his life.

"My career. I'm a firefighter."

Her brow rose in confusion. "And?"

His chest squeezed. He took a deep breath and trudged on. "That won't change. I'll always be a firefighter."

"Okaaay." She drew the word out like she wasn't comprehending.

Dammit. He may be cutting his own throat but he had to know if Cassie was in this for the long haul. "Can you handle it?"

She took a moment to consider before answering, twisting his gut every second she remained silent.

"Are you asking me if I expect you to stop?"

"It's a dangerous job. But I'm trained. I—"

She covered his mouth with her palm. "Mike. I love you. I wouldn't change one thing about you. Seeing you help others, knowing others depend on you, some for their lives ... it amazes me. I admire you. I have every confidence in you."

She studied him for a moment and the love he saw in her expression, grabbed him by the balls.

"I need to tell you something," she said.

Good God, here it comes.

"Two years ago, my cousin's house burned to the ground. Don't look like that. It's a story I want to share."

That made him feel somewhat better.

"My cousin and her husband never had a honeymoon and on their tenth anniversary, her husband wanted to surprise her with a trip. I offered to stay with their son, who was eight. The fire was traced back to the dryer, so no one started it, but I woke to a room filled with smoke. I panicked. I tried to find my little cousin and couldn't. I couldn't even see. Thank God, he'd already made it outside and a firefighter carried me to safety."

Thank God. His heart stopped at the thought of Cassie being in a fire.

"Since then, I cringe when I hear a siren. It's not with the fear I felt while I was in that burning house. But the fear that someone else is suffering the same thing. Someone's house is burning and I wonder if they will get out alive." She cradled his cheek. "Mike. I'm in awe of your profession. Without men like you, people would die. I would never want you to change who you are."

He searched her eyes for the truth.

"I can't say I won't worry," she continued. "I'd probably worry if you got a cold. But I don't expect you to give up something I know is important to you."

Maybe she meant it now. But would she change her mind? He captured her hand with his.

"My mom left my dad because she couldn't handle the pressure. I was just a kid. I haven't seen her since. She never came back."

"I'd never do that," she said. "I love you. I'm in this for always. I believe in forever. I'll love you forever."

His eyes blurred, his emotions too much to stomach.

"Woman. You know how to make a man feel like a man." He flipped her onto her back and proceeded to show her just how much she meant to him.

CHAPTER 26

A car door slammed. Mike stepped from the back of the rig to see who had pulled up at the bay door.

"Hey Chuck." This guy could be mistaken for Jared, since they shared sandy blond hair and had a penchant for Ray-Ban sunglasses.

"Mike." Chuck gave a nod.

"What brings you—" Then he suddenly remembered the Spurs game and Chuck had promised him some tickets. "Oh, you have those tickets?"

"Nah. They're at home. I'm here to see your Captain."

Uh oh. If he'd used the title Captain, instead of Shep, it must be important. Chuck had the look of bad news. Mike could be wrong, but he didn't think so.

"Cap's upstairs in his office."

Chuck gave another nod and stepped inside the bay. "You think I can see him?"

"Sure. I'll take you up."

Chuck removed his sunglasses and fell in behind Mike without saying another word. Guess he wasn't in the mood for chitchat.

Shep opened the door before Mike had a chance to knock. He stepped back in surprise.

"You got something for me, Mike?"

Mike pointed a thumb over his shoulder. "Chuck's here to see you."

Shep's expression did not change. "Come on in."

Mike stepped back, unsure whether he was invited to the party. Chuck solved the puzzle real quick.

"You can come in, Mike. This concerns the entire department."

"You here officially?" Shep asked.

"Investigator Hooley is on the Wimer property case. He shared some information with me."

While Shep walked behind his desk, Mike stepped inside and closed the door. Chuck took a seat and Mike figured he better take one too.

"There's a detective in our department working closely with the fire inspector and Hooley asked for me to help with his investigation."

Shep sat down and leaned back in his chair, waiting for Chuck to continue.

"I've never known Hooley to ask for help before and you can bet I was surprised when he asked for me."

"I'm not," Mike said. "You're one of the best guys on the police force. You're meticulous, but fair. You've been on the force for how long?"

"Nine years. Seems more like twenty."

Mike wanted to laugh, but Chuck's job wasn't funny. He put his life on the line every day not knowing what to expect on any call that came through dispatch. Sure, firefighters fought fires, but at least they knew what they faced heading out on a call.

Chuck could go on a domestic call and end up getting shot. It happened too frequently.

"Does that mean you're working on the case now? Did you get promoted?" Shep asked.

"Congratulations, man," Mike added.

"No. I did not. I'm staying in uniform and working—I guess you could say—undercover."

"Undercover? Holy shit!"

"I'm working the street, watching traffic, looking for anything unusual. Keeping an eye out for strangers. Hooley showed me the film."

"You saw the film?" Mike shot a glance to Shep then turned in his seat toward Chuck.

"He wanted another assessment from a cop's view. We size people up and look for details a normal citizen might overlook."

"That sounds reasonable," Shep said with a nod. "So, tell me, Chuck. You have any idea who that guy is?"

Mike held his breath waiting for Chuck to answer. If anyone could figure out who the prick was, it would be Chuck.

"I couldn't get a good look. Most of his face was hidden by the protective mask. He knew where the camera was and kept his head turned."

"That fucker was right there in plain sight of everyone." Angry and frustrated, Mike stood to pace the room. Son-of-a-bitch. The guy was a cocky bastard.

"That tells us something."

Mike spun around on his heel.

"Tells you what?" Shep asked in a calm voice. At least the Captain was keeping his shit together.

"We think this guy is a pro."

The bottom fell out of Mike's stomach. "You think he's a firefighter?"

"Not necessarily. He's cool. Composed. Unruffled." Chuck turned his head and met Mike's gaze. "Like you said, he was right in the middle of the action. Walking around like he belonged there. Wearing Station Nine's gear."

"Bold mother—"

Chuck kept talking as if Mike hadn't spoken. "The guy has balls. At some point, he walked right into Station Nine and stole their gear. A smooth operator. And if he can do that, there's no limit to what this guy might do."

"So that you will know, I've talked to my men and instructed them to be alert. Mike has the idea, if this character got away with sneaking around one fire station, what's to keep him from hitting the others?"

"That man has a brass set. But if he comes in Station Eight, he's going to get his ass kicked." Mike flexed his arms.

"Like I said," Chuck stated, "this guy could be capable of anything. I think you need to be prepared for that."

For what? What the hell did Chuck mean?

He faced Mike. "Did you see anything, anything at all? The way he walked. Did he talk with anyone?"

"No. Nothing." Wilson had been running the show and all he remembered was the number nine on the asshole's helmet. Nothing looked out of place.

"This guy doesn't belong to Station Nine and he certainly doesn't hail from here. No one remembers anything suspicious. He doesn't have to be a firefighter, or an EMT. But he could be in the prison system."

"Prison, huh?"

"Like I said. He could be a professional. A criminal."

"Why are you here, Chuck?" Shep's graveled tone made the hair on Mike's arms stand.

"For whatever reason, this guy has targeted the fire department. He's already proved he's dangerous. There were five teams on sight that day. He could be pursuing any of them."

"You think we have a target on our backs?"

"It's possible. That's why Hooley brought me in. I cover every scenario, every possibility. The Wimer house exploded. Firefighters were hurt. It was no coincidence. Hooley found evidence of gas, propane, and explosives. Those items do serious damage. This guy isn't playing games. He's out for blood."

"You said is."

"The Wimer property is isolated. Our perp did his research and more than likely made several visits to the site. From what I understand, the timing was precise. He had to enter the property and set things in motion for the explosion to go off at the exact moment. That takes detailed planning. And accuracy."

Mike's eyes locked onto Shep's. Without any outward sign, dread came through loud and clear in his troubled gaze. After a lengthy silent communication, Shep turned back to Chuck.

"What aren't you telling us?"

Chuck scraped a hand over his jaw. "I don't like this, but I feel you need to be prepared. Especially after the incident downtown. The bullet to Mike's helmet may not have been an accident. I hope to God I'm wrong, but this perp could be a killer. One of you could be his next victim."

***

"Hello."

"Oh my God. Cassie, I had to call. I'm so excited."

"I can't tell." Cassie rolled over, trying to read the numbers on the clock. Seven AM. On a Saturday? What the heck had Tammy so wired she had to call and get her out of bed this early on the weekend?

"Wake up!" Tammy shouted. Or maybe it seemed that she did since Cassie was still half asleep. "I couldn't wait."

"All right, I'm awake," she grumbled and punched her pillow, then dragged herself up to lean against the Cannonball headboard.

"You'll never guess."

"Tammy, I'm in no mood to play guessing games at seven in the morning," she huffed.

"Don't get your panties in a bind. Uh-oh. Is Mike there? Oh, Good Lord. I'm sorry. I should have known."

"Tammy. Tammy!" When Tammy kept talking, Cassie shouted again to get her attention. "Mike isn't here. He's at the station."

"Then what's your problem?"

My problem? Should she count to ten before she bit Tammy's head off?

"My problem is being woken up from a sound sleep on a weekend when I can sleep late."

"Get over it."

"My, my. What's got you so freakin' cheery?"

"I saw Shep yesterday."

So that's it.

"And I'm just now hearing about it?"

"Complain, complain. We went to see his brother, the lawyer."

She had Cassie's full attention, now.

"Right. How did it go?"

"Great, Cassie. Great. Shep is *such* a gentleman. And I thought chivalry was dead. I think he is out of his time. He must be from the sixteenth century. I've never seen a man with such manners. And Eddie is so nice."

"Eddie?"

"Yes. Shep's brother's name is Eddie. He was so easy to talk to. He looks a lot like Shep. He's got that sexy silver at his temples. And he told me to call him Eddie."

It sounded like Tammy had a crush on Eddie.

"I'm glad you like him. Can he help?"

"Oh, Cassie. We talked for hours. Well, it seemed like hours anyway. Shep said his brother would listen and he did. Gosh, they're both so nice."

"Okay, we've got the *nice* covered. Will he knock Steve on his ass?"

"I think so. Shep says he can. Not in the same words you used, but he did say Eddie was a good lawyer and he would not be intimidated by anyone. Eddie said he wouldn't let Steve take my boys away from me. I'm so relieved."

"Tammy, that's wonderful."

"I had to call. I had to let you know my good news. Now do you forgive me?"

"Absolutely. I'm happy for you. I hope Shep's brother grinds Steve a new A-hole."

"I know you're a grizzly before your coffee, so I'll let you go. Bye." The line went dead.

In like a tornado and out like a light switch. Her friend was a hoot. Cassie couldn't remember the last time Tammy sounded so happy.

Why had she waited until this morning to give the good news? Why hadn't she called last night? She hadn't even given Cassie a chance to tell her about Mike.

She'd taken a chance.

She'd told him she loved him.

She'd finally found someone who loved her, someone she could trust. Someone who made her believe in herself, restore her confidence as a woman.

Placing her feet on the floor, Cassie stretched her arms over her head, cracking her back, feeling like a new woman.

***

"Hey, babe." Mike grabbed Cassie and poured his heart out in a kiss he'd been aching for all day. "God, you feel good."

The best thing in his life filled his arms. How could he be so damn lucky to have the most amazing woman in the world? Cassie kissed him like a starving wolf seizing a piece of meat. Good God, the woman could drive him insane.

He inhaled her sweet fragrance. Not too sweet. More like fresh rain water and a hint of something alluring that was hers alone. His chest swelled with pride. She belonged to him. Every enchanting inch of her. He shoved one hand through her hair and cradled the back of her neck, holding her while he pillaged her mouth. He tangled his tongue with hers and reveled in her moan of delight. Each sensual caress was meant to entice her further, make her ache in the very place she rubbed against him.

His cock thickened. He kissed her possessively, greedily, like he'd never kissed her before. They broke apart, gasping.

"Do you have any idea how you make me feel?" he said in a heaving sigh. "You kiss me and squeeze me like I'm the only man on earth. Like you can't get enough of me. God, Cassie. I love it when you do that. I love you."

He hadn't meant to pounce on her so quickly. But her touch, her taste, and he suddenly became a man driven. She returned his advances with equal measure and he couldn't help himself.

He tongued the curve of her ear, while he pulled her shirt down, exposing her glorious breasts. She squirmed against him and he knew what she needed. He thumbed her nipple, then seized it in his mouth, sucking greedily. He loved the way she moaned and tugged his hair, urging him on. He explored further, his hand drifting over her ribs and belly, stroking, caressing, seeking.

He found her wet and ready for him.

"God, Cassie. You're so wet. For me. Only for me," he growled.

"Yes, Mike. Only for you," she gasped.

His fingers teased her honey spot and suddenly her hand was on him, massaging his erection through his jeans. He was near to bursting. Things had never been so hot, so fast, so demanding between them. He growled and pressed into her hand.

Her fingers tugged at the waistband. He pulled back, flipped the snap and jerked the zipper allowing his bulge to breathe. When she dove into his briefs and pulled, he thought he'd go mad from sheer pleasure.

He tore at her clothes. She tore at his. When they were completely naked, he hoisted her up against the wall. There was no thought, no time to go anywhere else. He needed her now. She wrapped her legs around his waist, letting him know it was okay with her. Holding her just so, he slid between her folds and drove deep inside her.

Dazed with sensation, he froze in awe at the emotions rolling through him. Each intimate moment was like their first. Every precious touch was a phenomenon he ached to experience again and again.

"Cassie. God, Cassie. Mine. Only mine."

He tried going slow, but it was useless. His need fierce, he pounded her against the wall. She clung to him as if the world would end tomorrow. His mind reeled, sensations flooded his nerve endings. He claimed her, mated his soul with hers, and then ... a low growl formed in his chest as Cassie shattered, her cry ringing in his ears, his pounding release hammering through his body.

Cassie's short breaths keened in his ear. Indescribable emotions flooded him. A sense of home and belonging invaded his soul. This woman was his entire world. He'd never let her go.

Her heart battered his chest. When her head fell to his shoulder, he smiled, feeling all the love in his heart, and just held her.

Moments passed and he realized he had to move.

"One of these days we might make it to the bedroom first," he murmured.

"I'm not complaining."

No, she never objected. She accepted him at any moment, every time he touched her. Such trust ... what a privilege she'd given him. Fortune had surely blessed him with an angel.

"Hold on."

"I don't know if I can."

He shifted. She drooped like a wet noodle, causing a snigger to escape his lips. He scooped her into his arms and carried her down the hall to her bedroom, then gently laid her upon the comforter. He feasted his eyes on her golden hair in disarray on the pillow, the languorous expression in her eyes, the satisfied smile on her face. He quickly shed his clothes and stretched out beside her and gathered her next to him, throwing his thigh over hers.

Peace. Contentment. Happiness. All the things he'd feared he would never have.

He thought she'd fallen asleep. She surprised him when she spoke.

"Mike?"

"Hmmm?" He rubbed his chin over the top of her head.

"I love you."

He smiled, his heart swelling. "I know. And I love you."

CHAPTER 27

Kathy's restaurant was a favorite for breakfast. With a cozy atmosphere and fantastic food, the place was usually packed. Today was no different. Cassie stared out the window over the rim of her coffee mug. A silver streak zoomed into the parking lot making her catch her breath.

She could do this.

Cassie and Mike had talked for hours. She told him about her mom, her dad, her sister, who had gotten her all worked up into a stew. Mike talked her through her grief regarding her dad and said he wanted to meet her mom. He'd even convinced her to make amends with her sister. God, how she loved that man.

Even though her sister agreed to meet, Cassie's stomach churned with nausea. They'd talked, apologized, then Jennifer had suggested breakfast. So, it shouldn't be but so bad. Still, Cassie couldn't calm her nerves.

Jennifer entered the restaurant, spotted Cassie and headed straight for their table.

"I'm starved," she said plopping down into the booth. "I had to take Ranger out for a walk, then I took a shower and my stomach growled all the way here."

Just like Jennifer to take charge and act like nothing was out of sorts. Cassie welcomed it. This was better than being at each other's throats.

"That's because you were looking forward to blueberry pancakes."

"Is there any other kind?" Jennifer asked with a roll of her eyes.

The waitress came to their table carrying a pot of fresh coffee. She poured a cup for Jennifer then refilled Cassie's and took their orders.

"I'm glad you called yesterday. I knew you wouldn't stay mad long."

Here we go.

"We both said some pretty heavy things," Jennifer continued. "I'm sorry, too."

The air escaped Cassie's lungs and she stared at her sister in amazement.

"Oh, don't look at me like that," Jennifer said with a wave of her hand. "I can shoot my mouth off with the best of them. A lot of what I spew is just me venting. I've always done that."

"You do it with style."

"What's that supposed to mean?"

"Your words, most of the time, are precise. Like you're dictating. You don't sound like me when I vent."

"You did a fabulous job of it at the hospital."

"I was pissed."

"No shit."

The waitress brought coffee for Jennifer and then took their order. Jennifer lifted her mug and blew across the surface before putting it to her lips. She set the cup down and met Cassie's eyes. "We're sisters. That will never change. What you said really hit me."

At the time, Cassie had meant every word. But Jennifer was right. She couldn't stay mad. Especially if her sister was being sensible. Which was not like her at all.

"You looked like you could kill me."

"I was pretty mad."

"I didn't mean half of what I said."

Cassie knew better than to point out Jennifer had said *half*. Some of the things they'd shouted were true.

"I know."

"Especially the part about my ex. That was just stupid."

"I'm glad to hear you didn't believe that. I had no interest in—"

"You don't need to say it. All men stare at you. Your chest, anyway."

Heat crawled up Cassie's neck, but she managed to keep her mouth shut on that subject.

"Look," Jennifer said with a shrug, "what's done is done. "Besides. That's history. He's gone, I remarried, end of story."

The waitress appeared with their food. "Scrambled eggs for you," she said, placing a plate before Cassie, "and blueberries for you." The waitress set a plate of pancakes piled with blueberries and whipped cream in front of Jennifer, then pasted a big grin on her face. "You make me want to get an order for myself."

"Blueberry pancakes and whipped cream are my favorite."

"They're my favorite, too. Can I get you ladies anything else?"

"Thank you. I'm good," Jennifer said, reaching for the syrup.

"Thank you." Cassie picked up a piece of bacon and took a bite.

"I could hardly wait to get here and get my pancakes."

"Kathy's serves the best."

"Mmm, she has great breakfast food." Jennifer tried to chew and talk at the same time. Cassie laughed.

Jennifer froze. "That's better than the last time I saw you."

"What?"

"Nothing. I want to talk about Mom."

"We both care for her."

"She's doing well and getting around really good, now."

"Yeah, she's completely recovered from the surgery and happy to be back in her own house. Thank you for taking care of her during her recovery."

"No thanks necessary. I know you would have brought her to your home if you didn't work."

A few minutes of silence ensued while they both devoured their food. Cassie lifted her mug just as Jennifer spoke.

"You think it's true that a person can wither away pining for their spouse or is it just crap?"

Where did that come from?

"I guess ... if you really love your husband or your wife ... I've known some who couldn't live without their mate."

"You mean soul mate?"

Cassie shrugged. "I guess. If you really love—"

"So, you believe in that?"

This wasn't like Jennifer. Where was this coming from? Cassie wanted to tell her sister about Mike, but Jennifer had something on her mind.

"Yes. I do."

"Hmm," Jennifer mumbled and took a big bite of pancakes.

"Do you believe in that kind of love?" her sister asked hesitantly.

Jennifer was quiet for a long while. Cassie chewed her food and waited.

"I thought about what you said. About my current husband and how he would leave me too."

Uh oh. She'd forgotten that. She prepared herself for the sermon she was about to receive.

"I do care for Eric." Jennifer lowered her eyes to her plate. "I didn't realize how much until you said what you did."

"Jennifer, I'm—"

"It got me to thinking. I don't want to lose him."

Oh shit.

"Is your marriage in trouble?"

Her gaze shot to meet Cassie's. "I never thought so. But it's not what it could be."

A real conversation, with her sister. Miracles did happen.

"You can work on that."

"How?"

I can't believe she's asking me.

The last twenty-nine years of oppressiveness floated from her shoulders. Jennifer was her sister and this could be the beginning of what Cassie wanted—a new relationship.

"Explore your feelings. Pay more attention to your husband."

"Are you kidding? He's never home."

"When he comes home, what do you do? Do you greet him with warmth? Tell him you're glad to see him? Fix him a special meal?"

"When he gets home at bedtime?"

"You don't think he's having an affair, do you?"

"No. But I wouldn't be surprised if he stayed at work to avoid me." Her shoulders slumped and she placed her fork beside her plate. "He says he has to keep me satisfied. And he's not talking about the first thing you'd think. He means money."

By her sister's actions, it was easy enough to believe all Jennifer cared about was money. Diamonds graced each of her fingers, she drove a Porsche and bragged about her possessions to anyone who would listen.

"You can fix that," she told her sister. "Take notice of what he wants. What he might like. When was the last time you did something for him?"

"I picked up his dry-cleaning for him yesterday."

"Not that, Jennifer. For him personally. It could be anything from bringing him coffee or—I know. Have a drink ready for him when he walks in the door. If he gets home late, he has to be exhausted. You could take his briefcase or his coat. Give him a drink, lead him to the couch and rub his shoulders."

"He'd think he was in the wrong house. Or with another woman."

"Point made," Cassie said with intensity. "Show him more attention. Give him a reason to come home."

"I can't change overnight."

"But you can try. You've already noticed your marriage can be better. You seem willing to do something about it. Why not spruce it up a bit?"

"You want me to get a see-through negligee and lie on the couch naked?"

"If you want." Cassie shook her head, wondering if her suggestions were pointless. "A simple gesture might go a long way."

"Where do you get all of your great wisdom?" Jennifer said sarcastically.

Cassie immediately thought of Mike. Her pulse quickened and her face heated.

"I can only tell you how I feel."

"Oh my God. You have a man in your life?"

"Don't act so surprised," Cassie grumbled, then picked up her fork and cut her scrambled eggs, taking her frustration out on them.

Jennifer slammed her palms on the table. "You do. The only reason I'm surprised is because you don't date. Hardly ever."

"Well, I do have someone and it's serious."

"Really?"

Cassie leveled a glare on her sister. "Really."

"Tell me about him. How did you meet? Wait. Is he that fireman? Tammy told me about him when she came to pick up the boys."

"He's a firefighter. And he's everything to me."

Her sister's fork stopped mid-air and never reached her mouth. "You can't be serious. You just met the guy."

"I'm very serious, and if we"—Cassie moved her fork between the two of them—"weren't so busy fighting, you'd know about him."

Jennifer stabbed a blueberry. "Tell me about him, then."

Cassie's chest squeezed a little. Partly just because she loved Mike and partly because her sister was willing to listen.

Mike knew all her secrets and loved her anyway.

"He's the most wonderful man I've ever met and he loves me." Saying the words made her believe them even more. Mike did love her.

"For now, anyway."

Irritation made Cassie's muscles tense. "Must you always be so discouraging?"

"Do you forget there is a word called divorce? Forever doesn't mean *for- ever*," Jennifer said with a shrug.

"It can. With the right man."

"Who's to say there is such a thing as the right man?"

"Can you say you had the same feeling for Ronnie that you claim to have for Eric now? You didn't love your first husband."

With a shrug, Jennifer stuffed more pancake into her mouth.

"You've mentioned you'd like to fix things with Eric. At the very least, make them better so you don't lose him."

A flash of discomfort flickered in Jennifer's eyes.

"Think about what I said." Cassie lifted her mug. "You can have forever with Eric if that's what you want. I want forever. One of these days, I'll be married."

Jennifer choked on her food. "What?" she gasped.

"You think you were the only one with marriage plans?" Cassie asked.

"You're getting married?" Jennifer shouted.

"Lower your voice." Cassie could feel the stares from the other patrons. "I will one day."

"How soon?"

"Why? What's wrong with my wanting to get married?"

"Have you told Mom?"

"I haven't told anyone. I haven't been asked."

"But you're thinking about it."

"Look," Cassie said, placing her mug on the table and leaning forward. "I've fallen in love. I'm crazy about Mike."

"Mike, is it?" Jennifer leaned back with her cup in her hand.

"Yes, Mike Armstrong. I can't imagine my life without him."

"Wow. That's pretty heavy."

"I don't know when or how soon or even if we're getting married. But he feels the same way I do."

"In that case, I'd say it won't be long."

The way Cassie felt about Mike, she'd marry him today. Since they were on the subject, she might as well get a certain issue out of the way.

"Jennifer, I'd like you to be in my wedding, but you know Tammy will be my Maid of Honor."

"Are those darling boys going to be in it?"

The storm Cassie had expected did not come. Jennifer had spoken in a reasonable tone and actually seemed to accept the idea. Cassie needed to be sure.

"You're okay with Tammy being my Maid of Honor?" she asked cautiously.

"*Matron* of honor," Jennifer corrected. "It figures. She's been your best friend forever."

Cassie released a sigh of relief.

It was nice to have a conversation with her sister without dreading a scene.

CHAPTER 28

The morning sun rose, shining its light on a brand-new day. Cassie's spirits soared higher than they had in a long time. She had to be the luckiest woman alive.

She padded to the kitchen, made another pot of coffee and called Tammy. When Cassie mentioned her breakfast with Jennifer yesterday and their big discussion, her friend rushed right over.

"So, Mike is the reason you called Jennifer?"

Cassie placed the coffee pot back on the burner. "Mike and I talked about Jennifer and how much control I've allowed her to have over my life. He thought I would feel better if I dealt with her. He told me I should call her and square things."

Tammy's eyes flew wide with surprise. "He doesn't know her."

"I told him. And he also told me if that didn't work to tell her to go to hell."

Tammy hooted. "I like your man."

"So, do I." She stared at the third finger on her left hand, imagining a ring there. "How did I get so lucky?"

"I still can't believe you had a normal conversation with Jennifer. Is she setting you up for a fall?"

"She seemed genuine." Cassie cut a slice of pound cake to go with their coffee. "Thanks for bringing over the cake."

"You're welcome. Is she bipolar?"

Cassie chuckled. "She doesn't have mood swings. She speaks in the same monotone, snooty voice all the time."

"How can you be monotone and snooty?"

"Well, just uppity, then. Although, she did act different at Kathy's."

"Different how?"

"I don't know," Cassie said handing Tammy a fork. "Almost human."

"Mmm, this is good, if I must say so myself." Tammy should pat herself on the back. Her cakes were awesome.

"It's a good thing I don't bake. I've put on ten pounds since I met you."

"So, are we planning a wedding?" Tammy asked before shoving a bite of cake into her mouth.

"Aren't you putting the cart before the horse?"

"Just a matter of time," Tammy replied. "He will ask. I just hope you have the sense to say yes."

"What do you mean by that?"

"Come on, girlfriend. Your insecurities. Thank God he's just as stubborn as you."

Cassie waved her comment away and stabbed another fork of cake. "I'm too happy to care. I love him and he loves me and yes, I plan on getting married."

"To one hot firefighter. I'm happy for you."

"You'll be my maid of honor."

"I better be." Tammy stared at her for a moment, then surprised Cassie. "You deserve Mike."

"I wish. He's everything to me. I didn't know it was possible to love someone so much." Only weeks ago, she'd been alone. Content with her teaching during the day and quiet evenings at home. Now she knew she couldn't face another day without Mike. He made her days brighter. He made her feel alive.

The doorbell rang.

"That's Mike. We're going to see my mom. It's time she met him." Cassie rose to answer the door, but Tammy grabbed her hand.

"Cassie?"

"Yeah."

"I'm really happy for you." Tammy stepped forward and nearly crushed Cassie with a fierce hug.

The doorbell rang again. Cassie broke free and ran to the door. Mike stood there with his cropped black hair and designer shades, looking like sin in his comfy jeans. She struggled to breathe.

"Hello, beautiful." As had become his habit, Mike grabbed her and sealed her lips with a sensual kiss. She melted into him. He smelled so damn good, she snuggled, wanting to crawl inside his skin.

"Don't let me interrupt."

Mike was in no hurry to pull back. He glanced at Tammy. "Hi."

"Hi yourself." Tammy smirked, then picked up her purse. "I'm outta here. You kids have fun."

Cassie tugged Mike inside. Before she could close the door, he spoke.

"If you want me to meet your mom, we better leave *right now*."

***

Cassie's mom had recovered from her surgery and returned home two weeks ago. She'd gone off the pain medication and the soreness in her back grew more tolerable each day. She still needed to take it easy for a while.

A man friend from her church visited regularly and on his first visit he'd brought roses. Cassie suspected a romance brewing there. Even so, her mom did not spend her days alone, which eased Cassie's mind considerably.

Mike held Cassie's hand as they stood on the front porch of her mom's house. The front door opened. "Hi sweetie. Come in, come in." Mom's eyes lit up when she saw Mike. "And is this your man?"

Mike's chuckle eased Cassie's tension and let her know he liked her mother's comment.

"Yes, Mom. This is Mike." Her chest swelled with pride as he took her mother's hand.

"How wonderful to meet you."

"It's my pleasure to meet you, Mrs. Peters." Mike filled the doorway with a big grin on his handsome face.

"Call me Dorothy, please."

Cassie leaned in and placed a kiss on her mother's cheek while Mike closed the door, then he followed them into the living room.

Mom sat in her usual spot, a rose winged-back chair. She smoothed her hands down the sides of her skirt. "A fireman. Oh my. What an impressive profession."

"It's just a job," Mike answered as he settled on the sofa beside Cassie.

"Oh, surely not. It's an honorable career. Putting out fires. Saving lives."

"I go where I'm needed. I do what I have to do." He said it casually, almost embarrassed.

The big strong firefighter who saved lives didn't like being called a hero. But, he was a hero. Her hero.

"I would say it takes a special individual to be a fireman."

"It's *firefighter*, mom. They say firefighter now."

"Oh? It's still a very dangerous occupation."

"Mrs. Peters, I assure you ..."

She waved her hand in a quick motion, brushing his comment away. "I'm sure you are quite capable. And I can see you love my daughter."

Mike glanced at Cassie with a raised brow. Maybe she should have warned him her mother was not only good at reading people, but also a bit outspoken.

"Why don't I get us some tea? And then you can tell me all about yourself, other than your job."

"Yes, ma'am."

Cassie squeezed his hand.

"Come with me, dear." Her mom rose and turned toward the kitchen. Cassie couldn't wait to see what her mom thought of Mike.

"I'll be right back." She whispered and he gave a nod of understanding.

As soon as they were in the kitchen, her mother started talking. "He's quite handsome. And quite large."

"Thanks, Mom."

"For complimenting your man?"

Your man. That's the second time her mom had referred to him that way. First Tammy and now Mom. Cassie loved the idea. Mike belonging to her.

All she had to do was believe in herself. And in Mike.

"Like the sound of that, do you?"

Cassie glanced to her mom in question.

"Your face lit up like the bright bulbs on a Christmas tree. And you've been glowing since you walked through the front door. And no man looks at a woman like that young man in there looks at you, unless he's been intimate with her."

Cassie wanted to crawl under the table. She never could hide anything from her mom.

"I'm not a fuddy dutty. I was young once too. Although in my day, marriage came first." Her mom took three glasses from the cabinet and placed them on the counter, her rebuke as calm as if they were discussing the weather. "Get the ice, will you dear?"

Cassie opened the freezer door, collected the ice and then dropped a few cubes into each glass. She replaced the container and when she turned around, saw her mom braced against the counter with her head down.

"Mom?"

When she looked up, tears glazed her eyes. "I wish your dad could be here."

"Oh, Mom. I'm so sorry."

"Don't be silly." She sniffed and focused on pouring the tea. "I just wish your father could meet your young man. He so loved his baby girl."

"Me, too," Cassie said.

Mom's voice broke. Then she took a deep breath as if she needed it to hold herself together. "He couldn't give up those darn cigarettes."

Cassie wrapped her arms around her mother.

"I have something to tell you that will make you feel better."

Mom took a tissue from her pocket and dabbed her eyes. "More good news?"

"Jennifer and I met at Kathy's yesterday and had a long talk over pancakes."

"You did?"

"We talked about a lot of things, Mom. Really talked."

"Whatever in the world … how … I need to sit down."

Cassie pulled out a chair for her mom and took the one beside it. Cassie took her hands, giving her comfort.

"I called Jennifer and we went to breakfast. She opened up to me. We talked like we've never talked. It was good, Mom."

Her mother squeezed back. "Cassie. You've made me so happy. All I've ever wanted was for you and your sister to get along."

"I know. She's older and she's always bossed me around. She married money and brags about it." Seeing her mother's expression, Cassie wished she'd not mentioned that part.

"That's your sister, dear."

Yeah, that had been her sister all Cassie's life. She would have liked to kick her ass, but she'd never tell her mother that.

"I love you, Mom. I'll always be here for you."

"I know, dear. Enough of that, now." Her mom swiped at her cheeks and shoved out of her chair. "There's a handsome young man in there waiting for his tea. Splash some water on your face and let's go see if I think he's good enough for my daughter."

Cassie smiled and her heart lifted at the grin she received from her mother. When she entered the living room, Mike studied her face. One thing she couldn't hide, her red, puffy eyes.

"I was starting to get a little worried about you two," he said in a low voice.

"We talked about Jennifer and Dad."

Concern etched his brow. "Are you okay?"

"Better than okay." She smiled in assurance.

Seeming to believe her, he nodded. She handed him his iced tea.

"Thanks."

"You're welcome." As always, his low hum sent shivers down her spine. She leaned in for a kiss. Her heart did that funny little leap, the one it did every time Mike touched her. She clung to this wonderful man she loved with all her heart. Just as he began to kiss her back, her mother came into the room.

"Now then." Excitement flashed in her eyes. "Tell me, Mike, how you won my daughter's heart."

EPILOGUE

Revenge was a warm companion.

He didn't need friends, although some of his acquaintances provided some handy benefits. Like the new ID with a false name.

No one in this town knew him. His target would find out soon enough, but Seth preferred to stay under the radar.

He had a plan.

Payback had a price.

The End of Book 1: Mike.
Be sure to read on for a sneak peek of Book 2: Shep!

Passions soar and desires burn hot, yet each is afraid to surrender to love. 5 Men - 5 full length books. Together, the hero and heroine overcome their inner conflict to achieve love completely unaware there is a more dangerous peril—one man's revenge.

Shep, the captain of Fire & Rescue Station #8, devotes his time and energy to fighting fires and rescuing victims. At the age of thirty-six, he's spent the last fifteen years without a woman turning

his world upside down. Tammy needs his help. And damned if he doesn't like the idea of being tormented by the sexy redhead.

Tammy's ex threatens to take her boys away. She needs a lawyer – fast. Through her best friend, she finds an attorney. But his brother is the one she wants. A hunk and a firefighter who creates a burning flame in her.

Keep Reading for an Excerpt from
Shep: The Firefighters of Station #8 – Book 2

SHEP

CHAPTER 1

The Pitt Stop sign glowed above the brightly-lit building centered in the middle of a huge parking lot. Shep shoved the gearshift into park and shut off the headlights. After the day he'd had, a cold beer sounded mighty fine. Too many unanswered questions. An unexplained explosion weighed heavy on his conscious. The fire investigator had not found any leads and his squad, the men he was responsible for, had gone back to the training site on their own. If his profession didn't kill him, worry would. Yep, he needed just one hour free of his current problems.

"Smell that?" Mike, one of the firefighters in his squad, puffed his big chest out as he inhaled. The smell of charcoaled beef drifted through the door at the front entrance. "Aren't you glad you agreed?"

Yep. Shep's taste buds tingled, but right now he wanted a cold drink more than food. He gave a nod and followed Mike into the noisy bar. Loud voices, laughter and the jute-box blaring a country song made him glad for the disruption. Even though

The Pitt Stop had great food, it was better known for music and dancing. Bands played every weekend and when they didn't, the jute-box stayed operational making the place lively.

"Hi Mike. Shep. Two beers coming right up."

Since he and Mike were regulars, Sam knew what they wanted without question. Shep didn't drink a lot, but he frequented the place as much as anyone. Not to mention, the firefighters were well known and always welcome.

"Thanks, Sam. Put it on his tab," Shep nodded toward Mike.

"Guess that's only fair, since I talked you into coming."

"Sure thing." Sam grinned and moved down the bar to take another man's order.

Shep leaned a hip against the bar while he surveyed the crowded room and twirling bodies. Been a while since he'd been on the dance floor, but he was one of the few men who actually liked to dance. Women liked a man that could boogie, but then they got other ideas in their heads. So, most of the time, he just watched.

"Well, I'll be damned."

Shep turned to the sound of Mike's voice, seeing a huge grin on his face. "What's up?"

"I see someone I know."

Shep searched the room looking for the person responsible for putting that expression on Mike's face.

"Cassie and her friend," Mike said before Shep saw them.

"The school teachers?"

"Yep. Right over there." Mike gestured with the bottle in his hand.

Shep saw a blonde and a redhead, giggling like a couple of teenagers. He recognized them from the Mexican restaurant the team had gone to after the training exercise. Mike had been keeping company with the blonde for a while now and seemed to be getting attached.

"From the Mexican restaurant?" Shep asked, even though he already knew.

"They're the ones."

"I seem to remember Jared taking a fancy to the redhead." Shep had noticed her right off. The woman had an inviting smile and her eyes had sparkled while she'd flirted with Jared, another member of his squad. The team called him *Pretty Boy*. He had the looks and the personality to warrant the name. Jared had seen the women first. Being his normal cocky self, he'd swaggered over to their table and moved right in. For the first time in years, Shep had almost felt the pangs of jealousy.

"Naw," Mike said. "Jared recognized her flirting as innocent. I think she was just having fun. Not trying to pick him up."

"Hmmm."

"Come on. They look a little too buoyant. Let's see what they're up to."

Again, Shep followed Mike. He weaved his way through the dancers toward the booth with the laughing women. Mike leaned against a post at one side, so Shep stood alongside the opposite one. The blonde took a huge bite of her burger and closed her eyes.

"Mmm mmm. Heaven," she said. Damn if she didn't look like a woman having an orgasm. She opened her eyes and froze, her gaze fixed on Mike.

"Heaven?" Mike teased in a sensual tone.

Shep knew his buddy had the same thoughts he did. Now, the woman looked like she might choke. Mike let her stew for a few seconds but Shep knew he wanted to laugh.

"This is Shep," Mike said to both women. "Shep, this is Tammy. And this," Mike angled his beer at the blonde, "is Cassie." Her face turned red and she dropped her burger.

"It's a pleasure, ladies." Shep glanced to the redhead who stared back at him with devilment sparkling in her beautiful green eyes.

"Hello Shep. You a big strong firefighter, too," Tammy asked with a hint of sexual innuendo. She'd propped her head in the palm of her hand, her elbow resting on the wood. He wondered if her provocative behavior might have been prompted by the empty shot glass in front of her. Even so, she was too cute for words.

"Why, yes ma'am. I am."

"Well, come on over here, fire-hero, and tell me all about yourself."

Chuckling, he slipped into the booth beside her. She acted all silly and cuddled right up next to him. Mike had warned him about her flirting, but he figured the alcohol was a contributor. Normally, he did not engage in such things, but she was fun. And he couldn't help playing along.

"When Mike mentioned coming to this place, I almost suggested going somewhere else," Shep told her. "At the time, it didn't make any difference to me. Now I'm glad we came here."

"Is that so?" Tammy's glassy eyes peered up at him, drawing him into their charming depths.

"Yes, ma'am."

"Please don't call me ma'am," she said, rolling out her lip in a sexy pout.

"My mother taught me manners."

She perked right up. "I can appreciate that."

He couldn't help but add, "The evening had promised to be another boring one for me. Not so, now."

"Really. How come?" Her breath tickled his cheek. "Because I met you."

"I have met you before. Well, not actually met," she said waving her hand. "But I remember you from El Puerto's."

Tammy remembered him? She'd been flirting with Jared.

"The whole fire department showed up there," she said with some awe.

"Yeah. We had training that week. Several County units gathered for drills and preparation exercises. On that particular day, we went out for some dinner." He didn't add the reason. An explosion at the training site had shaken the men. Station Nine had been in charge so, Shep being the Captain at Station Eight, he'd stayed at the firehouse. Once he heard everyone's versions of what happened, the men decided to go out to eat. Dumb luck, they ended up at the same restaurant.

"You men in your blue uniforms caused quite a stir." Tammy leaned closer to him and smiled in adoration. He recognized the look. He'd seen it enough. Still, he didn't move. He kind of liked the attention.

"We get that a lot."

"I love a man in uniform."

He chuckled, wondering how much she'd had to drink.

"Here ya go, gals." A waitress placed two shot glasses of dark liquid on their table. "You said keep 'em coming."

Now he understood. *Shots.*

The sexy waitress propped a hand on her hip. "What can I get for you boys?"

"What's that?" Mike said, pointing to the drinks.

"B52 bombers."

"Sounds good to me," Shep said, thinking why not. The girls were having fun. They must be celebrating. He didn't mind keeping an eye on the lovely Tammy. He was sure Mike felt the same way about Cassie. "Two more."

Mike raised his brows. Mike knew Shep didn't drink hard liquor. And he wasn't exactly planning on starting now.

"Are you ladies celebrating?"

A cloud of darkness screwed up Tammy's face and he wished he could take back his words. Cassie quickly filled the silence.

"We, uh, received some troubling news."

Shit.

"And we're here to forget." Tammy lifted one of the shot glasses. "Bottoms up." She glared at Cassie as if daring her. Shep wondered what kind of shit storm he opened up.

"Why don't you take mine?" Cassie slid her glass across the table to Shep.

"Oh, no. I couldn't take yours." He shoved it back. For one thing, he didn't want it. For another, if these girls were trying to forget bad news, what better way than drowning out their problems. For the moment, anyway.

"Bottoms up," Shep echoed Tammy.

"We agreed that ..." Cassie started, then stopped as Tammy flung back her head and the contents of the shot-glass disappeared.

She gasped as if the liquor had stolen her breath. He lifted his beer and offered it to her. He didn't expect her to take it but she grabbed it and gulped.

"What the hell." Cassie shrugged and tilted her own glass, draining it.

Shep grinned and he saw Mike's shoulders shake. Just then, the waitress placed more shots on the table. Shep couldn't resist. He held up his fingers. "Two more."

"How you doing on beers?"

"Another round, please. And two more burgers." He needed food.

The Pitt Stop served man-sized burgers. Damned if he wasn't hungry. Looked like he might be here a spell.

"Oh, yeah." Cassie looked at her burger as if she'd forgotten it.

"I love a woman with a good appetite," Mike said.

"See? I told ya." Tammy shouted.

"Told her what?" Shep asked, turning to Tammy.

"She was worried about eating a juicy burger in front of a hunk like him." Tammy pointed her finger directly at Mike.

Cassie made choking sounds. Mike patted her on the back.

Time for some space.

Shep lightly grabbed Tammy's wrist. "Can you two-step?" Her eyes flew wide and she giggled as he tugged her from the booth.

Once on the dance floor, he took her hand in his and slid his arm around her back. Tammy packed some pretty sexy curves. She didn't resist when he tugged her close, just gave him another one of her beaming smiles as he led her around the dance floor. Her adoring gaze gave him a funny feeling in his chest. He liked her looking at him as if he were the greatest thing since chocolate. Like maybe she wanted to take a bite

Before his reaction could cause a stirring below his belt, he spun her in a circle. Damn if her arousing laugh didn't do what he'd tried to avoid. Ignoring the sensation, he stepped faster to the Charlie Daniels tune.

Tammy was fun and lively and laughed like a tinkling bell. Her face was getting flushed and he wondered if it might be from him spinning her around. She was out of breath when the song ended.

"This guy knows how to dance," Tammy told Mike and Cassie as she skidded into the booth. Shep slid right in behind her.

"I grew up in a house with four brothers," he explained. "My mom believed we were made for dancing and took great pleasure in torturing us." He faced Tammy, lowered his voice and directed his words to her. "Which is the way we thought of prancing around, until we found out girls liked boys who danced. A girl will pick a guy that can dance over the best-looking guy in any place."

"Like you have anything to worry about." Tammy walked her fingers right up his chest.

Christ. He might as well give up on trying to control his arousal. He doubted Tammy would notice anyway. The woman was well on her way to getting tanked. He'd never take advantage either. He slowed his breathing trying to calm things down and ignore the heat from her fingers scorching his chest. Let the women have their fun.

Trying to get her to eat was a bigger chore than he'd anticipated. When his burger came, he coaxed her to take a few bites of his. Damn, Tammy was sexy. She crooned and nibbled, at least she swallowed something other than alcohol. She was bound to have regrets in the morning.

He thought about that. Guess he should feel guilty. He didn't. Whatever the bad news had been, she deserved to have a moment—or a night—of fun. A moment where she didn't have to worry over her problems, stress free of whatever had happened.

After all, he'd come here with Mike looking for an hour of peace this evening? He glanced at his watch. *Hell.* Three hours? He chuckled in amazement. He'd gotten his hour and more.

"What do you think?" Mike asked.

Shep glanced between the two women. "I think it's time to take these girls home. Which one of you ladies has keys?"

Tammy pointed across the table.

"I do." Cassie giggled and dug into her purse. "I'm not sure I should drive."

Hell no, she shouldn't drive. Mike would see to that. Tammy snuggled into Shep's side where she'd been plastered pretty much all evening.

"I want my big handsome," hiccup, "fire guy ..." She hiccupped again. Wasn't talking too plain either.

"Come on, Sweetheart," he said, pulling her from the booth. He kept one arm around her since she wasn't too steady on her feet.

"You taking me home?" Her sparkling green eyes peered up at him. He was glad she'd eaten something. Hope she didn't puke in his truck on the way home.

Since Tammy was all wobbly, he had to help her into his SUV. The woman might have carried a few extra pounds—sensual curves—but he lifted her easily. The problem was, she kept clinging to him and he couldn't untangle himself quick enough to get the damn door shut. Finally, he clicked the seatbelt, closed the door and turned to find Mike standing behind him.

"Woman's got more arms than a squid," he said.

"Cassie's already asleep." Mike gave a nod of his head toward her car.

Shep chuckled again. He hadn't laughed this much since, he couldn't remember when.

"You aided and abetted."

Shep wrinkled up his forehead.

"Bottoms up," Mike mimicked.

"Don't worry. They won't remember a thing in the morning." He still didn't feel guilty ordering more shots for the girls.

"I'll take Tammy home, put her in bed and leave. I won't even undress her. She's a school teacher." He said the last part as if he needed to remind himself.

Shep glanced at the woman in the truck, blowing him kisses. Damn, his face might crack from this constant grinning. "I figured if the girls wanted to cut loose, let them. Better with us than some other guys that could have happened along. At least with us, they were safe."

"The distressing news was Tammy's."

"You know what happened?"

"Yeah. Her ex. Cassie said she needs a good lawyer. Said she needed to get drunk."

"Well, she managed that."

"With your help."

Shep chuckled again. This was a habit he could get used to.

Order your copy of
Shep: The Firefighters of Station #8 – Book 2
Scan the QR code below!

ABOUT THE AUTHOR

Samanthya Wyatt writes sizzling hot romance with suspense. Intensely emotional characters with a deep passionate love for friends, family, and most importantly—between the hero and heroine. Although her first love is historical romance, this award-winning author also writes contemporary romance under the pen name S. R. Wyatt. Additionally, she has written a book of one family's struggle based on true life events.

Samanthya left her accounting career and married a military man traveling and making her home in the United States and abroad. She now lives in the Shenandoah Valley. On a sunny day, you can find her and her husband driving on the Blue Ridge Parkway or going to car shows in their 1969 Mustang convertible. She loves long walks, and a book to read on a sandy beach. Starbucks is her favorite drink and she likes hearing from her fans.

She invites you to lay the worries of the world off your shoulders and get lost in the pages of a romance, where you embark on a journey with the hero and heroine, become involved in a dream, plunge into a world of fantasy, and live an adventure your heart can share.

To find out more about Samanthya Wyatt and her books, please visit her website: https://samanthyawyattauthor.com/